The Other Side

of the

Island

David Frazer Wray

By the same author

A Fool's Pilgrimage

To Kjersti and Owen

Foreword

An island is a microcosm of human society, as too is a village, a town or a city. You could argue that we are all islanders in some way.

However much these societies differ, they all share one thing in common – they consist of human beings. And all of us share at least some characteristics. We are born more or less in the same way. If we are lucky, we will fall in love. If we are even luckier, that love will endure until old age. And then we will die.

Our fellow islanders may have disagreements, quarrels and fights. They may be unreasonable, bigoted or prejudiced. They may be victims of the sins of others. They may be cheated and dispossessed. And yet they may also create beauty.

They can laugh, dance and sing.

And even if they can do none of those things, they can honour this planet with their very existence, with their own innate, inimitable beauty.

This may all sound pretentious, yet, for all that, it is true.

In writing these simple stories, I have tried to reflect this diversity and sameness. So, the stories are not about a particular island or particular people.

I hope we are all there. The island is us.

A lot of people have contributed to bringing this little book to its audience. In particular, I would like to thank Trevor Moore who was the first to recognise that I have a certain obscure talent for the short story. Peter Cawley sharpened my prose and mitigated my addiction to adverbs. My dear wife Kjersti was the best editor of all.

And, of course, I would like to thank everyone at Sparsile Books, especially Stephen Cashmore and Lesley Affrossman for their consummate professionalism.

Oslo, 2024

Contents

Gift

Evangelos did not hold the honour of being the poorest man on the island, yet he must have at least been a serious contender. Few people, however, had the opportunity to judge his lack of wealth for few people ever visited him on the lonely cape that the locals call Faneromeni after the chapel of that name that perches at its tip.

Evangelos lived in a tiny, two-room house. He got water from the well, fish from the sea, and milk, cheese and meat from his herd of goats. He would get up when the sun rose and go to bed when it set.

Evangelos lived alone but this had not always been so. Once there had been three of them living on the barren peninsular. But his father had passed away when Evangelos was ten years old and then there came the day when his mother fell asleep in her chair in the sun and never woke up again. Evangelos had been thirty-five at the time. In fact, she went to her final sleep on his thirty-fifth birthday.

Yet in spite of the fact that the population of Faneromeni had been reduced by two-thirds in the space of only twenty-five years, Evangelos never yearned for company. He would meet other people when he loaded up the donkey with cheese and freshly killed goat and took the long trek to the village and back. There he might enjoy a game or two of tavli with some of the other men, drink a little too much tsikoudia, and then head for home tired from the hustle and bustle of city life. And once a year, the villagers would come to him when they celebrated the holy day of Panagia Faneromeni by coming to the peninsular by boat, attending a service half in and half out of the tiny chapel, and then partying in the lean-to shelter next to it.

Evangelos never considered himself poor. To do that, you need some sort of yardstick and he had none. Although there were already computers and televisions in the village, Evangelos either did not notice them or, if he did, simply took them for granted as yet another part of village life that he did not understand. As he had no television or radio, he was never exhorted to buy a washing machine or a DVD player. And even if he had, it would have been almost impossible for him to install it as electricity had not made its way to Faneromeni, and he would have been unable to read the instructions.

Normally, Evangelos would spend his day tending his goats and fishing. Tending the goats did not require a great deal of effort but fishing was always an absorbing occupation, if not a very profitable one. His great-grandfather, Alexandros, had built a sturdy little boat that could still weather all but the fiercest of storms but even the best and biggest of boats is of little use if there are no fish to catch. Evangelos probably would not have understood the term "over-fishing" had he heard it, but he did know that there were far fewer fish in the sea than when he was a boy and that those fish that had survived were wily creatures that could be caught only with patience and great skill. So, the fact that he managed to catch any at all is testimony to the fact that he had patience and skill in equal measure.

In fact, Evangelos was so isolated from the outside world, and so innocent of its vagaries, that it came as a very great surprise to him when, one day, he received a gift.

It was on one of his visits to the village. After selling his cheese and goat's meat, Evangelos followed his usual habit of going to the *kafeneion* for a game of tavli and a glass or two of tsikoudia. It was, as he remembered later, after his second game of tavli and his fourth glass of tsikoudia that Giannis, the owner of the *kafeneion*, approached his table carrying a large, brightly wrapped package.

"For you," he said.

Evangelos put down his glass of tsikoudia and squinted at Giannis and then at the package.

"For me?" he said.

"For you," repeated Giannis.

Evangelos became aware that every other man in the *kafeneion* was looking at him. The tavli boards had ceased to rattle. There were no more sounds of cards slapping against tables. Faces were turned towards him. Some were smiling. Some men were holding their hands before their mouths as if embarrassed by his good fortune.

Giannis placed the brightly wrapped package on the table next to Evangelos and stood back. Evangelos gazed at it with wonder and yet with a certain trepidation.

"Well, aren't you going to open it?" asked Giannis.

Evangelos continued to gaze at the package.

"What is it?" he murmured.

"A gift," replied Giannis, smiling at him with his soft, brown, twinkling eyes.

"A gift," repeated Evangelos. He knew, of course, what a gift was, but he had never actually received one. His mother had painted eggs at Easter and given them to him. Had they been gifts too? No, they were not wrapped in bright paper, so they could not have been gifts.

"Who gives me this gift?" he asked, finally.

"I don't know," said Giannis hurriedly, as if he wanted to be shot of the whole business. "Someone left it here. For you."

"Who?"

"I don't know," snapped Giannis, with a touch of irritation. "Someone. A woman, I think."

"A woman!" exclaimed Evangelos, with a force that brought forth a murmur of amusement from the other men.

"Well, open it then," insisted Giannis.

Evangelos stared at the brightly wrapped package. He was confused. Part of him wanted to grasp the package, tear it open and see what was inside but a nagging voice told him that this was not the place to do it. Not in the presence of all those others. Not in the *kafeneion*. And certainly not when it came from a woman! This was something that he should do in his little house at Faneromeni. It should be a private occasion that he could savour, not an indiscriminate moment in the noise and bustle of the *kafeneion*.

Not that there was, at that moment, anything noisy or bustling about the *kafeneion*. In fact, at that moment, it was arguably one of the quieter places on an extremely quiet island. The eyes around him gazed in expectation. Smiles still creased the faces of some men. Others laughed silently at his confusion.

"I'll open it at home," said Evangelos, firmly.

"What?" exclaimed Giannis, nonplussed.

"I'll open it at home."

"You mean not here?" asked Giannis, apparently quite shocked at the decision.

"That's what I said," said Evangelos, calmly and deliberately. "I'll open it at home."

There was a murmur of disapproval in the *kafeneion*. Somebody shouted, "Go on, Vangeli, open it!" but Evangelos ignored him. And soon the cards and tavli were resumed and, apart from the occasional glance in Evangelos's direction to make sure that he had not opened the brightly wrapped package anyway, business at the *kafeneion* went on as usual.

That night, Evangelos rode his donkey back to the little house at Faneromeni with a feeling that he had never before experienced in his forty-eight years of life. Tied to the saddle was a brightly wrapped package that had been given to him, and him alone, as a gift. Evangelos was still confused but now his confusion focused not on whether or not to open the package—for he was going to do that as soon as he got home—but more on what the package might contain and, more particularly, the identity of the mysterious woman who had given it to him.

Evangelos racked his brain to think of a likely woman, but he could not recall anyone who had shown particular interest in him and no one for whom he had done a favour that might merit a gift. Perhaps Giannis had been mistaken and it had been a man and not a woman. But he could not recall ever having done a favour for a man either, unless this was some sort of recognition for the excellence of his goat's cheese.

Admittedly, Evangelos's powers of reasoning were not greatly helped by several glasses of tsikoudia, a few of which had clearly been given to him in the hope that he might feel tempted to open the gift, but it was nevertheless an imponderable mystery.

At the house, Evangelos lit the oil lamp, placed the package carefully on the table and sat down on the bed. It was a windless night, stiflingly warm. The only sound he could hear was the gentle lapping of waves on the beach outside. Gazing at the package on the table, Evangelos felt almost frightened—scared for the first time that he could remember. Never before in his life had there been something he could not really understand. The televisions and computers in the village were not intimidating because he knew that they were perfectly understandable to the people who had them. Even the depths of the sea were understandable, in a way, as they had always been there and, although there were many places where you could not see the bottom, you could be confident that everything there was as it should be. Some families from the village had gone to live in Australia and America. These countries were at the other side of the world, but Evangelos was quite confident that they existed and that people there were also fishing and tending goats.

But this brightly wrapped package was different. It was not as it should be. There should be no brightly wrapped package for Evangelos.

And, with that thought in his head, Evangelos extinguished the oil lamp, curled up on his bed without undressing, and went to sleep.

The following morning, the first thing that Evangelos saw was the brightly wrapped package on the table. In the light of dawn, it looked less spectacular. The bright wrapping, which he now saw had pictures of leaves and berries on it, was rather crumpled and dog-eared. Carrying it tied to the donkey had probably not helped. Yet now was surely the time to open it.

Evangelos grasped the package in both hands and looked around for a knife. However, in those few seconds, the package had grown mysteriously heavy. This perplexed Evangelos because, as he remembered it from the night before, the package was really quite light. In fact, it was so light that it might have contained nothing at all. He replaced it on the table, sat down opposite it and stared.

Perhaps the package did not want to be opened. Perhaps it contained a gift that preferred to remain concealed.

Evangelos pondered this for a time but then dismissed the idea. Packages have no feelings! They do not decide who will open them or when, let alone if. And yet, opening his gift there and then seemed to cheapen it. The opening should, at the very least, be accompanied by some sort of celebration—roast goat and a bottle of tsikoudia, for example. It was something to be savoured and enjoyed and not a banal event in the greyness of morning.

So Evangelos took his customary breakfast of bread, olives and goat's milk and went out to tend his flock. It is true that his thoughts returned to the package several times throughout the day, yet something told him that these were inappropriate times to consider the matter. And Evangelos did not kill a goat that day. When he was sure that the goats were watered, he returned to the house, packed a loaf of bread and a flask of water, and went fishing. It was not a good catch, but how often had there been a good catch since his mother died? There was enough to make a meal and so, as the sun began to dip towards the horizon, he slowly rowed his old boat back to the shore.

However, there was pleasure and anticipation in his rowing. He was not, as before, rowing home to an empty house. Inside, there was a promise. A temptation. An element of passion and danger. Waiting for him, on the other side of the wind-battered door, was something of delicacy and elegance.

The package was there on the table, just as he had left it. Evangelos poured himself a mug of milk, sat down at the table, and admired his gift. There was no question of opening it now for there was no roast goat, no bottle of tsikoudia. Also, he felt that opening the package could be better combined with another event: Easter perhaps, his name day, or the anniversary of his mother's birth. After all, as he understood it, the giving and receiving of gifts was generally related to an event. And there had been no event that might have prompted a mysterious lady to give him a gift. If she had taken a fancy to him on one of his infrequent visits to the village, then she had certainly taken her time in responding and would, presumably, not object to waiting an equal length of time for a reply. Or perhaps longer. When all was said and done, time was not an important consideration at Faneromeni.

And so Evangelos cooked and ate his fish and went to bed.

Over the following days and weeks, the pattern of that day was, in general terms, repeated. There was the occasional time when Evangelos felt very tempted to rip the package open and finally satisfy his curiosity, but he always refrained and his mood quickly passed. At other times, most times in fact, he would return home and give the package no more than an affectionate pat. Was it not better to imagine what might lie inside the wrapping of leaves and berries than to face the possible disappointment of discovery? After all, until Giannis had presented him with the gift, Evangelos's life had been pretty short on mystery. Everything that surrounded him had been as it was for as far back as he could remember. The sea and the sky could change colour infinitely, one minute dull gun-blue and the next a shower of silver and gold splinters, but this mutability was unceasing and therefore comfortingly normal. The land followed the age-old pattern of the seasons and there was nothing extraordinary about that. On the other hand, his gift remained the unknown. Its bright, cheery wrapping, decorated with berries and leaves, might hide bitter disappointment or unbounded joy. And it would take only a few movements of a knife to reveal it.

"Did you ever open that package you got?" asked Christos, as he rolled the dice into Evangelos's side of the tavli board.

There were three other men from the village watching them play. Evangelos noticed that one of them scratched his head and appeared not to remember his gift, one smiled vaguely and the third smirked behind his hand. Christos looked up at Evangelos with innocent dark eyes.

"The gift," he said.

Evangelos was confused. It had never occurred to him that someone might eventually ask such a question and, now that Christos had done so, he did not have a ready reply.

Christos moved his stones on the tavli board and seemed in no hurry to receive a response, but Evangelos was suddenly consumed by panic. If he said no, they would certainly ridicule him, but if he said yes, they would also want to know what the package contained. And perhaps they already knew.

"What gift?" he replied, casually, trying to buy a little extra time.

Christos regarded him levelly.

"You know," he murmured. "The one Giannis gave you a few weeks back. The one from the lady."

"Yes, of course," said Evangelos. "Of course I opened it."

"And?"

Evangelos was having to think quickly. Duplicity was not a skill that was needed at Faneromeni.

"It was as it was," he replied, and smiled in a way that he hoped might be taken as either complicity in a shared joke or the natural reticence that a lover might have in recounting an affair of the heart.

However it was taken, his answer seemed to have a beneficial effect. Christos shrugged his shoulders, the other three looked slightly disappointed and the game of tavli continued without any further reference to the package.

Evangelos returned home from the village angry with himself. How could he have been duped by a woman? What female could have stooped so low as to give him a gift that he dared not open? He would show them! He would show *her*! He would go home and rip the package apart, reveal the gift and have his revenge on all of them!

By the time he reached the little house at Faneromeni, the effects of the tsikoudia were starting to wear off a little yet Evangelos was still firmly set on his path of revenge and determined to open his gift. He burst through the door of his cottage, struggled with the matches to light the oil lamp and grabbed a knife. In the yellow glow of the lamp, the gift on the table looked exotic and enticing.

Evangelos attacked the gift in a calm fury. Yet even that fury, calm as it was, was swiftly tempered. And that happened precisely when the sharp knife sliced through the outside wrapping of leaves and berries and came into contact with the cardboard below.

In his life, Evangelos had killed many things—goats and fish, of course, but also rabbits, snakes and other creatures. And he had done so without remorse. It was natural that he should kill in order to live himself. And to perform that killing, Evangelos had mostly used his knife. Cutting the throat of a goat and feeling the steel rub and slice against its bone produced no sense of horror in him at all. On the other hand, the contact of his knife with a few millimetres of cardboard immediately brought a sense of revulsion.

He paused. In front of him, the delicate skin of leaves and berries had been split and violated, revealing a stripe of coarse bone. Evangelos caught a glimpse of his shadow cast by the flickering oil lamp, knife poised to cut deeper. And all anger drained from him.

Evangelos threw the knife aside and collapsed sobbing onto the chair. Had he stooped so low that he would slice open such a beautiful object simply to satisfy the curiosity of a few drunken tavli players? The beautiful object? The delicate, womanly, beautiful object?

And so it was that in the remaining days of his life, which were many, Evangelos touched his gift on only one further occasion. Until then, it continued to represent many things for him. It was pretty and delightful to come home to after a day's work. On a Sunday, which was observed even at Faneromeni, he would watch it glow under the mantle of dust that was slowly accumulating on it. When winter storms blasted around the cape and rain penetrated the walls, the gift would somehow stand aloof from the violence around it, offering comfort and security. Evangelos rarely thought of the lady who had given it to him but, when he did, he most often thanked her silently for giving him a gift that offered everything that a man could most desire in life.

One day, in late October when the sea was still warm from the summer's heat, when the grapes had been harvested in the valley and fashioned into bright, strong wine, Evangelos did something that he had never done before. He reverently picked up the gift from its place on the table, brushed the dust off carefully, and carried it out into the sunlight. He noted how the berries and leaves of its wrapping had faded into dull blotches and how the gash that he had ripped with his knife so many years before had never healed.

Evangelos took his chair outside into the sun, just as his mother had done, and carefully placed his gift on the ground beside it. In front of him, the sunlight sparkled on the dark water. Behind him, he heard the tinkling of a bell from his flock of goats. Evangelos looked briefly at his gift lying intact and inviolate beside him and smiled. And then Evangelos fell asleep.

Car

"Just look at that, will you?" exclaimed Pavlos, smiling proudly. "What a beauty! Mercedes Benz 240D! Two-and-a-half-litre diesel engine! Sixty-five horsepower! Sunroof, leather upholstery, air-conditioning and heated seats!"

Costas stared at the huge, white car. It was only ten o'clock on a June morning, yet the sun had already turned the jetty to a hotplate. The heat was soaking through the soles of his shoes. A trickle of sweat seeped from under his blue cap, ran down to the tip of his nose, and dropped to the concrete.

"Heated seats?"

"This car will do one hundred and fifty kilometres an hour, Costa," persisted Pavlos. "And it's a diesel! That means it's reliable. This car will never let you down. It's a Mercedes!"

Costas wiped his brow.

"If you say so, Pavlo."

Pavlos gave Costas a withering look.

"What do you know about cars anyway?" he said, shaking his head.

"Not a lot," admitted Costas, spitting into the water. "But I know you won't get it onto that boat."

The boat in question was a small *kaiki* moored next to the jetty. It had been used as a way of ferrying farm machinery from the larger island to the smaller island for many years now and had been modified accordingly. Its deck had been stripped clean and its gunwales widened slightly to take the wheels of a vehicle; brightly coloured rag carpeting had been laid to increase traction and hold the vehicle in place. However, it had never been called upon to carry anything quite as long and wide as a Mercedes Benz 240D.

"According to the handbook, the Mercedes Benz 240D is 1.446 metres wide," declared Pavlos, with an air of authority. "The boat is 1.5 metres wide. I've measured it."

Costas shrugged and caught Christos's eye. Christos raised his eyes to a seagull that was wheeling through the sky above him. He reached into his pocket for his tobacco and papers.

"Maybe the handbook is wrong," he said.

"It's a German handbook."

Christos nodded his head as he began to roll a cigarette. In his experience, the Germans had been precise about most things.

"And it's too heavy," continued Costas. "How much does that thing weigh?"

"That 'thing' weighs about one-and-a-half tons," said Pavlos. "According to the handbook."

Christos whistled and continued rolling. Pavlos glanced at him in annoyance, but could not help himself from also glancing at the two thin planks that were intended to convey the one-and- a-half-ton monster from jetty to *kaiki*.

"Have you emptied the boot?" asked Costas, helpfully.

"Of course I've emptied the boot," replied Pavlos, his moustache bristling at the insult. "Toolkit, spare parts, everything!"

"Spare parts?" said Christos, innocently.

"And a toolkit," added Costas, rather less innocently. "Sounds like they were expecting trouble."

Pavlos stroked his moustache reflectively. This was not the time to engage in an argument with the two men who were going to help him bring his new car to the island.

"The spare parts were thrown in by the previous owner," he said calmly. "The toolkit is standard."

"So they *do* expect trouble," said Costas, spitting again. "And to think it's a Mercedes!"

"I told you it comes as standard!" snapped Pavlos, momentarily forgetting himself. "All expensive cars come with their own toolkit!"

Christos lit his cigarette and gazed at the car. He could not imagine why an expensive car, which was presumably less likely to break down, should come with its own toolkit, while cheap cars, which were presumably more likely to break down, did not.

"Why—" he began.

"Look, let's get moving, shall we?" said Pavlos, in a grating voice. "I promised to take the Mayor and Papa Grigoris for a drive this afternoon. And my wife too, of course."

"Drive?" repeated Costas. "Drive where?"

"To Agios Nikolaos."

"The other side of the island?" said Costas. "Good luck!"

The road to Agios Nikolaos was the only road on the island. Or at least the only road that was usable for any vehicle other than a tractor. Yet strangely, or perhaps even perversely, this was a fact that Pavlos had entirely ignored when he decided to buy the big, white Mercedes. It was not even that he could claim to be unaware of this, since many people, not least his wife Maria, had been more than ready to remind him.

"Where on earth are you going to drive it?" she asked, as she peeled the potatoes for dinner. "There's only one road."

"We can go to Agios Nikolaos and eat in Bennos's taverna," replied Pavlos, without raising his eyes from his newspaper.

Maria put down her knife and potato.

"Why?"

"What do you mean, why?"

"I mean, why go to Agios Nikolaos to eat in a taverna when there are tavernas here?"

"Bennos's Taverna is one of the best on the island! Everyone knows that!"

"Everyone who likes fish knows that," corrected Maria. "And I don't like fish."

"Then you can eat vegetables."

"Ha!"

Maria began peeling furiously. "All the way to Agios Nikolaos to eat vegetables!"

Pavlos was aware that the possibility of his ever actually owning the car would be put in severe jeopardy if he pursued this particular tack.

"The car has air-conditioning," he added, in a gentle, almost seductive voice.

"Does it?" asked Maria, slightly impressed that they might actually possess the first fully-functional air-conditioning unit on the island, even if it was in a car. Her peeling became a little less furious.

"And it has heated seats," added Pavlos, soothingly.

"Heated seats!" exclaimed Maria. "Heated seats here?"

"Ah," said Pavlos. "Just imagine gliding down the road in the winter rain, with our bottoms gently warmed. Or speeding through the summer heat in the comfort of our air-conditioned interior."

"To eat vegetables!"

However, Maria's opposition to buying the Mercedes gradually waned. This certainly had nothing to do with the honour of having the first car on the island, or even the prospect of owning the first mobile air-conditioning unit. Maria's eventual capitulation owed itself to a combination of two things: Pavlos's inexhaustible persistence and her own soft heart. After all, her husband was a hard worker who had built up a successful, if modest, hotel business. He was entitled to his bit of self-indulgence.

"Why did you have to buy this thing?" exclaimed Costas, sucking the blood from a deep scratch on the back of his hand. "I mean…a car…okay. Fine. But why did it have to be so big?"

"Shut up and push!" snapped Pavlos, as the sweat stung his eyes.

The Mercedes had progressed in its journey from jetty to boat. Although its rear wheels were still firmly on the jetty, its front wheels were now, not quite as firmly, on the two thin planks leading onto the *kaiki*. In fact, one wheel was now very close to losing contact with its plank altogether.

"Forget it!" shouted Pavlos to Costas. "You lift, I'll push!"

"Lift?" echoed Costas. "Lift what?"

"The car, you bloody fool! What else?"

Costas risked a glance at the huge white object looming over him.

"I can't lift that!" he protested. "It'd take a crane to lift that!"

"Just do your best."

And so his best is exactly what Costas did, and it is a tribute to a life spent in the open air and the smoky interior of the *kafeneion* that he managed to summon the strength to elevate the Mercedes by a matter of a centimetre, which was all Pavlos needed to push the plank firmly and centrally under the offending wheel.

"Okay!" he exclaimed. "Now it's just a question of steering it down the planks and onto the boat."

"And turning it onto the gunwales," added Costas, pessimistically.

"And turning it onto the gunwales, as you say," repeated Pavlos, equally pessimistically.

However, it suddenly occurred to Pavlos that steering the car was a relatively easy job and that the really tricky part was making sure that the planks did not spring out from under the wheels.

"Christos! You steer!"

"Eh?"

"You heard me! Get in the car and steer."

Christos, who had been supervising contact between the other wheel and its appropriate plank, shrugged his shoulders, jumped onto the jetty and got into the car.

"The other side!" yelled Pavlos.

"Eh?"

"You're not a passenger; you're steering! The steering wheel is on the other side!"

"Oh."

Christos scrambled out of the car and took his place behind the steering wheel. He had never sat behind the steering wheel of a car in his life, and it felt very grand. The upholstery had the opulent smell of saddle leather, the mahogany trim reminded him of a boat.

"Shall I start the engine?" he shouted hopefully through the window.

"No!"

Actually, this came as some relief to Christos, who had no idea how to start the engine anyway. There should, he theorised, be some sort of red button somewhere but he could not see one.

"Just steer," commanded Pavlos. "No, don't steer, just keep it straight."

"How do I keep it straight?" asked Christos.

"Just keep the wheel where it is now."

This did not seem like proper steering to Christos. He had seen the motor racing once. It was like the horse racing but then longer, and with cars.

"Can't I just turn the wheel a little bit?" he shouted plaintively.

"Only if I say!" shouted Pavlos.

Christos shrugged and puffed at his dead cigarette. Surely driving a car could not be more difficult than riding a donkey. After all, a car is a machine and will always do what you tell it.

Little by little, the Mercedes inched along the planks. Finally, each of the front wheels was resting on a gunwale.

"Now!" shouted Pavlos to Christos. "Turn the wheel."

It took four hours for the breakdown truck to arrive. The actual journey time between its depot and the jetty was only twenty minutes but prior to this was a full hour's shouting between Pavlos and Christos, with occasional attempts at mediation from Costas, a walk to the nearest telephone, a long consultation with directory enquiries, a wait until the call was answered, a further wait until the driver of the breakdown truck could be contacted and persuaded to leave the comfort of his local *kafeneion* to help some idiot move a big car, and an even longer wait as the driver of the breakdown truck argued about his bill in the *kafeneion*, phoned his wife and explained that he would be later than expected, promised his wife that he was not chasing after some foreign woman, failed to start his moped, took his moped for repair, borrowed a friend's moped and finally turned the key in the ignition of the breakdown truck.

Thanks to the large crane on the back of the breakdown truck, it was finally possible to rescue the Mercedes from its position of being slightly half-in and half-out of the *kaiki* and place it squarely on the gunwales. Pavlos paid the driver of the breakdown truck, who, by that time, was by no means as disgruntled as he had been on arrival. In fact, the sight of a large, white German car spread-eagled across the little ferry like a huge, gleaming fish that had not been fully landed, had reduced him to tears of mirth.

"Don't you think we should secure it with something?" suggested Costas, when the driver had gone.

"Secure it?" replied Pavlos. "On that boat, it's not going anywhere."

As it happened, this prediction turned out to be true. Although the breeze had freshened since the early morning, causing the *kaiki* to roll and pitch on its passage to the island, the Mercedes stared stolidly and steadfastly ahead with the uncompromising gaze of a military commander.

Nor was it as difficult as expected to retrieve the car from the *kaiki* once they had made landfall. Reluctant to trust to Christos's steering ability a second time, Pavlos recruited the help of twenty-three men who lifted the Mercedes bodily onto the quayside.

"So that's it, is it?" observed Maria, eyeing the car suspiciously. "What took you so long?"

"We had a problem loading it," said Pavlos, hurriedly. "Just listen to this though."

He swung into place behind the wheel and turned the key in the ignition. There was a sharp grating sound and the electric starter began to crank. Pavlos smiled at Maria as the starter turned and turned. Finally, there was a loud explosion from the exhaust, a cloud of choking blue smoke, and the engine roared into life.

"Just listen to that!" crowed Pavlos, triumphantly. As the crowd of admiring villagers applauded loudly.

In fact, there was plenty to listen to. As with most diesel engines of that age, the Mercedes-Benz was by no means silent even when factory new. But, in this case, it was also accompanied by a highly rhythmical range of clicks, bangs, whistles and rattles that would have put many a Brazilian samba band to shame.

"What about the air-conditioning?" Maria shouted above the din.

Pavlos stared intently at the dashboard, and then made a few adjustments that Maria could not see.

"There!" he shouted. "Twenty degrees!"

Maria smiled for the first time since the arrival of the car and nodded her head graciously at the assembled villagers.

"Air-conditioning!" she announced. And the assembled villagers looked duly impressed even though many of them did not fully understand.

"And heated seats!" added Pavlos, grinning.

By this time, Costas had had quite enough of the Mercedes and retreated to the shade of a nearby café. Christos, on the other hand, was absolutely enthralled. Not only was the Mercedes huge and white and shining but it was also impressively noisy. He ran his hand over the paintwork with an almost proprietary air and also smiled graciously at the rest of the village.

Pavlos stepped out of the car and addressed no one in particular: "It is now time for the inaugural drive!"

Those invited to the inaugural drive were, of course, Mayor Tzavaras and his wife Anna, the local priest Papa Grigoris and his wife Maria, Pavlos's wife Maria and, as a gesture of forgiveness, coloured by a slight feeling of sympathy, Christos.

Naturally, it was only fitting that Maria should sit next to her husband. But, indeed, fitting proved to be a problem in the case of the other passengers. Given a width of 1.446 metres, the back seat of the car could theoretically have held five people each with an average width of 0.2892 metres; however, Papa Grigoris alone significantly exceeded that limit. Fortunately, Mayor Tzavaras suggested that his wife sit on his lap. Maria Tzavaras regarded this as a little below her dignity, and strongly suggested that Christos should forego his first drive in a car in the general interests of comfort. Nevertheless, her husband prevailed. And so it was that the Mercedes Benz started out for Agios Nikolaos with a complement of seven.

They glided smoothly out of the village. Christos was entranced. Although the Mercedes was noisy on the outside, it was surprisingly quiet on the inside. Almost as wonderful were the opulent leather seats. Until then, Christos had never sat on anything more comfortable than cane, rush or plastic. It was true that Mrs Tzavaras's back and bottom tended to crush him against the door every time Pavlos avoided a large rock or pothole, which was every few seconds, but Christos felt that this was a very small price to pay for being ferried to Agios Nikolaos in the luxury of a chauffeured limousine.

For her part, Mrs Tzavaras was not quite as entranced by the experience. It was bad enough to suffer the indignity of sitting on her husband's lap but infinitely worse was her unpleasant contact with Christos as Pavlos manoeuvred along the road. Matters were not helped when, to complete his idea of luxurious living, Christos lit a cigarette and proceeded to puff away happily with both hands in his trouser pockets.

Apart from Christos and Pavlos, Mr Tzavaras was possibly the only entirely happy person in the car. Naturally, he did not care a jot about the Mercedes and he did not particularly want to go to Agios Nikolaos to eat fish. However, it was many years since Mrs Tzavaras had last consented to sit on his lap and he was grateful to Pavlos for providing a suitable pretext.

Papa Grigoris had not wanted to come on the inaugural drive at all. He had been in many cars in his life. He admitted that, as a means of getting from A to B, a car was both efficient and relatively safe. However, these were two qualities that were not generally shared by their drivers.

And he also very much doubted that Pavlos had a driving licence, which, indeed, he did not.

Mrs Grigoris shared her husband's dislike of the inaugural drive, but she was used to disliking many of the activities forced on her as a consequence of his vocation. She disliked boat trips to an obscure part of the island to celebrate the festival of some equally obscure saint who happened to have a chapel named after him or her. She disliked having to listen to lengthy and unintelligible speeches delivered by visiting dignitaries. In short, she disliked being married to a priest, but then Papa Grigoris had not been a priest when she married him.

Now that Maria was actually in the car, coasting rather un-smoothly towards Agios Nikolaos, any lingering doubts about the wisdom of buying the Mercedes had been dispelled from her mind. What could be more fitting for the wife of an up-and-coming businessman than to travel in the luxury of a limousine? It was unfortunate that the radio no longer seemed to work, but Maria reasoned that this was not necessarily a disadvantage as it was a German car and German was one of the many languages that she did not understand. On the other hand, the air-conditioning was definitely something to savour! In fact, it was not until they had been travelling for around ten minutes, during which time they had covered a distance of some four kilometres, that she realised that the air-conditioning was not working.

"The air-conditioning…" she said, leaning over towards Pavlos. "It is on, isn't it?"

Pavlos glanced at the controls.

"Twenty degrees exactly!"

Maria fanned herself with her handkerchief.

"Well, perhaps we might have a window open too," she suggested. "Just for a breath of fresh air?"

"If you open the windows, the air-conditioning won't work."

"Oh."

But now that Maria's attention was more closely focused on the question of bodily temperature, she also realised that her bottom was beginning to grow very warm indeed.

"Pavlo?" she asked, in a small voice. "You did say that the car has heated seats, didn't you?"

"Yes," replied Pavlos, aware for the first time that his own bottom was beginning to glow a little.

"Are you sure they're not on?"

Pavlos glanced at the switches. "No, they're off," he replied.

"Oh."

In fact, the question of temperature was one that was now beginning to vex everybody in the car to some extent, with the exception of Christos, who was now puffing contentedly on his second cigarette and revelling in the feel of warm leather. Apart from Maria, Mr Tzavaras was definitely the passenger who was starting to suffer most, insulated as he was by his wife.

"Pavlo!" he called. "Maybe it is a good idea to open a window. What do you think?"

Typical politician, thought Pavlos. Why not say it straight out instead of asking me what I think?

"The air-conditioning doesn't work if you open the windows," explained Pavlos, patiently. "You okay, Christo?"

"I'm fine," grunted Christos, contentedly snuggling down between the door and Mrs Tzavaras. "Nice and cosy!"

However, the temperature in the car continued to rise. Not only was there solar heat conducted through the solid steel coachwork of the Mercedes but also, and increasingly, warmth generated in the depths of the car's opulent leatherwork.

Pavlos punched the seat-heater switches repeatedly off and on but it did not make any difference. He also fiddled with the controls to the air-conditioning but, either as a result of ignorance or malfunction, this did not seem to make any difference either.

Papa Grigoris was inclined to put the situation down to ignorance.

"Do you know how to operate this car, Pavlo?" he inquired, in a loud voice.

"Drive it, you mean?" replied Pavlos, his moustache bristling with indignation. "Of course I do! I have read the handbook!"

"It comes with a toolkit," added Christos, helpfully.

"Just as well," muttered Papa Grigoris.

By this time, Mr Tzavaras was beginning to get short of breath. For a politician, this is a serious problem and therefore, with the characteristic, no-nonsense attitude that had raised the Tzavaras family to its position of prominence in the island's society, he was quick to act.

"Pavlo! I really do suggest that we open a window!"

This time, Pavlos did not demur. Attempting to look as reluctant as possible, he wound down the driver's side window. Immediately, a stream of dusty, scalding air shot past him into the rear of the vehicle.

"Shut the window, for God's sake!" shouted Papa Grigoris, coughing.

"You just told me to open it!"

"I didn't tell you to open it!" retorted Papa Grigoris. "It was this fool of a mayor!"

"Who are you calling a fool, you idiot priest?" shouted Mr Tzavaras, with his voice slightly muffled under a heavily sweating wife.

"Don't you call my husband an idiot!" yelled Mrs Grigoris, galvanized from her customary apathy.

"Let us calm ourselves, children," interposed Papa Grigoris, vocationally. "It is not every man who can go to Corinth."

"We're not going to Corinth, you dimwit!" shouted Mr Tzavaras, through a face full of hair. "We're going to Agios Nikolaos!"

It was at this point that Pavlos acted in a way that befitted his ancestors, the simple fishermen whose daily encounters with the hazards of the sea had provided him with the foundations of his blossoming business empire. He stopped the car.

"Right!" he shouted. "Everybody out!"

And everybody did get out, with the exception of Christos, who, dead cigarette in mouth, was now comfortably asleep.

It was a very hot afternoon but to the passengers it seemed as if they had stepped out into a fresh spring morning.

"My God!" exclaimed Papa Grigoris, and he turned to Pavlos. "Is a Mercedes Benz always that hot?"

"I think there may be something wrong with the air-conditioning," admitted Pavlos.

"And the heated seats," added Maria, bitterly.

"And the heated seats," confirmed Pavlos, sadly.

"And this fool of a mayor," snapped Mrs Grigoris.

"Are you calling my husband a fool?" retorted Mrs Tzavaras, who was nevertheless very relieved not to be sitting on her husband's lap.

"Look," said Pavlos, reasonably. "I'm sorry about the heat."

That seemed to satisfy everyone, at least for a few minutes. As if guided by a common impulse, they retired to the adjacent dry-stone wall and leaned over it, gazing at the gun-blue sea below.

"Perhaps we should turn back," said Pavlos, contritely. "I can get the seats and the air-conditioning fixed and we can do this another day."

At first, nobody answered. Maria, Mrs Tzavaras and Mrs Grigoris were fanning themselves with their handkerchiefs. Papa Grigoris and Mr Tzavaras were leaning with their backs against the wall, legs apart, taking every advantage of the slightest cooling breeze.

"Let's push on to Agios Nikolaos," said Mr Tzavaras finally. "When we come back, it will be cool and then we will need the heated seats. After all, it's still chilly in the evenings."

41

"Oh, that's fine, isn't it!" exclaimed his wife. "So I have to go the rest of the way there and all the way back sitting on your knee!"

"What's wrong with that?" protested Mr Tzavaras, innocently. "We're married, aren't we?"

"It's undignified!" retorted Mrs Tzavaras. "I am the mayor's wife, when all's said and done!"

"Well, I'm the mayor and I don't mind," said Mr Tzavaras.

"Let *her* sit on her husband's knee instead!" shouted Mrs Tzavaras, pointing at Mrs Grigoris.

"I," answered Mrs Grigoris, drawing herself up to her full height of five feet, "am the priest's wife! I do not sit on knees."

"She's right," confirmed Papa Grigoris, sadly. "She doesn't."

However, once Mr Tzavaras's proposal of continuing to Agios Nikolaos had been accepted by all, or at least a majority, everyone resumed their seats in the Mercedes Benz exactly as they had done when first embarking on the inaugural drive.

"Are we there yet?" asked Christos, sleepily, as Mrs Tzavaras thrust her backside into his ribs with indignant force.

"Shut up!" she growled.

It would be pleasing to report that the rest of the journey to Agios Nikolaos went without a hitch; however, this was not the case. Certainly, the warmth generated by the heated seats was, to some extent, mitigated by opening all of the windows and the sunroof, but the moderation in temperature was inevitably accompanied by a constant flow of hot dust which, by-passing those in the front, settled evenly and without particular discrimination, on those in the back.

What is more, the road to Agios Nikolaos, although relatively smooth at the outset, became progressively more difficult to negotiate the further they ventured away from the village. Closer to the village, countless generations of islanders had removed the larger rocks and stones—not, of course, on any organised basis—resulting in a road surface that was picturesquely uneven though still relatively serviceable. However, there had been no such attempt at road improvement further on. After all, most people who went to Agios Nikolaos went by donkey, mule or motorbike, and the presence of a large boulder rising to a height of one or two feet above the road surface did not pose a problem for any of those conveyances. You simply went around it.

However, you cannot go around such a boulder in a car that is 1.446 metres in width. The best you can hope for—and, in fact, the wisest thing you can do—is to keep one side of the car on the flatter surface and climb over the boulder with the wheels on the other side of the car. This was the tactic that Pavlos employed in the vast majority of cases, with some success, it has to be said. Gradually the inaugural drive edged towards Agios Nikolaos.

It is one of the ironies of life that major hazards, because they are major, are often easier to avoid. It's the minor hazards, or rather the medium-sized hazards, that tend to cause problems. One underestimates their ability to cause considerable damage. And considerable damage is generally what they cause.

It was when Pavlos decided that the smooth-sided boulder ahead of him did not pose any appreciable threat and judged that it would pass safely under the car, that disaster finally struck. Unfortunately, due to another irony of life, it was not a disaster that was immediately recognised as such. Had the Mercedes been travelling at a speed in excess of five kilometres per hour, the disaster would have been directly apparent. As it was, there was simply a grating, crunching noise and the car came to a stop. Pavlos cursed and got out to inspect the damage.

The Mercedes had beached itself evenly on the top of the boulder. Frustratingly, Pavlos could see that it was a matter of only one or perhaps two centimetres at the most. In fact, had the car not been carrying seven people, it would certainly have negotiated the boulder without any problem. And, having realised this, Pavlos immediately saw the solution.

"Everybody out!" he shouted.

"What's the matter, Pavlo?" asked Maria, anxious that her air-conditioning system, faulty as it was, might end up at the roadside far from the village.

"Just stuck, that's all," said Pavlos breezily. "There's no need to worry."

"Are we there yet?" asked Christos, opening his eyes.

"Just shut up and get out," said Mrs Tzavaras. Christos got out, and took the opportunity to roll a cigarette.

"Stuck then," he observed, licking the paper together. "Second time today."

Naturally, when relieved of its burden of passengers, the Mercedes crossed the boulder with ease. Everyone resumed their positions in the car and the inaugural drive continued. Soon they had turned the final bend. Below them, the sunlight twinkled on the waters of the bay and the car could coast downhill, albeit with an ominous clunking sound, to Agios Nikolaos and Bennos's Taverna.

The Mercedes pulled up in front of the taverna to be greeted by an admiring Bennos and his wife and children, and such was the universal joy that nobody noticed a rock that completed the damage that the large boulder had initiated. Neither did anyone notice the thin trail of oil left by a cracked gearbox.

"Beautiful!" exclaimed Bennos, running his hand over the dusty coachwork. "It must have cost a packet!"

"Quite a bit, yes," said Pavlos proudly, glancing at Maria to see whether the mention of money had caused any reaction. Fortunately, Maria was far too busy helping Mrs Tzavaras and Mrs Grigoris to rid themselves of the layer of dust that had accumulated on their clothing to pay much heed to the conversation.

"It's a fine car," added Mr Tzavaras. "Very comfortable."

"As cars go," confirmed Papa Grigoris, in a gesture of Christian largesse.

"You will want to eat now, I suppose," said Bennos, eyeing Pavlos slyly. "And drink, eh?"

"You're right, Benno," replied Pavlos. "We'll eat and drink and I shall pay for all. What do you have today?"

"Fish."

It had been a tiring day for everyone. A day that had caused dissent between husband and wife, and even church and state. But soon, all of these petty annoyances were forgotten around the table at Bennos' Taverna. There was even an adequate supply of vegetables for those who did not like fish. And naturally, there was Bennos's incomparable tsikoudia to wash it all down!

"It was a fine idea, this drive," admitted Papa Grigoris, late in the evening. "In great attempts, even to fail is glorious! But you did not fail, Pavlo! Your car is the finest on the island!"

There could be little doubt that it was the finest, if only because it was the first, but Pavlos accepted the compliment in the spirit in which it was given and, indeed, it was a perfect evening in which any differences between husband and wife, church and state, seemed to have been set aside, temporarily.

The evening was drawing on and, in spite of the fact that it was now generally accepted that the car was a fine thing and that Pavlos was very much to be admired for purchasing it, no one was particularly relishing the journey back to the village in the darkness.

Yet, after a further two bottles of tsikoudia provided on the house by Bennos, it was time for the travellers to resume their seats in the Mercedes for the journey home.

Sadly, the journey home took much longer than expected. In fact, after the Mercedes failed to leave Agios Nikolaos, it was only as the light of dawn turned the sea from empty blackness to a miracle of grey and pink that the seven travellers finally trudged into the village. The journey had succeeded in re-establishing the petty squabbles between husband and wife, church and state that appeared to have been eliminated forever in Bennos's taverna.

The car, the beautiful Mercedes Benz 240D, remained in Agios Nikolaos. It was, forever, the first car on the island and, indeed, for many years it continued to be the finest. It was also the most expensive, if only in terms of the potential cost of repairing it.

Pavlos's wife Maria, although the first woman on the island to have an air-conditioning system, was also the first and only woman to lose one. Nevertheless, she was of a pragmatic turn of mind and her loss was more than compensated as Pavlos's infatuation with his car ended on the rocky road back to the village. For many years after the road had been blasted clear of boulders and resurfaced with tarmac, he steadfastly refused to buy another car, preferring a moped instead.

However, Maria was not the only person to benefit from the demise of the Mercedes. Christos, who had sat quietly at a corner of the table in Bennos' Taverna and had walked uncomplainingly back to the village, retained a glorious memory of falling asleep in the leathery comfort of a chauffeur-driven limousine.

Bennos obtained an unexpected benefit. On the morning after his guests' departure, he wandered barefoot out to the Mercedes, sat behind the wheel, and experimentally turned the key in the ignition. Several lights glowed on the dashboard and finally, after some coughing and choking, the engine started. He knew the car was not going to move and, in fact, he had really not expected it to start. However, as he sat there, with the engine hammering away, he noticed that the heated seats had ceased to work. He also became aware of a gentle flow of cool air.

And so it was that Bennos became the island's second owner of an air-conditioning system. Yet, unlike Maria, he continued to enjoy it. On the hottest days, when the bay at Agios Nikolaos shone like a mirror and the sky was powdered with heat haze, he would retire to the car with a newspaper, a cigarette and a glass of tsikoudia and relax in the leather seat in the cool air. And, thanks to the occasional purchase of a can of diesel, he continued to do that for many years.

Dance

The Compagnie des Mines de l'Ouest Oriental had just taken over the mine when Tanga arrived. The British company that had been digging calamine out of the island since the nineteenth century was bankrupt and the French had immediately stepped in. The new company firmly believed that it could succeed where its predecessor had failed. It was simply a matter of more manpower, better technology and more favourable economic circumstances.

Tanga neatly fitted the first two points. He had been mining in South America for an Argentinean-British consortium and was an expert user of the one-man drill. Although Tanga never actually admitted it, it was an open secret that he had been offered a fairly large amount of money to move to the island and this was probably true since he had left Greece in his late teens and would surely not have returned without an adequate financial reason.

For the islanders, Tanga was far more exotic than the Frenchmen, Spaniards and Portuguese that the mining company also brought with it. First of all, he was not from the island yet he was Greek. And, being Greek, his exoticism was understandable. Secondly, he spoke Greek with a slightly foreign accent and a certain stilted delivery that he was never to lose entirely, but which added to his charm. Thirdly, and most importantly, he had been to places that, for most of the islanders, existed only as strange names on the faded map in the village schoolroom. Tanga had been to Argentina, Brazil, Chile and Bolivia. He had trekked through the Andes, hacked his way through the Amazonian jungle, worked his passage on dirty tramp steamers. And he had danced in Buenos Aires.

He had danced the tango.

In the years that were to follow, the origin of Tanga's nickname became lost. Some said that he took it from the one-man drill that he used in the calamine mine, which, in its confined depths, deafened his fellow workers with its constant "tanga-tanga-tanga". Others believed, equally firmly, that Tanga was a corruption of tango, the dance of Argentina. The truth, quite simply, is that his real name was Andreas Tanganis.

Yet one cannot blame those who thought that Tanga was a corruption of tango for he was a master of the dance.

"Tanga! Tanga! Tanga! Your gramophone!"

Tanga crushed his cigarette under his heel.

"Who wishes this?" he asked, raising a supercilious eyebrow.

"I wish it," came a voice.

"And I," came another.

Tanga pulled aside his shirt and scratched his chest. The evening was warm. Sweat dug channels across a skin still coated in dust.

"I do not dance with men," he said. "What woman wants this?"

The women crowded about him.

"Me, Tanga! Take me!"

And so Tanga left the miners' hut and returned with the gramophone.

The gramophone had a huge, brass, tubular horn that bore a picture of a dog listening to an identical tubular horn; the case was polished mahogany. With it were heavy shellac records in paper cases bearing strange inscriptions.

In the midst of a hushed crowd, Tanga placed the gramophone reverently on a table, selected a record, cranked the handle and lifted the needle. There were a few seconds of loud scratches.

De noche, con la luna, soñando sobre el mar
el ritmo de las olas me miente su compás.

Tanga grasped the arm of a girl and led her through the door to the flat area of crushed rubble outside. There, the hillside was bathed in moonlight, turning the calamine rubble to marble. The scents of wild oregano and thyme washed their dance floor in a sea of fragrance.

Tanga did not dance the refined tango of ballrooms and formal competitions; he danced *milonguero*, the tango of the slums, the tango of the mining camps and dockyards.

As they danced, even before they had started dancing, the crowd in the miners' hut came out to watch. The miners and the women stared in fascination at Tanga and his partner.

His body entwined with hers, forced her into movements that she had never known before, and yet his feet slid and floated over the rough stones as if they belonged to a different person. It seemed as if the passionate, brutal Tanga of the mind was betrayed by the delicate, sophisticated movements of his body.

Yet she, the unknown girl, followed his every movement, twisting when he twisted, halting with head thrown back. And as the dance progressed, as Tanga's skin glittered with sweat and calamine dust, the girl was no longer in a miners' camp on a forsaken hill on a forgotten island.

Bailemos este tango, no quiero recordar.
Mañana zarpa un barco, tal vez no vuelva más.

Suddenly the dance was finished. There remained the scratchy tock-tock of the needle.

"*Opa!*" came a shout from the crowd, followed by clapping and whistles. "*Opa*, Tanga!"

Tanga smiled at the unknown girl, as she leaned back over his arm.

"You dance well," he said. "Good."

The girl released herself from his grasp and stood back from him shyly, smoothing down her skirt with both hands.

"I've never danced like this before," she said. "It's a new dance."

"No, it is an old dance," replied Tanga and bowed to her. "As old as men and women. Come."

Not waiting for a word of acquiescence, and to a chorus of ribald cheering, he took her by the wrist and led her away from the pool of light into the darkness below.

"Wait!" she said. "I'm not one of those girls!"

"And I am not one of those men," replied Tanga. "I have something to show you, that's all."

They stopped a short distance down the hillside and Tanga released his hold on the girl's wrist. She immediately drew aside and looked at him with a mixture of curiosity and suspicion. Tanga removed his blue cap, brushed invisible dust from a rock.

"Sit down," he said.

"I'm fine just where I am, thank you," murmured the girl.

"No, sit down," Tanga insisted. "It's all right."

"I told you. I'm not one of those girls."

"And I told you I'm not one of those men. So now that we are clear about that, sit down."

The girl smiled, glanced around as if to be sure that no one was watching them, and daintily seated herself on the rock. She was then slightly relieved to see that Tanga was in no hurry at all to sit beside her. She had not really wanted to come up to the mining camp at all and would certainly not have done so if her friends had not insisted. There was so little to do on the island.

"Just look at that!" exclaimed Tanga, pointing upwards.

The girl searched the night sky but saw only the moon and a few stars twinkling over the sea.

"Look at what?" she asked.

"Why, the moon of course!" exclaimed Tanga. "Look at it!"

The girl looked at the moon. It was beautiful, but no more beautiful than a full moon ever was. She felt a pang of anxiety. What did this strange man, this Tanga, want her to say? And why was she so anxious about giving the right answer?

"It's beautiful," she offered, hesitantly.

"It is full," Tanga corrected. "It is full and complete. It is like a dance. A dance has a beginning, a middle and an end. And when the dance has finished, it is full. Like the moon."

He spread his arms wide to embrace the entire night sky and then dropped them to his sides, as if overcome.

"The moon is always full. Even when you do not see it. Finally, its dance is always complete. But sometimes your own dance is less than perfect. You can trip. You can fall. You can fall off the moon. Your dance cannot always be full like the moon."

Tanga sighed, as if he had unburdened himself of some great secret that could be imparted only to the girl and to no one else. Suddenly the vigorous, irrepressible Tanga seemed drained of energy. He gazed at the moon for a few moments, rubbed one hand over his stubbly chin and then seated himself on a rock opposite the girl.

"Full. Like the moon," he repeated. But he said it in a small voice. The voice of an embarrassed child.

The girl looked at the moon again and then she looked at Tanga.

"Yes," she said simply, in a voice even smaller than Tanga's. "A full moon is a dance that is complete."

It was not long before the Compagnie des Mines de l'Ouest Oriental finally acknowledged that more manpower, better technology and more favourable economic circumstances were no more likely to make the island's calamine mine profitable than the outdated methods of its British predecessors. The mine was closed, the equipment removed and the French, Spanish, Portuguese and Greek miners moved on to further employment elsewhere.

But not Tanga.

One evening, when almost all of the other miners had gone, Tanga walked down the hillside to the same spot where he and the girl had sat together not so many months before. The moon had, once again, completed its dance. It gazed down on him in its fullness, turning the sea to spun quicksilver and the hills to filigree.

I shall find that girl again, he thought, and if she is not married, I will marry her. And I will stay here. To complete my dance.

Tanga found the girl. In spite of the diminutive size of the island, it was not such an easy task, for he had never asked her name. In fact, all that he could remember about her was that she had danced the tango as if she understood it and had known that a full moon is a dance that is complete. Fortunately, Tanga was a very strong man and he did not mind walking back and forth across the island to find her. And he did find her, and he discovered that her name was Maria, and they were married soon after.

Just as he had done on their first evening together, Tanga continued to surprise Maria in the weeks following their betrothal. She had always assumed that miners must be very poor, for who else but a poor man would risk life and limb below the ground? But Tanga was by no means a poor man. While hacking his way through the Amazonian jungle, trekking through the Andes and working his passage on dirty tramp steamers, not to mention his work for the Compagnie des Mines de l'Ouest Oriental, he had managed to put aside a tidy sum of money. Which was just as well since Maria's parents were genuinely poor and could offer very little in the way of a dowry.

The second way in which Tanga surprised Maria was in his firm decision to give up hacking, trekking, tramping and mining forever and become, of all things, a farmer.

"But what do you know about farming? she asked.

"What did I know about mining until I started?" he replied. "It cannot be any more difficult and, God knows, it is a lot safer. Besides, when I have farmed, I will be full."

"Full?"

"Full. Like the moon."

Tanga and Maria bought land. Naturally, those who owned the best land were not in a hurry to sell it so Tanga reasoned that if they could not have quality, at least they would have quantity and bought as much land as he could. However, once they had built a house, it swiftly became clear that Tanga would not be able to apply the same degree of mechanisation to farming as he had formerly done to mining. Very little of his savings were left. There was no question of buying even an old tractor, for example, so they contented themselves with a plough and a mule.

On a small island, outsiders, even if they are married to insiders, are always considered fair game when it comes to driving a bargain. So, the mule that Tanga eventually bought was not a beast in the prime of its life. Neither, on the other hand, was it a decrepit travesty of the species that someone would be too embarrassed to sell. It was young. Very young.

"It's very young," said Maria, eyeing it for the first time.

"It will grow," replied Tanga, a trifle defensively.

"I just hope we don't starve before it does," said Maria. "What's its name anyway?"

"Name?" repeated Tanga, staring at the mule.

The mule stared back. It was a rather philosophical stare for such a young, unsophisticated animal.

"Its name," said Tanga, "is The Moon."

Maria quickly brought her hand to her mouth to stifle a laugh.

"The Moon?"

"Yes. The Moon. Or at least it will be The Moon. When it is complete."

Young as it was, The Moon could draw the plough. Soon it could pull it without struggling too much and within a few more months it could draw the share effortlessly through the stony soil.

"The Moon is good," said Tanga one day. "He will make us rich."

"Not rich," replied Maria. "But if we aren't poor that will be full enough."

And The Moon did get full. Whether the animal's fullness owed itself to cosmic influence, an inherited predisposition or sheer greed, Tanga could only guess, yet over the years The Moon gradually began to resemble its namesake.

"Do you think he's pregnant," asked Maria once.

"How can a he be pregnant?" replied Tanga. "Have you ever heard of a pregnant moon?"

Indeed, Tanga had no grounds for criticism, for as The Moon waxed, so did he. The once lithe, agile, muscular Tanga developed a belly that became the envy of many a man in the village for, as we know, a man's prosperity can be measured by his girth. And to give credence to this, The Moon was finally replaced by a tractor for drawing the plough and, from then on, he was reserved exclusively for Tanga's daily visits to the village.

Tanga soon became a familiar sight. The Moon's heavy footfall was his first advertisement and commonly this would soon be followed by The Moon itself with the rotund, moustachioed, behatted figure of Tanga riding it side-saddle. But although The Moon could already be heard far down the street, it was never long before it made its appearance for, in some strange, osmotic way, the quick nimbleness of step that typified its rider seemed to have been passed on to his steed. Many were the unwary tourists who were saved from being trampled underfoot only by a loud bellow from Tanga.

However, in spite of his nickname and the reputation that continued to linger among the older islanders, Tanga had never been seen to dance since his last evening at the miner's camp. It would be true to say that few people had even seen him walk, let alone dance, as Tanga's visits to the village were almost entirely confined to Moon-back and the only occasions when he dismounted were to unload his produce and load his purchases or to take his seat in the *kafeneion*. In fact, the gramophone, which had begun to acquire a certain antique value in addition to its mythical status, had been donated to the *kafeneion* fairly soon after Tanga and Maria were married. For a few years it saw regular service, but the advent of electricity and the introduction of the cassette player soon relegated it to a storeroom and thence to a shelf behind the bar where it kept company with an antique Turkish coffee pot and a box wrapped in faded Christmas paper. It frequently drew the admiring glances of nostalgic tourists.

Tanga and Maria had two sons and two daughters. Much to Maria's surprise, Tanga did not seem at all inclined to give them astronomical names, settling quite happily for Andreas, Giannis, Maria and Despina. In the fullness of time, they were all married and quite advantageously so. When asked if he and Maria had ever considered having more children, Tanga simply answered, "The family is full."

Sadly, Maria did not live to see her youngest daughter married. She died at the age of fifty-two from septicaemia following a burst appendix. Tanga confronted the bare fact of her death with his customary stoicism. It was clear to him that her life had completed its dance, even if the music had stopped before the final steps.

Maria's passing did little to change Tanga's daily routine. After all, what is a single death when measured against the constant waxing and waning of the seasons? Every day, he would wake early to milk the cows and goats. Every day, he would tend his fields, sowing and reaping. And every day, he would still climb onto the back of The Moon and trot into the village. However, his visits to the *kafeneion*, which had once been fairly perfunctory, were now extended somewhat. It was not that he took to drink, as many a widower has, but more for the human contact that the *kafeneion* afforded. Unlike most of his contemporaries, he had no fondness for tsikoudia and preferred to drink rum, a beverage that he had grown fond of during his years in South America. And occasionally, although he did not usually smoke, Tanga would invest some of his hard-earned money in a fat Havana cigar.

There are times, rare times, when a convergence of phenomena that are almost insignificant in themselves can have a cataclysmic result. One such rare event was to happen on a warm night in July when the moon was full.

In the urban west, where the moon is often hidden behind cloud or, even when bright and full, lies dim and distant behind a veil of pollution, its lunatic effect on people's minds is hardly perceptible. But on a small, largely barren expanse of rock like the island, where the atmosphere is as transparent as polished glass and the full moon looms huge, bathing rock and bush in its silvery glow, its effect is as real and tangible as that of a sunbed on a South London car salesman. And, given that fact, the night of a full moon is not always the best time to have a party.

The party in question was to celebrate the name day of Maria. As roughly fifty per cent of the island's female population shared that name, there were various small parties taking place simultaneously. However, at least half a dozen of those parties eventually spilled over into the main square of the village where the participants found that they all shared a common interest and informally decided to combine.

For Tanga, the name day of his deceased wife was hardly a cause for celebration but he felt, obscurely, that it should be marked in some way. And so, instead of returning to the farm after a few hands of cards and a glass or two of rum, he bought a cigar in honour of Maria and sat down with his broad back braced against the outside wall of the *kafeneion* to watch the young people enjoying themselves.

The village square was crowded to overflowing for this was not only a festival of Marias but also the tourist season. That being the case, Tanga would not normally have lingered there for very long, as the din of rock music from the surrounding bars made conversation almost impossible. In fact, Tanga's feelings on the matter were shared by many of the older generation of islanders and notably by Giannis, the proprietor of the *kafeneion*. Giannis disliked rock music at the best of times but, more than that, he resented the competition that his *kafeneion* had to face from those upstart seasonal bars run by young, smooth-talking Athenians. However, his answer to the problem, was to fight fire with fire. In this case, it meant playing his own music at a level that single-handedly matched the entire combined output of his competitors. As Giannis was rarely able to venture out of the *kafeneion* on such evenings and therefore heard no music except his own, he happily assumed that he had successfully drowned out the opposition. Unfortunately, this strategy meant that anyone on the square would find himself seated precisely at the interface of at least three and possibly as many as five different sound systems. The fact that Giannis's taste in music extended little further than the bottom ten of the Greek top-twenty did not help matters.

But as usual, no one seemed to mind the cacophony, at least, at first. Tanga, who was quietly admiring the young Marias, ordered a third glass of rum and puffed contentedly on his cigar. His thoughts turned to his own Maria and he felt a sharp jab of pain. She had completed her dance before the music had stopped. He could not help feeling that this was sadly ironic for a woman who had danced so perfectly, so instinctively, always knowing when to step forwards or back, when to bend and when to resist.

Tanga looked up through the strings of coloured lights at the scarred face of the moon. Maria had completed her dance, yet she had never been full.

It was then that Tanga's attention was diverted by some sort of dispute taking place at the bar inside the *kafeneion*. He twisted awkwardly in his seat and looked through the window. Inside, a boy and two girls appeared to be arguing with Giannis. Voices could be heard even above the din. Although he could not clearly hear what was being said, Tanga assumed it must have something to do with the music as the boy was pointing dismissively at Giannis's music centre and the girls were nodding their heads in agreement. Finally, Giannis banged the zinc of the bar with the flat of his hand, turned abruptly and pulled the electric plug out of its socket.

The effect of this was not, of course, silence but the noisy equivalent of silence. If, for example, you were to stand next to a busy street and instantly all the cars, buses and taxis were to disappear, leaving only motorbikes, the result would be comparatively the same.

"Then there will be no music at all!" bawled a red-faced Giannis. The boy to whom he addressed these words shrugged, the girls scowled and the three of them turned their backs on the outraged proprietor and slouched out of the *kafeneion* to rejoin their companions.

Tanga returned his gaze to the square and chuckled. "Well, it was not exactly the tango," he muttered, "but all the same…"

Strangely, although there was still plenty of noise in the square—you could not call it music—Giannis's action seemed to have dampened the atmosphere somewhat. It was not just the youngsters who had complained about his choice of the less fashionable end of the top-twenty and who were now subdued and grumbling; the various interrelated Maria parties also seemed to have lost their sparkle, and even some tourists looked about uncertainly, realising that things were not as they usually were.

Now that the first flush of his indignation had waned a little, Giannis himself was also beginning to question his wisdom. Music was good for trade. Most of the people in the square were young and therefore they inevitably liked music. Even more worrying was that if he failed to supply them with music, they might well resort to the neighbouring bars. On the other hand, he had a right to choose the music he played and if people did not like it, so much the worse for them. If he started playing requests, there would be no end to it.

Although Giannis was no stranger to a good idea, as was evinced by the charming strings of coloured light bulbs swaying over the square, he was, shall we say, an infrequent visitor. However, it was at this point that his true genius intervened, or rather his eyes, which, sweeping around the *kafeneion* in desperate search of anything animate or inanimate that might rescue him from his dilemma, alighted on an inanimate object behind the bar.

Quite unexpectedly, a more complex time signature intruded into the chaotic mix of four beats to the bar. It was one that strutted and halted. Fuelled by bandoneon and double bass, driven by piano and violins and caressed by the moon, the tango lurched into the square.

De noche, con la luna, soñando sobre el mar
el ritmo de las olas me miente su compás.

As powerful as the ancient gramophone still was, it could never have competed with the modern sound systems of the surrounding bars had Giannis's genius not smiled upon him. Simply by switching on a primitive amplifier and placing the microphone—which was generally used by the mayor or a visiting dignitary—in the horn of the gramophone, Giannis had succeeded in producing a volume of sound that would have been the envy of many a rock band.

The overall effect of this on the people in the square was nothing short of stunning. All conversation instantly ceased. All eyes turned to the window of the *kafeneion* from where the horn of the gramophone protruded, dribbling its length of microphone cable. And all ears recognised that this was not simply a war of noise but a totally different statement.

Yet the music had its most profound effect on Tanga.

At first Tanga, was confused. Shocked. He felt a stab of pain akin to that of remembering Maria. And then he recalled the bars and brothels of Buenos Aires and La Plata, the mining camps of San Juan, and lastly the night on a moonlit mountain side when he had led and Maria had followed.

Tanga knocked back his remaining rum in one gulp and puffed mightily on his cigar. His fingers drummed on the sticky tabletop.

Bailemos este tango, no quiero recordar.
Mañana zarpa un barco, tal vez no vuelva más.

"Tanga, Tanga, Tanga!"

Tanga looked up to see Giannis smiling at him, clapping his hands in time to the music, eyes innocently, imploringly wide, anxious to follow up his advantage.

Tanga looked away. And then a thought occurred to him. His dance was not complete. The moon was full, but Andreas Tanganis was not yet full. He pushed the table away and stepped forwards.

Despite his bulk, no one in the square took much notice of an old, grizzled farmer getting up from his chair. They did not notice him as he plodded heavily towards a space free of chairs and tables. They did not notice him as he plucked the dead cigar from his mouth.

But then Tanga began to dance *milonguero*.

At first, it was not easy. His feet quickly found the old rhythm but his body had changed since the last time he had danced. He could no longer arc backwards with his old suppleness; every dip of his body had to be carefully judged if he were not to lose his balance. Yet just as Tanga had quickly adapted to the other vicissitudes of life, he adapted to this too. After only a few seconds, he began to glide across the dirty flagstones.

Nevertheless, the tango is not like a Greek dance. It is not a solo dance. Neither does the tango dancer dance with other men.

Without breaking step, Tanga grasped the wrist of a blonde woman. If he was going to dance the tango, why not dance it with a foreigner? The tango is a foreign dance.

The woman did not know the tango and she was not Maria. She was embarrassed, flattered and amused but at least she let herself be led. Tanga led but she did not always follow. When he leant his body into hers, she leaned towards him and not away; she did not twist when he twisted. Yet the skill of a good dancer also lies in hiding the faults of your partner for few partners are equal to each other.

As Tanga and the blonde woman danced, all eyes were on them. Even the music from the surrounding bars was turned off as more people heard this new rhythm, were aware that something extraordinary was happening, and left to investigate.

…tal vez no vuelva más.

The needle hissed and then clacked noisily.

"Bravo! *Opa*! More!" came the shouts above the noise of applause. And Tanga smiled, bowed, kissed the hand of the blonde woman and then shuffled to his seat, once more an old man.

"Bravo, Tanga," said Giannis, gratefully. "You are still the best! Come now! Dance again!"

Tanga picked up his empty glass and looked at it absently.

"No," he said, replacing it. "Now I am complete. I do not need this."

Honour restored, so too was the music from the Greek top-twenty. The spectacle concluded, people returned to the bars to dance and get drunk.

"I am full," Tanga muttered, smiling, as he pushed himself out of his chair and slowly walked to the outside of the square where The Moon was tethered. As he approached, The Moon favoured him with his ancient philosophical look.

"I am full, The Moon," repeated Tanga as he clambered up the dry-stone wall in order to mount. As he threw his legs over the mule's back, he caught a glimpse of The Moon's namesake grinning ironically at the foolishness of men. And then, very strangely and very slowly, the moon bowed to him.

Ham

He had not wanted to buy ham. At least, he had not set out with the express purpose of buying it.

The fat man had rented a room for the summer. In the early days of tourism, accommodation was not easy to find but a friend in Athens had visited the island the year before and had been full of praise for a small room set high on a hillside overlooking the village. He claimed that it was idyllic, and indeed it did have a magnificent sea view, but the reality was that the room was actually a remote, one-room house with no amenities. No electricity and no plumbing. It was no more than a kilometre or two from the village but that might as well have been twenty. Yet it had a shady veranda and the view was magnificent.

The fat man had not always been fat. In his youth he had been lithe, agile and athletic but a love of food and his position as a minor though allegedly valued civil servant had conspired against him. Although he strictly adhered to a traditional Greek breakfast—a cigarette, cup of coffee and a newspaper—this was increasingly followed by an extended lunch, a siesta and then a late but rather calorie-laden dinner. Over the years, his tight abdominal muscles had atrophied and built up a protective layer of fat, a process that had gradually extended to the rest of his body.

On the advice of his doctor, the fat man had decided to moderate his eating habits, and his visit to the island seemed an ideal opportunity to try out this new regime, away from the temptations and invitations of Athens.

Breakfast would remain unchanged, but dinner would now consist of grilled meat and fish with salads. Lunch, however, which had always been a leisurely, indulgent affair, posed a problem. His response was to buy a couple of bread rolls from the baker, and then fill them with sliced cheese and perhaps tomato, before heading to the beach for some energetic swimming. After a few weeks on the island, this change of diet was already showing results: if he leant forwards slightly, he could now see the tips of his toes.

At that time, there were only two sources of food on the island apart from the pitifully few restaurants. One was a well-stocked grocery shop near the port and the other a small but singularly uninviting establishment at the opposite end of the village. The problem with the shop at the port was that not only was it too well stocked but also it was too close to the restaurants. There it was far too easy to succumb to temptation and spend an afternoon in the company of a succession of appetisers and associated beers, and idly watch the world go by—not that there was much of a world to go by in those days.

He had succumbed on several occasions.

The other shop was austere to say the least. There were no signs outside advertising suntan lotion or invitations to buy giant-size washing powder with a free plastic rain hood in every pack. In fact, there was not even a sign over the door and the windows were barred with a curious iron lattice that recalled the stained glass of ancient North-European cathedrals, but without the staining and, in some cases, without the glass. Although the building was small and painted white, it was monolithic and forbidding. It did not look like the sort of place where you could buy *paté en croûte*.

On the other hand, it was safely away from temptations, and, indeed, radiated the sort of severe inflexibility that was appropriate to a strict dietary regime. And so it was that after lapsing several times at the port, the fat man decided to grasp the nettle, take courage in both hands, and try the shop with the lattice windows.

In spite of the brilliant light outside, or perhaps because of it, the shop seemed very dark. A single, bare, fly-spotted lamp bulb dangling from the ceiling hardly compensated for the small amount of light provided by the dusty lattice windows. But there was a fragrance of fresh vegetables, herbs and other produce that elevated the atmosphere somewhat and seemed promising. There was nobody there. In a back room, behind a thin curtain, a black and white flickering suggested a television with the sound turned off.

"Hello!" shouted the fat man.

There was no response.

"Hello! Anybody there?"

He took advantage of the absence of any shopkeeper to look around the articles for sale. There was the usual stock of soap powder, without special offers, mousetraps, strange plastic culinary equipment, tinned foods, cheap brooms, brown wine in plastic bottles, and oil. There were several wooden trays full of onions, tomatoes and other fairly nondescript vegetables. Yet, there was also a modern cold display cabinet with a selection of cheeses, olives and cold cuts. The display hummed noisily in its attempts to adjust to the stifling heat.

The fat man perused it carefully. There was local kefalotyri, Danish blue cheese, feta swimming in brine, square slices of grey ham but also, to his immense surprise, a large piece of fresh, rosy Jambon de Bayonne.

He gazed at it in wonderment. Perhaps it was a fake. He had heard of food in the windows of Japanese restaurants that was made of plastic, designed to display the goods on offer to tourists. Perhaps this was a similar promotional gimmick. Yet it looked real enough. After glancing to right and left, he leant over the display case and sniffed in the fragrance of cheese, ham and olives. Somewhere within this heady mix was undoubtedly Jambon de Bayonne. How on earth had that delicacy found its way into this dark, fly-blown shop on a remote Greek island?

"Hello!" he shouted, towards the back room. "Anyone there?"

Again, there was no response.

"Hello!" he shouted louder.

"Yes?" came an answer from behind him.

The fat man turned around to see a smaller fat man smiling at him. The smaller fat man was considerably older than he, with thinning grey hair, a badly shaven chin and a thick moustache.

"I was in my garden," said the shopkeeper.

He stooped down and reverently placed two large handfuls of onions into an empty tray.

"Onions," he said, to dispel any doubts.

"Very nice," said the fat man.

"My own. From my own garden."

The shopkeeper straightened his back and winced.

"Old age is a terrible thing," he sighed. "It's a condition better suited to the young."

The shopkeeper made his way carefully to the back of the counter.

"It's hot today," he said.

The fat man agreed with this observation, although the day before had also been hot, and the day before that hotter yet. In fact, the weather had been hot ever since he had arrived.

"Yes. It is indeed hot. Now—"

"It was not like this last year," the shopkeeper interrupted. "Last year it was not so hot and we had more wind. Last year, July was very windy."

"I wasn't here last July."

"Just as well," replied the shopkeeper. "It was very windy."

For a moment, the two men stared at each other.

"Now, what can I do for you?" asked the shopkeeper, apparently getting bored with the staring business.

"I'd like a few slices of the Jambon de Bayonne," replied the fat man.

"The what?"

"This," said the fat man, pointing at it.

"Are you sure?" asked the shopkeeper.

This was not a question that any previous shopkeeper had asked. Normally, shopkeepers were only too ready to sell him anything he asked for, without warnings.

"Why would I not be sure?"

"Because no one has ever asked for it before."

"Why is that?"

"I don't know. How much would you like?"

"Perhaps four or five slices."

"Make your mind up. Four or five?"

"Five."

"Five it is."

As the shopkeeper lifted the piece of Jambon de Bayonne and placed it on the slicer, it was clear that he had not washed his hands after digging up the onions and it even seemed likely that he had not used a spade. Had this happened anywhere else, the fat man would have had no hesitation in drawing the shopkeeper's attention to this lack of hygiene and he might even have left the shop altogether. But here on the island, such a nicety as clean hands seemed almost irrelevant. The fat man reasoned that it was probably clean dirt, if there is such a thing, and that he could always wash it off in the sea.

Having secured the piece of ham on the ancient slicer, the shopkeeper paused and looked at the fat man.

"You said five slices."

"Yes."

"Then five slices it is."

The shopkeeper was just about to turn the handle of the slicer when he paused again.

"Where do you live?" he asked, as if this might have some bearing on the thickness of the ham.

"In Athens."

"Yes, I know that," replied the shopkeeper, impatiently. "That's perfectly obvious. I meant where do you live *here*?"

"Up the road. On the hillside."

"Which hillside?"

"The hillside up the road."

"Which road?"

It was the fat man's turn to pause. This was in danger of becoming a perpetual conversation that would defy the laws of physics. And the Jambon de Bayonne was no closer to being sliced.

Fortunately, just at that point, they were joined by a second customer.

"Good morning, Christo!" said the shopkeeper, beaming. "How are you today?"

The fat man turned to look at Christos. He was a small, thin man in a shabby suit with a blue, open-necked shirt. An extinguished roll-up protruded from one side of his mouth and his hands were thrust into his trouser pockets. He nodded at the fat man.

"Not too bad," he replied.

"Listen, Christo," said the shopkeeper, slicing halfway through the Jambon de Bayonne. "This gentleman here doesn't seem to know where he lives."

"That's awkward," said Christos, nodding his head.

"No," interposed the fat man. "I know perfectly well where I live."

"Problem solved then," said Christos. "Cigarette papers?"

"Here you are, Christo," replied the shopkeeper, reaching behind him and passing him a packet, now smeared with earth and ham fat. "But the question is, where does this gentleman actually live? He says, up the road and on the hillside."

"Which road?"

"No, we've already been through that. He's not sure."

"I *am* sure!"

"He says he's sure," said Christos.

"I heard what he said," said the shopkeeper.

"Then if you heard what he said, what's the problem?" asked Christos.

"Look, Christo," said the shopkeeper, scratching his moustache, "this gentleman is a tourist from Thessaloniki…"

"Athens," said the fat man.

"From Athens. Anyway, he has lost his way…"

"Not really."

"And we have to help the tourists, Christo. The mayor told us to, remember?"

"Yes," agreed, Christos, nodding sagely. "The mayor told us to."

The shopkeeper returned his attention to the fat man.

"This road of yours, sir. Can you be a bit more specific about which road you mean?"

The fat man reasoned that the only way to get his ham and proceed to the beach would be to supply the information that the shopkeeper was so anxious about.

"If you go up the main street and turn right just before you get to the bakery, there's a narrow street that goes up to the hillside."

"Which hillside?" asked Christos, pocketing his cigarette papers and spreading a few drachmas on the counter.

"The hillside that the road leads to," said the fat man. "I don't know what it's called."

"That's not much help," said Christos. "That road forks. If you take the fork on the right, it goes up the hillside."

"Exactly!"

"But if you take the fork on the left…"

"Yes?"

"It goes up another hillside. Eventually."

"You see!" said the shopkeeper triumphantly, and finished cutting the first slice. The fat man regarded this as, at least, some measure of progress.

It was just as the shopkeeper was about to cut the second slice of Jambon de Bayonne that further conjecture as to the whereabouts of the fat man's house was interrupted by the entrance of Madame Clara.

Madame Clara was a large, florid lady of doubtful age. She was not a native to the island but had lived there longer than most of the natives. Although it was said that she had been married and widowed several times, she eschewed the

traditional garb of widowhood—black with black accents—
and favoured extravagant patterned frocks with a dangling
of costume jewellery, excessive make-up, and a pink feather
boa, which was now much faded. It was also said that she had
once been the lover of the Prime Minister of Greece, although
exactly which prime minister, and when, was never specified.

"Ah, there you are!" she said to the shopkeeper, as if she
had been looking for him. "Onions!"

Christos removed his hands from his trouser pockets
and transferred his extinguished cigarette to the other side
of his mouth, as a token of respect.

"I'm just dealing with this customer here," said the shopkeeper nodding towards the fat man while successfully cutting
a second slice of ham.

Madame Clara looked at the fat man. He was clearly an
Athenian and a tourist. She smiled at him condescendingly.

"Onions!"

"All in good time, Madame Clara," said the shopkeeper,
and then paused again. "While you're waiting, perhaps you
can help us solve a problem. You see this gentleman here,
being new to the island, has lost his way."

"Well, I haven't…" began the fat man.

"So maybe you can help him out. He says he lives on the
hillside. Up from the main street if you take the right turn
just before you get to the bakery."

Madame Clara thought for a minute. It was obvious that
she was thinking because she held her index finger against
what had once been a dimple and looked at the ceiling,
fluttering her eyelashes. A fly entered the door of the shop,

buzzed around ineffectually, thought better of it and flew out again. The shopkeeper, the fat man and Christos looked at her expectantly.

"The right turn going up the street or the right turn going down the street?" she asked.

"Up," said the fat man, who was now starting to doubt whether he actually knew where he was living at all.

"And how long do you have to walk up this road before you get to your house, my dear?"

"About ten minutes, maybe fifteen."

The three men stared at Madame Clara in wonderment and expectation, but not all for the same reasons.

"And would I be right in thinking that your house is very small with a dead tree in front of it?"

"Yes."

"Maria Glaros's old house!"

"Who?" asked the shopkeeper.

"Maria Glaros. You remember, Christo; her husband died—rest his soul—and then she flew off to Chios with some big gypsy fellow. She always had a big appetite. Her son looks after the place now. Giannis."

"That's right!" exclaimed the fat man. "Giannis!"

"I told you so," replied Madame Clara. Folding her arms and shuffling her ample bosoms, which Christos much appreciated.

The fat man was much relieved. He now knew exactly where he was living and who owned it, not that he had been in any doubt in the first place.

"Thank you, Madame…" he began.

"Clara," said Clara, extending her hand, which the fat man felt duty-bound to kiss.

"Well, that's that sorted," said the shopkeeper, with a smile of satisfaction. "You did say four slices of ham, sir?"

"We'll, I said five actually," replied the fat man, "but perhaps that was a bit much, so as you've already cut two slices, I'll settle for that."

"As you wish, sir," said the shopkeeper, with a disappointed air, slowly tearing off a sheet of wrapping paper yet bundling the ham expertly. "And would there be anything else?"

"No," replied the fat man.

Tears

It was said by many on the island that Iacovina had been born crying. Although this may well have been true, and by no means exceptional in itself, the generally held opinion was that she never seemed to have entirely stopped.

As a baby, she cried incessantly. "She's hungry," was the usual suggestion, and so her parents would ensure that she was well fed. In fact, she was so well fed that she soon acquired a plumpness that, like her tears, was never to leave her.

The equally thoughtful suggestion of "it's probably wind" prompted Georgios and Maria to patiently pace up and down, gently patting Iacovina's back. But the ensuing burp merely punctuated her wailing. It very rarely stopped it.

Cures for colic were administered. The doctor was called in expensively regularly. Georgios and Maria spent many a long hour trying to keep Iacovina amused. Yet hot or cold, wet or dry, tired or not, Iacovina cried.

As the years passed, Iacovina's crying certainly became less frequent, yet it continued to be an unavoidable penalty for visiting the family home. Iacovina would cry several times a day, mostly for no apparent reason, and was never known to laugh.

Naturally, many people asked her why she was crying. Occasionally, Iacovina could point to some definite, understandable cause but, more often than not, she would simply shake her head hopelessly and continue to sob. It almost seemed—to some extent at least—that crying had supplanted talking. Or perhaps it had become a form of talking in itself.

Yet for all her crying, Iacovina was not really unhappy. In fact, for many years, her crying itself was the primary source of any unhappiness she experienced. On a material level, she had very little to lament. Georgios and Maria were comparatively well-off, and once they had accepted the fact that Iacovina would cry at the drop of a hat and more often without the hat being dropped at all, they treated her in the same way as their other children. For a girl growing up on a small Greek island in the nineteen-fifties, she received an adequate if limited education and there were few arguments if she wanted to spend a little money on herself.

Unsurprisingly, Iacovina did not marry. This was, of course, due directly and indirectly to her tearful disposition for, in spite of a certain plumpness, she was really not an unattractive girl. Financially too, she made a more than interesting match. However, every potential husband was quick to realise that even if she had been as beautiful and rich as Jacqueline Onassis, a lifetime in her tearful company would have been a poor investment.

This problem was not helped by the fact that many people regarded her as a bit touched—a judgement that appeared to have been confirmed beyond any doubt one spring morning when Iacovina was eighteen years old. Despina, a kindly but garrulous old widow, was returning homewards after feeding her hens when she came across Iacovina rolling about in a meadow and sobbing loudly.

"Iacovina!" shouted Despina, but there was no reaction from the young girl.

Despina hobbled through the long grass to where Iacovina was rolling and sobbing and saw that she was clutching handfuls of spring flowers to her tear-stained face.

"Iacovina, my dear! Is something the matter? What's happened?" asked Despina.

Iacovina looked up in surprise and saw the wizened face gazing down at her. The warm spring air was suffused with the perfume of bruised thyme.

"I...I...," she began and then convulsed with sobbing.

Despina lowered her old frame painfully to the grass and sat beside her. She bent over and gently stroked the girl's hair.

"There, there, child," she crooned.

Despina glanced hopelessly at the sea of flowers around her.

"I...I..."

Although old Despina was by no means evil tongued, she was not slow to tell her friends about the encounter and it was not long before almost everyone on the island knew of Iacovina's madness.

"Ah, poor girl!" Despina would say. "She'll be no use to anyone."

And the other old ladies of the village would shake their heads sadly.

Eventually, of course, the story, plus a few gratuitous embellishments, found its way back to her parents. They were quick to tackle Iacovina about it, but she merely burst into tears yet again, which was enough to dissuade Georgios and Maria from pursuing the matter.

So it was that Iacovina was relegated to the position of local curiosity. There was far too much competition for the role of village idiot to assure her of that status but, nevertheless, she enjoyed the major privilege allotted to that exclusive group of individuals: she was left alone. After the spring morning when Despina had found her rolling in the flowers, anyone who happened to see Iacovina crying simply put her behaviour down to her being a bit touched and left it at that.

Over the years, Iacovina withdrew even further into herself. Whether this was through personal choice or because fewer people wished to keep her company it is impossible to say. Usually, she could be found at specific parts of the island at specific times, always alone, and invariably crying. Of course, this also made it much easier for others to avoid her and in time she became no more than a familiar local curiosity and was rarely spoken about.

It was at one of these specific places, twenty-four years after Despina had found her rolling in the meadow, that she met Maeve Ahern. Or it would be more accurate to say that Maeve Ahern met Iacovina.

Maeve and her husband Donald had been regular visitors to the island for many years. They regarded it almost as a second home and, like most such visitors, they luxuriated in the fallacy that the fact that the islanders remembered their names and asked whether they had enjoyed a good winter was a mark of special status.

Not that Maeve and Donald were unfamiliar with islands, or islanders. In fact, they had lived on an island off the coast of County Galway for a little over thirty years. They knew what isolation meant. They were well acquainted with the pleasures and the perils of living in a small community.

However, they firmly believed that life on a Greek island was totally different. The most obvious difference was the climate, which meant that life was lived largely outdoors for at least nine months of the year. And then there was the open friendliness and hospitality of the people, which was, in fact, no more openly friendly and hospitable than at home.

It was also very easy to get carried away by the eternal holiday atmosphere of the place. By the ouzo, the tsikoudia and the juicy tomatoes. By the music and the dancing. And it was all too easy to reach that stage of inebriation where everyone is your friend for life and the island is the most perfect place in a perfect world.

And then, quite unexpectedly, Donald died.

Life in the closed community of a small island off the Irish coast soon became intolerable for Maeve. Naturally, everyone was supportive, occasionally excessively supportive; but all too soon this support became tinged with impatience. Yes, Donald was dead and gone and it was a great pity, but life goes on and it's time you pulled yourself together. And so Maeve felt herself obliged to rein in her tears and immerse herself in the practical, day-to-day concerns of her neighbours. She desperately wanted to talk about what a wonderful man Donald had been and about the naked unfairness of his death, but instead she found herself listening to home improvement plans and the perceived inadequacies of the Irish education system. These were issues that suddenly seemed quite irrelevant. In fact, the truth of the matter was that life on their island without Donald had lost its purpose, and yet everything and everyone she saw reminded her of him. There was no other choice but to leave the place for good.

One spring day, Maeve arrived on her Greek island, together with several large suitcases and instant access to an Irish bank account. She was greeted with surprise. Why had she arrived so early in the season? Where was Donald? Was he to come later?

On the face of it, the story of his sudden illness and death met with quite a different reception to what she had become used to back in Ireland. There was less stoic "you'll get over it and move on". People who she hardly knew received the news with grim faces; people who she knew rather better were moved to tears. There were hugs and kisses. However, recounting the story quickly ceased to become an exercise that moved Maeve herself to tears because she was obliged to constantly repeat it. Indeed, what more could you say about the pain? About the horrible, life-sucking moment of his death?

Finally, as her apparent calmness was mistaken for an ability to cope with the situation, the people around her rapidly became less mindful. Perhaps she was now expected to join the host of island widows, clad in black, mourning their spouses until their own time came. After all, the islanders were traditionally matter-of-fact about death. It did not lurk behind doors or in the dark places of the soul but stood in the open street at midday and touched all who passed.

Maeve bought a small house in the oldest part of the village. It was picturesque and dilapidated. Ridding it of cockroaches and spiders, whitewashing the walls and eventually furnishing it with the few objects that had been sent over from Ireland was a therapeutic exercise. The more she painted, the less vivid was Donald's presence. Unexpectedly, his presence had been even more intense on the Greek island than on the Irish one, for the Greek island had always meant total freedom from care while the Irish island was associated with day-to-day life, and death.

As the weeks passed and spring slid lazily into summer, she began to adopt a routine. She rose early and bought her groceries in the port, along with the other women in the village. She always ate at home, avoiding the increasingly noisy tavernas. She retired to bed early after listening to the BBC World Service while drinking a large glass of Bushmills to guarantee a dreamless sleep.

Although Maeve had been an avid reader, she now read very little. She could not face the emotional tensions of fiction, nor could she digest cold facts. Instead, she passed her time walking around the island, patiently awaiting the day when reading would no longer be difficult.

Walking also took her away from the company of friends and the forced jollity of tourists into the wildness of the island where her only companions were grasshoppers, seagulls and the occasional rabbit. When the wind allowed, she would scramble down to the rocky shoreline on the west side of the island, pick samphire and bathe in the crystal water, swimming with the wave-borne flotsam of plastic and orange peel. She seldom met other walkers there, and the islanders themselves rarely ventured into the hinterland unless it was for some specific purpose. So her surprise was great when, one day, she rounded a high outcrop of rock to see a lone woman sitting on the edge of the cliff.

Although Maeve had never seen the woman before, she looked like a local. Foreign tourists rarely went for walks without backpacks and Greek tourists rarely went for walks at all. The spot where she was sitting was several miles from the village along a tortuous and, at times, precipitous path. In fact, the path was so narrow that Maeve would have to pass within a few feet of her and some form of greeting, or at least acknowledgement, was inevitable.

"*Gia sou!*" called out Maeve, as she passed, smiling cheerfully.

The woman turned slightly to look at her and smiled weakly. Maeve saw that her eyes were red-rimmed from crying. Iacovina returned her gaze to the sea and sobbed.

Maeve stopped. She was not quite sure how to deal with this situation. Conflicting thoughts raced through her head. Why was a middle-aged woman perching on the edge of a cliff miles away from anywhere and so obviously distraught? Should she try to offer comfort? The woman would probably not understand her. Perhaps she just wanted to be left alone. Would Maeve be able to handle someone else's misfortune? Yet what if this woman was contemplating suicide and Maeve just passed by and did nothing?

"Are you all right?"

The woman did not acknowledge the question. Perhaps she hadn't heard or understood. Maeve approached to within a few feet of her.

"Is something the matter, dear?" she asked.

Again, Iacovina turned her head and gave Maeve a weak smile. She shook her head slowly.

The woman had a pretty face, Maeve thought. A bit over-weight perhaps but comfortable-looking. And kind. Whatever had made this woman unhappy, Maeve was sure was undeserved.

"Do you mind if I…?" she began, indicating that she wanted to sit down. Iacovina shuffled her skirt to one side to make more room and returned her gaze to the sea.

Maeve sat down next to her and followed Iacovina's gaze. Across a white-flecked sea, she could make out the misty outlines of distant islands. The sky, intensely blue when she looked above her, faded to powder grey at the horizon. Below them, the surf skittered across the shingle.

Iacovina sobbed and smiled.

"A man?" ventured Maeve.

Iacovina sobbed again and smiled, lowering her eyes.

"I thought as much. They're all bastards," said Maeve, sharply and conventionally. "Even the best of them. Who is he? Your husband?"

Iacovina sobbed quietly.

"Thought so. Mine's dead. "

Maeve took a long look at Iacovina. The Greek woman's face was turned to the horizon. Large tears rolled down her cheeks as she listened.

"A thief, that's what he was," continued Maeve, in a soft, hard voice. "He robbed us of our future. We were going to get old together, you see. No children so there'd just be him and me forever. And he took it all away, the selfish bastard."

Maeve paused and felt the tears welling. She was aware that the Greek woman was looking at her and smiling. Was it an ironic smile? Maeve's eyes were fixed on the horizon and she did not turn to see. Below them, a dazzling seagull skimmed low over the dark waters, wheeled, ascended effortlessly into the blue and hovered against the freshening wind.

"I shouldn't speak ill of him. He wasn't selfish really," she said in a low voice. "He was as kind a man as you'd ever meet. A bastard for leaving me but kind with it. Not that I'd ever make him out to be a saint, mind you. A saint he never was. Just human, like the rest of us."

The other woman had switched her gaze back to the view in front of them. There was something eloquent about her silence. Something that transcended all of the inadequate, well-intentioned advice that she had listen to so many times.

"I could have done more to help him. Dear God, if only I'd noticed the signs in time! If only I had, he'd be living yet. I didn't deserve the...I didn't deserve him. When I think of the times I was mean to him—really mean, mark you—I could die of shame. And now it's too late to say sorry."

Maeve sobbed. And the felt a soft hand stroking her hair. It was the slightest of pressures, like a butterfly alighting on a petal. The woman was still gazing at the horizon with its dusting of islands as the tears rolled gently down her cheeks.

"But what does sorry mean anyway? Just a word, isn't it? Fine words butter no parsnips. Real regret you feel in your heart and he must have known I felt it. Felt it just like he felt it. Because he could say things that were hurtful too, even though he didn't mean them. That's the trouble with words—they never describe how you really feel."

Quite gracefully, Iacovina gently withdrew her hand and replaced it in her lap. She gazed out over the sea with her wide eyes brimming with tears.

"*Oreia*!" she said.

"What?"

But the Greek woman made no answer.

"Oreya?" repeated Maeve.

Iacovina turned to her and smiled. It was a smile of understanding and a mutually shared truth.

Iacovina's smile persuaded Maeve that this kind lady was not about to launch herself over the cliff in a last expression of grief, rejection or unrequited love. There was nothing agitated or desperate about her. A fellow sufferer, her tearful companion was exorcising her demons in the same way as Maeve herself was doing.

"Oreya," she said again, and got up to leave.

"Thank you for this."

Over the weeks that followed, Maeve's thoughts often returned to that unexpected meeting on the narrow, cliff-top path. During that time, her life began to change. She rose later, went to bed later, and ate in tavernas instead of always cooking at home. She no longer avoided the companionship of her friends. Gradually, she began to read again.

Donald never entirely left her thoughts but her memories of him grew ragged about the edges. They were mellow and pleasant.

"Tell me, Anna," she said one evening to her oldest friend on the island. "What does oreya mean?"

"Oreya?" asked Anna. She arched her eyebrows and then laughed. "Oh! You mean *oreia*!"

"Whatever," said Maeve.

"It means beautiful."

It was several months later when Maeve found herself on the same spot where she had met Iacovina. The summer was over; the crowds had disappeared to their own lands in the north. Maeve had not set eyes on Iacovina since the day of their meeting and had not thought to ask about her. In fact, there was little to ask about as she did not even know her name. At the most, she could have asked after a middle-aged Greek lady who spoke excellent English, and that, she knew, would have led nowhere.

Maeve sat down on the narrow ledge bordering the cliff. She remembered, with regret, that she had never thought to ask after the real source of the woman's tears. Such is the egocentricity of grief.

On the horizon, the dusting of islands emerged from the haze and turned to gold as the sun completed its day's journey. The sky was empty and dark; the sea a black empress flecked with silver. Land, sky and sea merged.

That's the trouble with words—they never describe how you really feel.

"*Oreia!*" said Maeve.

And cried.

Football

Grigoris had never wanted to live on an island. He had never wanted to be a priest. At the time when this vocation was imposed upon him, he had been a talented defensive midfielder at the Iraklis Football Club in Thessaloniki. Far from aspiring to a bishopric, his ambitions focused on improving his dribbling and tackling, moving across town to join the far more successful PAOK F.C., and, perhaps, playing against Barcelona or Manchester United one day. Or preferably *for* them. To make matters worse, he had just married.

Maria was a pretty girl. She had screamed with joy when Grigoris beat two defenders, squared the ball to Sampras and volleyed the return pass into the top of the net.

She had groaned in anguish when Iraklis suffered another defeat.

She loved the idea of being a footballer's wife.

When his older brother, Apostolis, was killed in a car accident, Grigoris never imagined that this sad event would have a major impact on his chosen career. That became apparent only when he returned to the family home after the funeral.

"You know what this means for you, of course," murmured his father as he poured himself a glass of brandy. Family and friends had left; the only people remaining in the dark, heavily draped sitting room were Maria, Grigoris and his parents.

Grigoris's glass was empty. He glanced uncertainly at Maria, who was demure in black.

"No. What?" he asked.

His father reclined in his antimacassared armchair and sipped his drink. His mother stared at her husband with a mixture of anxiety and dislike.

"It means you will have to follow Apostolis into the church."

As if on cue, a car with a broken silencer roared up the street outside.

"You're not serious!"

His father glared at him. Out of the corner of his eye, Grigoris could see that Maria had frozen. Her mouth hung open slightly.

"Of course I am, Grigori! The firstborn son of this family has always gone into the church. You know that."

"But I'm not the firstborn. Apostolis was. I'm a footballer."

"And now you're a priest," said his father, without looking at him.

You did not argue with Grigoris's father. The Nazis had tried it once and had come off worse. Grigoris became a priest. Maria eventually reconciled herself to the fact that she would never live in Barcelona or drive a Ferrari, but she still entertained some hope of living in Athens and being the wife of a bishop.

Unfortunately, this too was a forlorn hope. At the age of twenty-five, Grigoris was sent to the islands.

"A godforsaken island!" a heavily pregnant Maria had shouted.

"I'm sure there are no places that God forsakes," replied Grigoris, with the adaptability that had made him an effective midfielder.

"It's the back of beyond!"

"We'll have to make the best of it."

And that is what they tried to do. However, for Grigoris, being sent to the island was like being consigned to a fourth-division team on a free transfer. If he had enjoyed a sense of vocation, had really believed in his ability to serve his congregation well, or had even believed wholeheartedly in God, his job might well have been easier. As it was, none of the above applied.

God was a thorny problem. Although Grigoris has been brought up in an extremely religious family, which had ultimately led him to his present situation, he had never regarded the hand of God as particularly effective, except in football. And even there he had seen players cross themselves before taking to the pitch and still be substituted in the first half, or even carried off on a stretcher. God so much loved his pious brother Apostolis that He saw fit to put a motorway bridge in his way at the precise moment when he lost control of his car. As a good priest, Apostolis had never worn a seatbelt. His fellow priests had assured Grigoris that this had been God's will, but Grigoris himself was doubtful.

Maria was embittered by what she considered a downturn in their fortunes. After their arrival on the island, she continued to brood, in the course of which she gave birth to two children. As the wife of the priest, she was expected to take an interest in local affairs, which she did somewhat grudgingly. When the children grew up and left for Athens, Maria's involvement in such affairs became correspondingly seldom. But most importantly, she had lost her respect for Grigoris. Why had he succumbed to his father's wishes so obediently? Why had he not renounced his holy orders instead of being sent out meekly to the island? It was bad enough to be married to a priest instead of a footballer, but to a weakling?

Grigoris himself adopted a different way of adapting to the setback. He conducted his official duties impeccably, from daily services to christenings, marriages and funerals and celebrated the Resurrection at Easter with all due solemnity. In fact, no one within living memory—which became correspondingly shorter as the years passed—had ever heard the liturgy performed better.

However, Grigoris considered that his duties to his congregation ended once he had left the church. At Iraklis F.C., it was normal to have a beer with the lads after training and especially after a match. Grigoris saw no reason to change this. Sadly, most of the islanders did not share his view. And the lads were not there. Grigoris continued to have a drink, usually ouzo, after the match but did so in the privacy of his home.

He never mentioned his previous life as a footballer and, unsurprisingly, no one ever asked.

Grigoris's one act of rebellion was the way he treated his parishioners when they came to ask advice. In the absence of counsellors or psychotherapists, this happened fairly often. Unless their problems were extreme, which was relatively rare, he did not particularly care about them. As advice, he fell back on the proverbs that he had heard as a child.

A good example is when Adonis the barber had difficulty with land that he wanted to sell to a foreigner. Adonis believed that the land belonged to him, while his brother equally believed that he was the rightful owner.

Adonis knocked respectfully on the door. It was opened by Maria, now a stout, energetic woman who looked Adonis up and down as if he were a Gypsy selling chairs.

"I've come to see Pappa Grigoris," mumbled Adonis, aware that all eyes in the village were on his back, which, of course, they were not.

Maria gave him a cold look.

"Then you'd better come in," she said, opening the door wider.

Grigoris was sitting at the kitchen table in his vest. In front of him, on the blue, plastic tablecloth was a plate of anchovies, a fork, a bottle of ouzo, a glass, an ashtray, a packet of cigarettes and a lighter.

"Adoni," said Grigoris, correctly identifying his visitor. "What brings you here?"

And so Adonis told him. Not in great detail but sufficiently to cover the main points. Grigoris paused to fill his glass and take a sip. He expertly speared an anchovy with his fork, ate it, lit a cigarette and inhaled. All six actions were undertaken with the smooth, almost seamless fluency that he had shown as a player.

"So, what is your question?" asked Pappa Grigoris, exhaling and munching his anchovy.

"Can you talk with my brother?" replied Adonis. "Make him see reason."

"Ah!" exclaimed Grigoris, and took another sip of ouzo. He gazed at the wall ruminatively. "In an honourable enterprise, there must be no delay."

"So, you will do it?" asked Adonis eagerly.

"Do what?".

"Talk to my brother?"

"I will think about it," Grigoris modified, scratching his beard. "Better to do a little well than a great deal badly."

"What?" asked Adonis.

"What?" replied Grigoris.

"You said something about doing a little badly."

"Did I?"

And then Grigoris turned suddenly confidential.

"Adoni," he said, slowly and deliberately, gesturing towards him with his glass of ouzo and raising an eyebrow, "when an oak has fallen, every man becomes a woodcutter. And sweetest is the life that is untroubled by thought."

"Pappa Grigori," said Adonis, in an attempt to turn the discussion from the proverbial. "My brother is cheating me. He has no right to this land. It was given to me by my father."

Grigoris's glassy-blue eyes focused squarely on Adonis. He reached out and touched him lightly on the arm.

"Listen to me, Adoni," he replied, in a tone almost of admonishment. "One cherry tree will not hold two jays."

"But we are not two jays!" protested Adonis. 'I am an honest man! It's my brother who is the thief!'

Grigoris helped himself to another forkful of anchovies.

"A bent log…can never be straightened," munched Grigoris, nodding his head sadly.

Adonis watched as Grigoris's head nodded slower and slower and finally settled comfortably on his chest. To confirm that the priest was indeed sleeping, a small, almost inaudible snore escaped his lips, from which the tail of an anchovy was still protruding.

"A bent log…" mumbled Grigoris.

Adonis stood up quietly and made for the door.

"Gold is useless to the dead!" boomed Grigoris, and then relapsed into snoring.

Strangely, no one ever complained about Grigoris's proverbs, although Adonis himself was far from satisfied. He very much doubted that his brother would admit to being a bent log, and express a belated desire to be straightened, thereby resolving the matter of ownership. But perhaps he had taken Papa Grigoris's advice too literally. When all was said and done, were not oracular pronouncements supposed to be impenetrable?

Although she had once hoped for it, Maria had never really expected her husband to become something big in the Church any more than she had actually thought it possible to move from Thessaloniki to the Costa Dorada, or even Manchester, and as the years passed, she more or less resigned herself to being the wife of a local priest. After almost forty years of marriage, they had settled into a routine. Although her lack of respect for Grigoris had not really diminished, it was by no means a preoccupation. Her affection for him outweighed that. She knew that basically he was the same long-haired footballer she had fallen in love with. His hair was as long as it had been then, longer in fact, although his boisterous, fun-loving nature was now hidden beneath a cassock and his smile beneath a beard.

It was just when Grigoris was starting to seriously contemplate the possibility of retirement that the local council announced that a football pitch would be built. As there were few level areas of the island that had not been built upon, a redundant car park was repurposed and resurfaced. The local children embraced this idea with enthusiasm and made great use of it, sometimes even for football. But it was considered that a new pitch needed a team to play on it.

It was not an easy matter to recruit eleven willing teenagers. First of all, there were not many teenagers on the island anyway and even fewer who were interested in football. Those who were fond of sports at all tended to favour basketball, and, in one case, golf. However, a team was duly formed, a bar owner was appointed trainer, and football kit was issued.

The island's new team was admitted to the football league for the surrounding islands and the first matches were scheduled. However, as Grigoris would certainly have appreciated, it is easy to lead a horse to water but occasionally a matter of the greatest difficulty to get it to drink. The island's new team ran out onto the pitch for their inaugural match, resplendent in their new kit and full of enthusiasm, to be eventually thumped 12-1. The "consolation goal" was actually an own goal scored quite deliberately by the opposition's goalkeeper, who felt sorry for his opponents.

Grigoris had not viewed the formation of the island's football team with alarm, but he did experience a little trepidation. Since he had joined the priesthood, he had eliminated football from his life entirely. Why torture yourself with what might have been? He never even read the sports pages, much less listen to, and later watch, football matches. Yet, despite his resolve not to pursue football, football appeared to have pursued him.

The island was a small community and the fortunes of the local football team became a regular subject of interest and speculation. The 12-1 defeat had been followed by a 7-0 drubbing and then an extraordinary 15-0 battering at the hands, or more accurately the feet, of the regional favourites. It was at this point that Grigoris decided to attend a game, if only to see how any team could possibly concede 34 goals in only three matches.

Fittingly, the day was overcast. It had rained earlier and the uneven bitumen, which constituted the pitch, was covered in pools of water whipped up by a gusty wind. These were by no means ideal playing conditions, but the opposition was not greatly deterred. The score line was flattering at only 6-0.

Grigoris watched from the touchline, his black cassock blowing in the wind. He watched as players were robbed of the ball, gave away the ball, failed to close down attacking play. And yet, here and there, were slight sparks of talent.

"If all the bees made honey, there would be enough for even Gypsies to eat," muttered Grigoris, as he trudged homewards.

"You went to the football," said Maria, pausing in her cooking.

"Yes."

"And?"

"Awful," said Grigoris. "Not many individual skills. Some of them have promise. They lacked passion."

"Passion?"

"Self-belief."

"Oh."

On the day of the following home game, the weather had improved. There had been no rain and the surface of the former car park was dry, but there was a bitter wind blowing in from the north-east. All of the players looked correspondingly miserable, particularly those from the home team, whose heads were down even before kick-off.

Come on, thought Grigoris. You can win this. You're not playing against Bayern Munich, for God's sake.

But a win seemed far away when the opposition scored, and then scored again.

By the sixty-fifth minute the onslaught had lessened a little. A watery sun emerged that seemed to taunt the home team. The defensive players passed the ball around aimlessly at the back. The island's lone striker—the best player—wandered around the opposition's half, bereft of a telling pass.

"Hoof the ball up to him!"

The shout came from a woman standing next to Grigoris. He looked and saw Maria. He stretched out his hand and she took it in hers.

Perhaps one of the island's defensive players heard her. Nobody was quite sure afterwards. Whatever the cause, the player hammered the ball skywards. Blown by the wind, it arced sideways, away from the frustrated striker, and directly towards Grigoris.

As the ball was kicked, Grigoris watched it rise and instinctively let go of Maria's hand to adjust his position slightly to the left. The ball had been kicked high and took a long time to reach him. As it descended, it was as if his life seemed to pass before him—the promising career, the bitter disappointment for Maria and himself, the difficulty of reconciling God and life.

The ball struck Grigoris in the middle of his chest.

Dulled for so long, his eyes became suddenly bright, piercing and focused. Expertly cushioned, the ball bounced slightly into the air before Grigoris, his black cassock and beard fluttering, swivelled, allowed for the wind, and volleyed it twenty-five yards over the head of the forlorn striker, beyond the reach of the goalkeeper, and straight into the top left of the net. His hat fell off.

Once he had recovered from the shock, the referee from Syros rushed up to Grigoris and brandished a red card. He must have surely realised that it was a useless gesture. Grigoris was not a member of the team or even its coach, and moreover he was a priest. If anyone was authorised to give him a red card, it was probably God.

"How did you do that?" muttered Christos, who was standing behind Maria.

"I don't know," replied Grigoris. "Maybe I learnt it at Iraklis. I used to play for them."

And then he looked at the island's weary players and smiled at Maria.

"Blessed are the poor in spirit."

Grigoris's goal being obviously disallowed, the island's team went on to record another defeat, yet this time it was only 2-0. A game later—an away match—they achieved their first victory, due in no small part to their new coach.

Rabbits

"Fish," said Captain Bennos, staring the fat man in the eye.

"Fish?" repeated the fat man.

"And grilled octopus, village salad, potato salad, tzatziki, taramasalata, aubergine, stuffed tomato…" Captain Bennos added absently, gazing across the empty tables to the far corner of his restaurant where six octopus dangled like ragged flags from a length of barbed wire. "…and that sort of thing."

"But, don't you have any meat?" asked the fat man, mopping his brow with a handkerchief. "Lamb, perhaps?"

Captain Bennos shifted his gaze back to the fat man and smiled the slightly sad, indulgent smile of a doctor who has just listened to a patient's attempt at self-diagnosis. He drew up a chair to the fat man's table and lowered himself onto the rush seat. He tossed back his head and clicked his tongue.

"Fish," said Captain Bennos, fixing the fat man with a penetrating stare.

The fat man was beginning to regret stopping at the little taverna. It had been a hot drive along the rough road that traversed the island north to south and petered out in a dusty delta of precisely and optimistically laid-out dirt streets that had, as yet, no houses. It had been a pleasant surprise to find that Agios Nikolaos offered any form of refreshment at all, let alone a taverna.

Admittedly, it had looked a fairly modest taverna to say the least, but it had a certain charm about it in a rough-and-ready way. There was no written menu to help out a simple tourist, not that the fat man had really expected one. In fact, the only concession to literacy at all was a fly-blown notice consisting of a leaf torn from a school exercise book and bearing the cryptic words "Trips round island with Captain Bennos. Ask me or him" written in English in black marker.

And now, this same Captain Bennos was staring at him with sharp eagle's eyes, his brow furrowed in concentration, waiting to volley an expected return of service.

"No chicken?" the fat man offered, weakly.

Captain Bennos was visibly disappointed. He could have been usefully prolonging his siesta without having to waste a prodigious talent for irony and metaphor on the fat man's pathetic attempts to procure something other than fish.

"No chicken," affirmed Captain Bennos.

The Captain raised his hand, lifted off his blue fisherman's cap and placed it carefully on the table. Then he slowly and very deliberately scratched his balding, white-haired head before replacing his cap again. Captain Bennos grinned, displaying a mouthful of disturbingly white, even teeth that were quite possibly false.

The man's certifiable, thought the fat man. He's as mad as they come.

As if reading his thoughts, Captain Bennos sprang up from his chair with surprising agility for a man of his years and, for a moment, looked as if he were about to confirm the fat man's opinion of his sanity. Yet instead, Captain Bennos disappeared into the kitchen to return a matter of seconds later with two plastic water bottles and two glasses, one small and one large, which he placed on the table in front of his customer.

"Thank you," said the fat man, slightly taken aback at this sudden, over-extravagant display of hospitality. Gratefully, he filled the larger of the two glasses and gulped down half of its contents at a single draught.

Now it is a regrettable fact that visitors to the island, particularly enthusiastic foreigners bent on sampling something uniquely Greek that is, probably for excellent reasons, virtually unobtainable abroad, rarely manage to get a good glass of tsikoudia. It is true that, when asked, virtually every bar and taverna will supply this local spirit, which shares some of the best and most of the worst characteristics of French eau-de-vie or Italian grappa, but invariably it is watered down. The semi-official reason for this is to prevent drunkenness on the part of the enthusiastic foreigners but the reality is that it extends the stocks of this sacred liquid by approximately thirty per cent.

Yet thirty per cent was a quite unknown concept for Captain Bennos. His tsikoudia was little changed since it had dripped like purest water from the still. And so it was that the fat man drank the pretty well unexpurgated version of Benno's Best at a single gulp.

It is a tribute to the fat man's stoicism and tenacity—that same stoicism and tenacity that had driven his ancestors to the far ends of the earth in Alexander's triumphant army and kept him pushing ever onward to the south of the island as the rear axle of his dented Lada groaned ominously—that he successfully managed to stifle any outward sign of his mistake. The tsikoudia coursed down his throat like a river of flaming magma but failed to transmit its glow to the fat man's cheeks. He did not cough and his eyes remained dry. The only indication that his glass had been full of anything but water lay in the slightly unnecessary force with which he replaced it on the table.

Since first entering the taverna, the fat man had not had occasion to speak very much. Those few words that he had uttered had mostly referred to vain attempts to order any sort of meat and beyond that he was not prepared to venture much further. This was just as well since, after a hefty measure of Benno's Best, he was now no longer in a position to venture anywhere.

Captain Bennos grinned and watched the fruits of his efforts with quiet satisfaction. The fat man may have been physically unprepossessing, with the verbal dexterity of a jellyfish, but he clearly knew a good tsikoudia when he tasted one. After all, he had distinguished it from the bottle of water at a glance. Grinning even more, with eyes twinkling, Captain Bennos generously topped up the fat man's glass.

Even though he had not drunk any tsikoudia himself, Captain Bennos found himself warming to the fat man. While it was undoubtedly true that no one but an idiot would expect to eat lamb or chicken at Agios Nikolaos, the fat man was clearly not just another snobbish, demanding Athenian. He probably deserved better.

For his part, after the initial shock, the fat man was actually starting to enjoy not only the tsikoudia, but also the taverna, Captain Bennos, Agios Nikolaos in particular, and the island in general. Captain Bennos grinned at the fat man and the fat man smiled back. And yet the question of the meal had remained unresolved and even in the midst of his euphoria, the fat man could feel the growing pangs of hunger. He took a further sip of Benno's Best.

"So there's no meat. Only fish," he said, after a long pause.

"Only fish," confirmed Captain Bennos, with a distinct note of apology.

And so the fat man ordered fish with village salad, tsatziki and stuffed tomato and sat back to await his meal. Captain Bennos disappeared into the taverna.

It was, indeed, a glorious afternoon, thought the fat man. The sun was sparkling on the sea in brilliant silver flecks. A warm, calm breeze whispered in the bougainvillea. Apart from the distant sounds of a dog barking and once, uniquely, the crack of a shotgun, he might have been alone at the end of the world. He sipped thoughtfully on the tsikoudia and emptied his mind of all the worries and anxieties that life in Athens brings with it.

It was just as the fat man's chin was beginning to nestle comfortably into his chest and thoughts of his imminent meal had given way to that delicious blankness that precedes a satisfying snooze that he was awoken by someone or something licking his hand. Startled, the fat man looked down to see a large, friendly dog. Its owner, who was just climbing over the wall that separated the taverna from the rest of Agios Nikolaos, was carrying a shotgun and a small, furry object.

"...and rabbit," said Captain Bennos.

Over the years, the story of Bennos, the fat man and the rabbit was retold innumerable times, mostly along with similar anecdotes that illustrated Bennos's odd behaviour and strange sense of humour. Many assumed that the story was entirely apocryphal, although most of the people who told it would go to great pains to assure their listeners it was not. Those who gave it credence felt certain that its source could only have been the fat man, for it was certainly not Bennos himself, nor was it the rabbit.

Bennos's taverna gradually extended its menu. This was largely due to road improvements. It was now possible to drive all the way from the village to Agios Nikolaos in little more than half an hour, and without the risk of substantial damage to the vehicle. As the taverna already had a well-established reputation for fish, Bennos reluctantly bowed to public demand and added goat and chicken to his bill of fare. This significantly increased his clientele. The addition of an infrequent bus service increased it even further.

Ten years after the fat man had or—according to some— had not eaten rabbit, Bennos sold his taverna to an Athenian. Up to that point, the restaurant had had no name at all and was popularly referred to as 'Bennos', or sometimes just 'the taverna'. Now it was officially called 'Taverna Bennos'. In fact, a large sign in blue lettering on a white background with artfully painted dolphins proclaimed it as such. According to village gossip, Captain Bennos had objected violently to this theft of his identity, but the new owner had maintained that he had bought the taverna as 'Bennos' and 'Bennos' it would stay. Village gossip also claimed that Captain Bennos had threatened to build a new taverna next to the old one and call that 'Bennos' too but, fortunately for tourists, this remained no more than gossip.

There were two main reasons for Bennos's decision to sell the taverna. One was that he was offered a lot of money for it and the other was that his failing eyesight was making it difficult to conduct his business efficiently, not that it had ever been conducted very efficiently in the first place.

It was fifteen years after the experience that had entered local legend that the fat man returned to Agios Nikolaos.

During the intervening years, he had not grown significantly fatter but he had become balder and wealthier. The direct descendent of the dented Lada that had almost failed to return from Agios Nikolaos was a new Mercedes, with heated seats that could be switched off and air-conditioning that worked.

Agios Nikolaos had changed too. The magnificent view was still the same, but the optimistically laid-out streets now hosted a smattering of villas with neat gardens. To the fat man's disappointment, 'Taverna Bennos' was much larger than he remembered from the days when it had no sign at all. There was a blackboard with 'Today's specials' written in English. Each of the modern tables had place-settings, upside-down wine glasses and vases of wilting flowers. Apart from a party of six blond-haired tourists at the far corner of the restaurant, he was the only customer. That was not surprising as it was late in the afternoon, too late for lunch and too early for dinner. The sun was rapidly descending towards the horizon, twinkling on the water and already tingeing the mountains with blue.

The fat man took a seat at a table in the corner and picked up the menu. It was bound in warm, brown plastic and felt like a book.

"Good evening, sir," said a young waiter. "Would you like some water while you decide?"

"No, thank you," he replied, while flicking through the menu. "Do you have any fish?"

"Of course, sir."

"Rabbit?"

"Sadly, not today, sir."

"Do you have any tsikoudia?"

"What?"

"Tsikoudia. Tsipouro. Raki."

"Oh, you mean local ouzo. No."

So, the fat man ordered a few small dishes from the menu, a small carafe of white wine, and sat back to wait. His wine arrived, which was perfectly chilled and not from the island, or even from the next island. The waiter poured it for him.

It was when he took his first sip that he noticed an old man sitting alone near the entrance to the kitchen.

The man was not eating. He was sitting next to an empty table, leaning on a stick, and staring at the bay and the islands beyond through large pebble glasses. Like fifteen years before, he was wearing a frayed, collarless shirt with the sleeves rolled up, a pair of dark trousers that might have been grey or brown with the cuffs rolled up, and a blue fisherman's cap pulled down at the front. His feet were bare.

Captain Bennos had aged considerably. His tanned, leathery face was a mass of wrinkles, large and small, radiating from his eyes and mouth. Small tufts of white hair protruded from his ears and from under his cap.

The fat man's first thought was to introduce himself and hope that Bennos would recall an afternoon long ago when he had tried to order meat. Yet, on reflection, it did not seem very likely that the old man would remember him, so the fat man ate his meal, ordered more wine, and watched the sun dip under the horizon. He was just about to catch the waiter's eye and ask for the bill when he saw Bennos lean on his stick and bend forwards, with every sign of standing up and leaving.

"Captain Benno!" he shouted.

Bennos slumped back onto his chair and looked around; the fat man eased himself from behind his table and approached him.

"Captain Benno. Remember me?"

Bennos squinted up at him. His eyes, unnaturally blue, seemed to swell to the size of the entire convex lenses in front of them, giving him the air of an alien in a cheap science-fiction movie.

"Yes."

"You do remember me?"

"Yes, of course I do. Did you like the rabbit?"

The fat man laughed.

"It was delicious. I think I told you so at the time. Although it took many hours to prepare, as I remember."

Bennos grinned his perfectly aligned grin.

"It takes no time at all to shoot a rabbit but a long time to cook it," he said, and gestured to the chair opposite.

"Sit down."

The fat man did as he was ordered.

"Are you in good health?" asked Bennos, gravely.

"Not too bad."

"And your wife and children?"

"I don't have a wife and children."

"Lucky for you."

Bennos removed his glasses and polished them on his shirt. The fat man noted that, for all that they might now be far less efficient than the new restaurant, his eyes still twinkled with mischievousness and sly cunning.

"I heard you have no rabbit on the menu now," ventured the fat man.

"It never was on the menu," replied Bennos. "Besides, it's not my menu anyway. It's not even my restaurant."

That seemed logical in view of his age.

"Tsikoudia?" asked Bennos, replacing his glasses with a sly grin.

"They don't have tsikoudia here."

"They do if you ask properly."

Whatever the proper way of asking for tsikoudia was, it duly arrived on their table in the form of an unlabelled one-and-a-half-litre plastic bottle accompanied by two Duralex glasses, which were made in France and practically guaranteed to bounce from a tiled floor.

"I remember you with more hair," said Bennos, filling the glasses. "*Gia mas!*"

The fat man brushed a hand over his smooth, sunburnt pate and smiled ruefully.

"*Gia mas*! I remember *you* without glasses."

Bennos carefully removed his spectacles, stared at them, and shrugged.

"I don't really need them," he said.

The fat man looked at the thick lenses.

"Really?"

"My eyes are certainly good enough to see those girls over there," chuckled Bennos, gesturing with his stick to the table of foreigners.

The fat man followed Bennos's gaze to the table of blond Scandinavians, all of whom were male.

"Not bad then," he agreed.

"They could be better," conceded Bennos. "If I could see perfectly, I wouldn't need these."

And he tapped the pebble glasses.

"I suppose there's no more hunting now," said the fat man.

"Hunting?" replied Captain Bennos, admiring the Scandinavian men at the far side of the restaurant, who had now paid their bill and were about to leave.

"Rabbits."

"I thought you meant girls," said Bennos, wistfully. "I'm getting a bit old for girls, to tell you the truth, but I can still look."

"No, I meant rabbits. You seemed to be a pretty good shot fifteen years ago."

"I still am."

The fat man coughed politely.

"Isn't your eyesight a bit of a problem?"

"Only for the rabbits."

The fat man smiled indulgently and took another large sip of Benno's Best.

Captain Bennos sighed in exasperation, knocked back his tsikoudia and refilled their glasses. He could see that the fat man had no readier a wit than he had had fifteen years ago.

"Let me explain," he said, carefully. "When is the best time of day to hunt rabbits?"

"I really don't know," replied the fat man, never having hunted rabbits, or anything else for that matter.

"At night," said Bennos. "That's when all the rabbits are out and about, doing whatever rabbits do. The trouble is that you can't see them. And that's why most people hunt in the twilight, just before it gets dark. Or in the early morning just before it gets light."

"I see."

"But because of my eyesight, I can hunt in the dark."

The fat man nodded.

"You can hunt in the dark?"

"Yes."

"How?"

"You may have noticed that I have a slight problem with seeing in the daytime. This is to be expected when you have a slight problem. But on the hillside at night, with my new glasses, my slight problem goes away and I can see as perfectly as an owl."

The fat man scanned Captain Bennos's face for any sign that he might be being teased but the older man stared back at him earnestly. To add further conviction, he wiped his glasses on his shirt and put them on.

"The rabbit is a mysterious animal," he said. "Beloved of Aphrodite. Wait here."

This was a rather unnecessary instruction as the fat man had not considered going anywhere at that point. Bennos got up from the table, with an energy surprising in a man of his years, and stomped into the kitchen.

It was a warm, still evening. The Scandinavian men had left. A young couple with a toddler and a baby hovered uncertainly at the entrance to the taverna before being intercepted by a young, enthusiastic waiter.

A mysterious animal beloved of Aphrodite? What sort of nonsense was that?

There were raised voices from inside the kitchen but the fat man could not hear what was being said. He thought back to fifteen years earlier when Captain Bennos had appeared with a small, bloody animal that was later cooked and served. This time, he appeared with a shotgun.

Bennos grabbed his glass of tsikoudia and downed it in one.

"Follow me."

The fat man would have liked to protest but there was no time. Shotgun in one hand and walking stick in the other, a half-drunk and possibly half-mad Captain Bennos led the way out of the restaurant and into the blackness outside, with the fat man waddling after him apprehensively.

He had every reason to feel apprehensive. Even when his eyes had adjusted to the dark, he had no other option than to follow in Bennos's footsteps. When Bennos barked his shins on a rock, the fat man barked his shins too; when Bennos stumbled into a gulley, he inevitably followed him.

It did not help that the fat man was not dressed for hunting, or even scrambling around on hillsides without hunting. When he had arrived at Agios Nikolaos and stepped out of his air-conditioned Mercedes, he had been wearing a linen suit, white cotton shirt and a blue, silk tie. After only ten minutes of walking, he stuffed his tie into his jacket pocket;

after fifteen minutes, he slipped off his jacket and slung it over his shoulder.

Half an hour later, they arrived at a juniper tree. Even though the fat man was panting and fearful of a heart attack, even though his shirt was sticking to him like a second skin and his linen trousers were ripped, he still paused to marvel. The juniper was magnificent. It seemed to draw the night sky down upon it. It was a tree that had thrust itself, twisting and bending, out of the arid, stony soil. A tree that had survived when all the odds were stacked against it.

"This is where we sit," said Captain Bennos, following the words with the action. He did not say this in the hushed tones of a hunter or a narrator of wildlife documentaries. He said the words at a normal volume and sat down with his full force and a curse. Greatly relieved, the fat man sat down too.

"Now, if you look behind that tree, you'll see a hole," said Bennos, rubbing his bare feet.

The fat man peered round the tree and saw only blackness.

"I can't see a hole," he whispered.

"Eh?" said Bennos. "You'll have to speak up, I can't hear you if you whisper."

"I can't see a hole," repeated the fat man, in a normal tone.

"And you think *I'm* blind!" said Captain Bennos. "It's over there to your right."

The fat man looked to his right and dimly but quite distinctly in the flitting moonlight, at a distance of about twenty metres, was what looked like a hole.

"Well, I can see a hole, I think," he said. "But I don't know whether it's the hole you mean."

"How many bloody holes do you think there are?" asked Captain Bennos, irritably. "Now, watch it until you see something move."

And having said that, Captain Bennos, leaned back against the juniper tree and lit a cigarette.

"I didn't know that you smoked," said the fat man.

"It attracts the rabbits."

An hour passed. An hour is a long time to stare at a hole in the dark and there were moments when the fat man became distracted. Chief amongst those distractions was wondering why he was on a hillside, in the dark, staring at a hole. However, it has to be said that there were moments when his attention wandered too far.

"You're not looking at the hole."

"Yes, I am!"

"No you're not. I was watching you. You can't expect to shoot a rabbit if you don't look at the hole."

And so the fat man continued to look. His bones ached; his right leg with the ripped trousers was raw and bleeding; he was hungry.

Bennos was on his third cigarette, when the fat man finally fancied that he caught a glimpse of movement.

"I think I can see something moving," he hissed.

"Can you?" replied Bennos, taking a long drag on his cigarette and stubbing it out on a rock.

"It could be a rabbit."

Bennos gave a long sigh.

"Then it probably *is* a rabbit. Which side of the hole is it on, left or right?"

"What do you mean which side is it on?" said the fat man, his former apprehension returning rapidly.

"Just tell me. Saves time," muttered Bennos.

"The left side."

Captain Bennos put down his shotgun, fumbled in his pocket and withdrew his pebble glasses. He put them on very carefully, bending the wire frames around his ears.

"Left side, you said?"

"Yes."

Bennos nestled the shotgun into his shoulder, steadied it against the trunk of the ancient juniper, and squeezed the trigger.

There was an ear-shattering crack that echoed around the mountainside and flew out across the sea. It was a much louder crack than fifteen years before, but it was unmistakably the same crack. The hole exploded in a puff of dust.

"Did you get it?" exclaimed the fat man, excitedly.

Captain Bennos laid down the shotgun and rested his back against the juniper.

"You'd better take a look," he said. The fat man caught a glimmer of white that was probably Bennos grinning.

It took a few minutes for the fat man to scramble up to the hole and return.

"Well done, Captain!" he crowed, holding aloft a large and perfectly dead rabbit. "What a beauty!"

"Eh?" said Bennos, removing his glasses.

Bennos stared at the rabbit in wonderment. The fat man stared at Bennos with admiration. The rabbit just stared.

In the faint moonlight, the fat man saw Bennos's chest convulsing. He began to make alarming wheezing noises.

"Captain Bennos!" he shouted, scrambling towards him across the hard rocks.

Bennos gave vent to a ghastly choking gurgle, and then exploded into laughter. His laughter was almost as loud as the crack of his shotgun and reverberated far across the moonlit hillside and back down to the taverna far below. He clasped both hands to his belly. Tears rolled from beneath his spectacles. Not content with that, he levered himself to his feet and performed an improvised sirtaki under the juniper tree.

"I hit it!" he sang. "I hit it, I hit it, I hit it!!"

The fat man stared at him dumbfounded.

"But didn't you expect to hit it?"

Captain Bennos removed his spectacles and wiped the tears from his eyes.

"Of course not," he replied.

The eight of spades

Almost all the land bordering the sea was barren. It was as if the island had wished to shake off everything that was infertile but had succeeded in moving it only as far as the shoreline. Ever since the island was first inhabited, millennia earlier, this continuous strip of rock and scrub had been a stark, scarred no-man's-land between the rich farmland of the interior and the wealth of the sea beyond. It had no value. It was worthless.

Worthless until the arrival of the first tourists. The tourists were not farmers, neither were they fishermen. To them, the sea was neither an enemy nor a source of income. It was, to the mystification of the islanders, an attraction in its own right. The foreigners would spend all day lying in the devouring heat of the sun, half or fully naked, until their bodies were burnt and painful. And they would literally rub salt into the wounds by constantly dipping in the sea. When they were not engaged in these bizarre practices, they would stare at the water for hours as if they expected something to emerge from it at any moment. At the end of the day, they would gather to watch the sun dip below the horizon, just as it had always done.

And naturally, when the richer tourists reasoned that building a house on the island was preferable to renting a room every year, when they wished to purchase a part of the island that they had come to love so dearly, they chose to site their new holiday homes as close to the sea as possible.

This was altogether to the satisfaction of the islanders. Suddenly the worthless strips of land bordering the sea had acquired considerable value. In fact, some islanders who had previously been counted as poor, because the only land they owned was the rocky, thorny littoral, became millionaires overnight. Drachma millionaires perhaps, but millionaires nonetheless.

This development did not escape the notice of Adonis. Admittedly, he noticed it relatively late in the day, when villas had already started to spring up all over the island, but he was by no means the last to jump on the land-selling bandwagon. For him, however, selling otherwise worthless land to foreigners was not simply a question of acquiring hard cash for its own sake: he needed the money to finance his plans. His ambition was to build rooms for the tourists on a small piece of land that he owned close to the village—an investment for the future. Apart from his own home, this plot and a small stretch of coastline was the only property he owned, or at least the only property that his parents had left him once his elder brother Vassilis had received his share. His father had died of a heart attack when Adonis was twenty-one; his mother died of a broken heart eighteen months later.

He had expected Vassilis to inherit the farm, although it did seem unfair. The farm provided his brother with a steady if unspectacular income, although it would have been slightly more spectacular if Vassilis had had any interest in farming and less interest in gambling. Vassilis won at cards regularly, and lost even more regularly. In fact, it was thanks only to his wife that he had not already gambled away the farm.

The two brothers had once been close but a five-year age gap had been significant. When Vassilis was conscripted into the army, Adonis was only thirteen. When he returned, two years later, Adonis was still at school, reading comics and listening to Led Zeppelin. By that time, thanks to the army, Vassilis was already hooked on gambling.

Apart from the endemic purchase of lottery tickets and a raffle when someone was lucky enough to catch a big fish, gambling was not widespread on the island, in fact there were only five or six men who met infrequently in the back room of Apostolis's bar in the port. They all fancied themselves cardsharps, but no one was particularly adept. All the same, large sums of money would sometimes change hands. Happily, because no one was particularly adept, the money would often work its way round to the original loser.

Adonis had had several girlfriends but, as the village barber, he was far from an attractive catch. He learned to cut hair when he followed Vassilis into the army and later fell back on it as one way of making a living for a man who did not own farmland or a boat. The women would take the ferry to the big island to have their hair styled but this was a needless luxury for the men.

Adonis always treated his customers with courtesy and respect, and as his customers included all those men who still had hair and chose not to have it cut at home, he soon acquired a reputation for politeness and honest dealing.

It would be untrue to say that Adonis resigned himself to being unmarried; it was more that he had not yet met a woman who was prepared to accept him for what he was without looking at his bank balance first. He still lived in hope, although it has to be said that his sights were set unrealistically high, as was evidenced by the dusty, creased picture of Sophia Loren, torn from a magazine and pinned next to the mirror in his shop.

Adonis found it relatively easy to sell his property. He constructed a makeshift sign and hammered it into the hard earth on the corner of his plot. It bore the words "For Sale" with his telephone number. He also mentioned the sale to virtually all of his customers, who promised that they would tell any foreigner who was inquiring about land. And as Adonis was well respected on the island, it was from this quarter that the eventual offer came.

The prospective buyer was Swiss—a retired businessman from Lucerne by the name of Moritz Huber. Herr Huber had been a frequent visitor to the island for many years and made it known, through an interpreter, that Adonis's plot of land commanded one of the finest views on the island. Adonis had never regarded the view as particularly fine but he was thrilled, and not a little surprised, that Herr Huber was willing to pay the asking price of fifty million drachmas. Adonis had very little understanding of the law, so he secured the services of a lawyer from a neighbouring island to conduct the sale.

Mr Margaronis was a tall, thin man with a nicotine-stained moustache. He struck Adonis as rather languid and off-hand, but then Adonis had no more understanding of lawyers than he had of the law.

Once the sale contract had been signed, Adonis could not wait to start developing the plot of land next to the village. After all, the fifty million drachmas were simply a one-off windfall; his future prosperity would be assured by the new rooms for the tourists.

So rather than wait to receive the fifty million drachmas from Herr Huber, Adonis decided to start work immediately. If the contractors worked efficiently and did not waste too much time drinking beer, some of the rooms would be ready to receive guests by the time next year's season began. However, Giorgos, the local contractor. was understandably reluctant to start work without seeing at least some money in advance.

"There are materials to buy," he explained. "And, of course, I have to pay my men."

"But I'll have the money soon. Why wait until then?"

Giorgos stared into the middle distance and sighed. Then he nodded his head.

"Look. Normally I would insist on half of the money now and the other half on delivery. But you're a good man, Adoni. I trust you. Tell me, do you have any money in savings?"

Adonis looked embarrassed. He was not used to discussing his private affairs.

"I have some money put by," he muttered. "Not much though. For my old age."

"Well, you won't need that now, will you?" laughed Giorgos. "Not when you have your rooms and apartments! How much do you have?"

"A hundred thousand drachmas. A little less," said Adonis, shrugging.

Giorgos sucked his teeth.

"A hundred thousand drachmas. Well, it's not much, but I suppose it will do as a gesture of good faith. Give me the hundred thousand now and the balance of the first instalment when you get it. We'll start work next week."

Adonis paid him and Giorgos was as good as his word. Early the following week, workmen descended on Adonis's plot of land near the village and began clearing away rubbish and digging up the boulders that a beneficent God had generously strewn across the island when it was created. When time allowed, Adonis would go to the building site and watch the work, occasionally asserting his proprietorship by making some quite unnecessary suggestion as to how it might be done quicker, more efficiently or, at the very least, differently.

However, there was no further news about the money from the sale.

Adonis telephoned Mr Margaronis frequently but the lawyer offered no explanation for the delay. What he did offer was invariably a long, complicated monologue on the various legal aspects of buying and selling property that was interspersed with equally long digressions on anything that took his fancy. After a relatively short time, Adonis began to suspect there was definitely something amiss and so he finally insisted on a personal meeting to find out exactly what was happening.

Mr Margaronis's office was a small room on the first floor of a nondescript concrete building in the biggest town of the neighbouring island. It was an oppressively hot day. In an effort to obtain some small ventilation, Mr Margaronis had opened the windows but by no more than a few inches for fear of the wind blowing away valuable documents that were scattered on every available space. Mr Margaronis was sitting behind a large heavy desk that was covered with papers and dusted with cigarette ash. His short sleeves were rolled up; his face was beady with perspiration.

"Adoni! Do take a seat!" said Mr Margaronis, indicating the simple wooden chair on the opposite side of his desk.

Adonis sat down and glanced about him. If Mr Margaronis's success as a lawyer could be measured in terms of the number of documents that his office contained, then his affairs were certainly in good hands.

"You've come about the sale of your land, of course."

"I've heard nothing," said Adonis. "About the money, that is."

Mr Margaronis coughed alarmingly. He reached into his pocket, withdrew a silk handkerchief and mopped his brow.

"Infernally hot, isn't it?" he said.

Adonis nodded but did not reply.

Mr Margaronis stared at a large, battered filing cabinet that was erupting paper and then, apparently, decided to cut to the chase.

"To be honest with you, we've hit a snag."

"A snag?" What sort of snag?"

"I was hoping that the matter would resolve itself but… that doesn't seem to be the case," said the lawyer, weakly.

"The Swiss does not want to pay?" asked Adonis, fearing the worst.

"No, no, no!" exclaimed Mr Margaronis. "It isn't that. It's more a question of ownership."

"Ownership?"

"Who owns what."

Adonis looked puzzled.

"I don't understand."

Mr Margaronis paused, slid a long cigarette out of a silver case, lit it and puffed a large cloud of blue smoke across the office.

"A claim has been made that you are not the outright owner of the land you are selling," he said, with some apparent relief at having got the unpleasant fact off his chest.

"Who says this?"

"Your brother," replied Mr Margaronis, regarding him levelly through the smoke.

"Vassilis!"

"He claims that your father left the land to him."

"This is not true, I swear it," protested Adonis. "He left me this land. He said so on his deathbed."

"Did your father leave a will?"

"Of course he didn't. No one on my island makes a will. We trust each other."

"Well, it seems that your trust was misplaced. Your brother is quite adamant that the land belongs to him and that you have no right to sell it."

"Then he's a liar!" shouted Adonis. "A liar and a thief!"

Mr Margaronis took a deep drag on his cigarette and then stubbed it out without finishing it.

"When your father bequeathed the land to you, were there witnesses?"

"I don't know…no…I was alone with him."

"That is unfortunate," said Mr Margaronis. "But I'm afraid it's all too common. There are many such cases. Sometimes as many as five parties or more lay claim to a piece of land. Naturally, the land in question rarely gets sold."

"This brother of mine is a liar," muttered Adonis.

"That may be so," said Mr Margaronis. "But, in law, your claim is no stronger than his."

"So, what am I to do? What about the Swiss? He will now look for land elsewhere."

"I have informed Herr Huber of the delay," said Mr Margaronis. "I told him that there was a small legal issue that would soon be resolved. He seems content to wait. He will probably buy the land anyway, regardless of whom he buys it from. In the meantime, I suggest that you talk to your brother and try to come to an arrangement."

"With Vassilis? You might as well talk to a donkey!"

"I can see no other alternative," said Mr Margaronis, with an air of finality.

There was a storm approaching. The daylight had turned a sickly yellow and the air in Mr Margaronis's office to warm treacle. Adonis stood up, shook a thin, bony hand and left.

"Talk to your brother," Margaronis had said. His brother Vassilis had smelt money to pay his gambling debts. There would be no talking to him but, indeed, what alternative was there?

"I was expecting you, little brother," said Vassilis, gesturing towards a seat.

Adonis did not sit down.

"You told the lawyer that you own my land," said Adonis bitterly.

"*Your* land?" retorted Vassilis. "Since when has it been *your* land?"

"Since our father gave it to me."

"Our father did no such thing," said Vassilis, smiling. "He gave the land to me. I heard it with my own ears."

"No he didn't!"

"Can you prove it?" replied Vassilis, calmly. "As I see it, you've taken my land and sold it to a foreigner."

Adonis could not help noticing that there was little of value left in Vassilis's home. Even the television set had gone.

"Fifty million drachmas is a lot of money, little brother, "said Vassilis. "Far more than you need to build those rooms of yours. So, I'll tell you what. Let's say to the lawyer that we have agreed to share the property fifty-fifty. You can build your rooms and we will all be happy."

"And your fifty per cent would be gambled away, I suppose."

Vassilis's lips crisped to a pencil line.

"How I spend my money is my own business, not yours."

Adonis turned and made for the door. But he paused at the threshold.

"But it is not *your* money, Vassili," he said, calmly. "God will judge."

"Good! Then I have nothing to fear, *malaka*!" shouted Vassilis at his brother's retreating back.

For a time, Adonis waited patiently for God to judge, however He appeared to be occupied with more pressing matters. To give Him a helping hand, he decided to visit His representative on Earth. However, Pappa Grigoris seemed even less inclined to co-operate.

"Short back and sides," muttered Christos, with a dead cigarette clamped firmly in his mouth. "And a bit off the top."

Christos visited Adonis's barber's shop every few months. Given the fact that Christos's lack of hair was roughly proportionate to his lack of money, Adonis cut it for free.

"So you've sold that land of yours," muttered Christos. The sale of the worthless strip of land bordering the sea was now common knowledge.

"No, my brother Vassilis says he owns it."

"Does he?"

"Yes."

"Tough luck," muttered Christos.

"No, I mean that's what he says," replied Adonis, pausing his comb and scissors. "He doesn't own it. Our father left it to me."

"Well, that's all right then," said Christos, brightly.

"No, it's not all right."

"Why not?"

"I have no proof that the land belongs to me."

"You just said your dad left it to you."

"He did, but I have no paper."

"Ah! Paper!"

Christos blessed his lack of literacy and the fact that his brother had died twenty years ago of acute dermatitis, or so he had been told. Adonis considered snipping some of the hairs protruding from Christos's ears, but thought better of it.

"Have you asked Pappa Grigoris for help?" suggested Christos.

Adonis laughed humourlessly.

"Pappa Grigoris? Yes, and I listened to the usual string of proverbs. He told me that one cherry tree will not hold two jays and that gold is useless to the dead. He also told me to talk to my brother, which I'd already done. It didn't work."

"He was right," murmured Christos. "One cherry tree will not hold two jays."

Adonis paused behind Christos's left ear.

"Have you ever seen a jay, Christo?"

"Maybe. I can't remember. What's a jay?"

Adonis was very tempted to take an accidental snip at Christos's left ear, but thought better of that too.

"Pappa Grigoris talks in riddles," he said. "He may be right about gold being useless to the dead, but I'm alive and so is Vassilis. As to the jays…"

Adonis set down his comb and scissors, slumped onto the wooden chair next to the barber's chair and held his head in his hands.

"Vassilis will settle for fifty per cent," he mumbled. "Perhaps I should agree. But it won't be enough money to build my rooms. And Giorgos has already started work; I've given him all my savings."

Christos took advantage of the break in hair-cutting to relight his cigarette. He took a deep drag and exhaled a plume of smoke against the cracked mirror in front of him. He reached over and ruffled Adonis's hair.

"What price is this foreigner paying for the land?"

"Fifty million drachmas."

"Fifty million drachmas?"

Christos thrust his hand forcefully into his trouser pockets and spat the remains of his cigarette onto the floor. Adonis stubbed it out with the toe of his shoe.

"That's half a billion lepta!"

"I suppose so."

Adonis was not only surprised at Christos's mathematical agility, but also that he chose to express the amount in the lowest denomination in Greek currency. On reflection, he assumed that Christos was more at home with leptas than with drachmas.

"So?"

Christos withdrew his hands from his trouser pockets. One of them clutched his tobacco tin and cigarette papers. He opened the tin, pinched a few strands of tobacco and began to roll them in a cigarette paper. He licked the paper, finished the rolling, reached for his matches, struck one, lit his cigarette, blew out a plume of smoke, and nodded his head thoughtfully.

"Adoni, listen to me. Your brother Vassilis likes to gamble. We all know this. He plays cards at Apostolis's bar in the port. In the back room. For high stakes."

Adonis inclined his head in agreement. Christos spat out a loose strand of tobacco and stared at his feet.

"Many years ago, I was a merchant seaman, Adoni. Nothing fancy. Not a captain or anything. I helped out in the kitchens. Did what I was told. Weeks at sea with nothing to do. Men would gamble to pass the time. I watched."

"Well?"

"They would win."

Christos paused significantly.

"And they would lose."

Adonis nodded his head. This was not a great revelation. Christos flicked his cigarette ash onto the floor.

"Are you going to finish cutting my hair?"

"Yes, of course," said Adonis, picking up his scissors and comb. He set to work again. He had not asked Christos for advice—why would he?—and now he just wanted to be rid of this simple old man as quickly as possible.

"Mostly, they lost."

"Really?"

"Yes."

Having successfully rendered the thin hair on the top of Christos's head even thinner, Adonis turned his attention to the sides.

"They never knew they were going to lose until they lost."

"Understandable."

"They always thought they would win."

"Well, they would think that."

"It's why they kept on gambling, even though they lost."

Adonis paused yet again and glared at Christos's reflection in the mirror.

"Is there some point to this, Christo?

Unfortunately, he could not point out that other customers were waiting, as there were none.

"The point is," said Christos, "Vassilis can't help gambling. If you wager your fifty per cent against his fifty per cent, he'll take the bet."

"Are you suggesting that I gamble with him?"

"Yes."

"Vassilis has been playing cards for as long as I can remember. The last time I played cards I was about five years old."

"I will teach you."

"You?" said Adonis, with a wry smile.

"Yes, me. I told you I watched people play. Not just on the boats. Also, in the back streets of Alexandria and Constantinople."

"Poker?"

"Yes, poker. But you will not be playing poker."

The room at the back of Apostolis's bar was practically airless and stiflingly hot. The only ventilation came from a tiny window giving onto the yard behind, covered in dirty mosquito gauze. Crates full of bottles, full and empty, were stacked against the wall. Illumination came from a single, naked light bulb hanging high above the card table.

Vassilis was already sitting at the table when Adonis and Christos entered. So too were some of his gambling cronies—all familiar to Adonis and Christos—who had come to watch Vassilis win twenty-five million drachmas from his younger brother, and perhaps have a few hands of poker afterwards. The room was blue with cigarette smoke. There was a bottle of Johnny Walker on the table, already half empty.

"Good evening, little brother," said Vassilis, with a smile.

"Good evening, Vassili," replied Adonis, taking the seat opposite him. Christos took up a position behind him and stuffed his hands into his trouser pockets.

Vassilis took a slug of whisky, wiped his mouth with the back of his hand and lit a cigarette.

"Are you sure you want to do this?" he asked.

"Why not, Vassili?"

"Surely, you must know I will win."

"There is always a winner and a loser, or so I've heard. There is always a chance. If I don't do this, there will be no chance at all."

"Of building your rooms?"

Adonis nodded. He was already sweating, but thankfully so were the others.

"Want a drink?" asked Vassilis, shoving the bottle of Johnny Walker towards him.

"Yes, but water. It's hot in here."

Apostolis duly provided a bottle of water and a glass. Adonis filled the glass to the brim.

"*Gia mas*!" he said, raising his glass and drinking its contents.

"*Gia mas*," replied Vassilis, doing likewise.

"Nervous?" he asked.

Adonis shrugged.

"Fine. Let's get down to business. You get to name the game. Poker? Straight, stud, draw?"

"No, not poker."

Vassilis leant his head to one side and squinted at his brother.

"Not poker? What then?"

"Three-card monte."

"Three-card *what*?"

"Monte."

This was the response that Christos and Adonis had hoped for. It had been a gamble, and perhaps it would turn out to be the biggest gamble of the evening. Since Vassilis had never left the island after his two years of national service ended, and had therefore never frequented the back streets of Alexandria and Constantinople, it was a reasonable assumption that he had never heard of three-card monte either, or witnessed its effects.

"I don't know the game."

"You don't?" exclaimed Adonis, with relief. "It's the simplest game in the world, big brother! I deal three cards face down. One of them is the ace of spades. I shuffle them around and then you have to pick the ace. If you guess right, you win."

"Are you mad? Where's the fun in it? We might just as well split the deck and the highest card wins."

"That's even less fun."

Vassilis looked his brother in the eye and grunted.

"There's got to be some sort of trick in this."

"How can there be a trick? Three cards. One of them is an ace. And you know all about tricks, don't you, Vassili?"

Vassilis bit his lip. Was his brother a complete idiot—as he had long suspected—or was he actually very smart? It was the second gamble of the evening.

"Look," said Adonis. "There are no tricks here, Vassili. Christo?"

"Yes, boss," replied Christos.

"Let's show my brother."

Adonis drew three cards from the deck, one of which was the ace of spades. Having shown them to Christos, he flipped them face down, deftly picked them up, two in one hand and one in the other, dropped them onto the table and shuffled them quickly. Vassilis watched intently.

"Which one is the ace, Christo?"

Christos bent over the table with his hands in his pockets and shook his head from side to side. Vassilis shuffled on his chair with the impatience of a schoolkid who knows the right answer to a question but is not called on to answer it. The other gamblers, and Apostolis, leant over the table.

"It's the one in the middle" said Christos.

Vassilis smacked his forehead with his hand and took another gulp of whisky. The other gamblers chuckled.

Adonis turned over the card in the middle.

"Sorry, Christo. It's not your lucky day."

"It was the one on the right, obviously!" said Vassilis, seeing his twenty-five million approaching rapidly.

"Let's see," murmured Adonis, turning over the card on the right.

"And it is! Good thing for you that you weren't gambling, Christo. And a pity that you weren't, Vassili."

Christos removed his cap and scratched his head. He looked at the ace of spades with a puzzled expression. The other gamblers laughed.

Vassilis topped up his glass and lit another cigarette.

"I've seen enough," he said. "Let's get down to it."

"If you're sure."

Vassilis roared with laughter.

"Sure? Of course, I'm sure."

And then he looked at Adonis solemnly.

"But are *you* sure, little brother. You never struck me as a gambling man. You will lose twenty-five million drachmas."

"Easy come, easy go," replied Adonis, nonchalantly. But he felt sick with fear. If the light in the back room had not been so dim, everyone would have seen his white face. If the room had not been so unbearably hot, they would have noticed his perspiration. Thankfully, his hands were not trembling.

"Then I salute you, Adoni!" said Vassilis, raising his glass. "*Gia mas!*"

"*Gia mas!*" Adonis responded and raised his glass of water.

He picked up the three cards, two in his right hand and one in his left. He did not need to remember what Christos had taught him because he had practised the moves hour after hour.

Vassilis's eyes never left the ace of spades.

Fortunately, Adonis had been a barber for many years. Cutting hair well was not only a matter of manual dexterity but precision. And the circumstances were also in his favour. The light was dim and a few glasses of Johnny Walker had further affected Vassilis's attention. The ace of spades, which Vassilis had watched carefully, did not drop in the place that he expected. It did not fall first, but last.

With a smile of satisfaction, Vassilis reached out and turned over a card. It was the eight of spades.

He froze.

"I could have sworn that…"

Adonis shrugged. Christos permitted himself a brief smile. Vassilis's bravado had instantly vanished. He glared at the cards.

"It looks like you have your land, little brother. Bravo."

And then Adonis said something that nobody in the room expected to hear.

"Best of three?"

Vassilis gazed at him in amazement, as did everyone else.

"You're giving me another chance?"

"Yes."

Christos looked sideways at Adonis. This had not been in the script.

Vassilis shook his head.

"You must be mad."

"You cheated me," said Adonis.

Vassilis picked up his glass and slammed it back on the table.

"I did not…"

"And I cheated you."

Christos took a step backwards from the table. This was not only not in the script; it seemed that, carefully crafted as it had been, the script had now been torn to shreds and tossed away.

"*You* cheated *me*?" said Vassilis, in a loud voice. "When? How?"

"Just now."

Vassilis looked bewildered. The befuddlement of Johnny Walker did not help.

"There is only one player who will win a game of three-card monte," said Adonis, calmly, "and that is the player who deals the cards."

"So you cheated!" shouted Vassilis, glaring at him.

"Yes, I cheated," said Adonis. "But you only have my word for that. Would you take me at my word?"

Adonis looked around at the spectators.

"Did anyone see me cheat?"

Someone coughed but said nothing. Apostolis feigned interest in the stacks of empty crates.

"No?"

He turned back to Vassilis.

"No one saw me cheat, Vassili. So perhaps I did not cheat at all, although I just told you that I did."

Adonis gathered the cards from the table and flexed them in his hands.

"Remember when we were young, Vassili?"

Vassilis had been about to raise his glass to his lips, but instead he replaced it gently on the table.

"I played with your old toys when you'd grown out of them. You taught me how to catch octopus in my hands. You used to chase me over the hills. Sometimes I chased you, but you were always faster. Do you remember?"

"Of course I remember," said Vassilis, gruffly.

"Since those days, we have lost each other," continued Adonis. "I regret that, and I think you do too."

Vassilis looked as if he were about to say something, but then just nodded.

"You cheated me and now I have cheated you. Only you and I know that. And about the land…it's pointless to argue about who was to blame—things are as they are. It's up to us to make the best of it. But whatever happens, we are brothers."

Vassilis lit a cigarette.

"What did you say this game is called?"

"It's not a game. It's called three-card monte."

"I would prefer one-card monte," laughed Vassilis. "Let's play it again."

"Are you sure?"

"I'm sure."

Adonis picked up the cards. This time, he ignored the lessons that Christos had taught him. When he dropped the cards, they fell naturally. A child could have followed the ace of spades.

Vassilis hesitated. He looked Adonis straight in the eye. It was not the sardonic, mocking look that he usually reserved for his younger brother. He reached out, without shifting his gaze from Adonis, and tapped a card.

Adonis turned it over. It was the eight of spades. Vassilis did not even look at it.

"The land is yours, Adoni," he said. "And with it comes my respect."

Christos smiled, nodded, and left the room.

Clara

When Madame Clara arrived on the island, she had just turned thirty-six. She knew the island from her childhood when she had visited it in the summer with her parents; when fishing boats had sails and donkeys were the only mode of transport. They had stayed in a villa—the first on the island—which her father had had built on an attractive location overlooking the port. It was quite modest but luxurious by the standards of Greek islands at the time. It had three bedrooms, a spacious living room and running water thanks to a well in the garden connected to an electrical pump powered by a noisy diesel generator. The generator also provided electric light.

Clara had fond memories of playing with the local children. They would jump from the jetty and splash about in the crystal water. She would invite her friends to the house to wonder at the bright miracle of electric light. They would make sandcastles on the beach, and dig channels so that the sea would flood them with moats, canals and lakes. And they would talk.

She would talk most of all to Eleftheria. Eleftheria, or Elly as everyone called her, was a smaller girl on an island of small girls. She was shy and bookish, to the dismay of her parents who were neither.

One day, when the boys had grown tired of throwing stones and leaping into the water and the sun was setting behind them, casting long shadows onto the bay, Eleftheria took Clara's hand in hers.

"I want to be an actress," she whispered.

"An actress?"

"Yes, like Melina Mercouri or Katharine Hepburn. Strong women."

Eleftheria was anything but strong.

"Why do want to be an actress?"

Eleftheria leant her head against Clara's shoulder and shuffled her feet in the warm sand.

"Because when you're an actress, you can be anyone."

Clara's visits to the island stopped when her father died. He was killed early on a Sunday morning on Vasilissis Amalias Avenue on his way to the family home in Athens' fashionable and expensive Kolonaki district. He had been drinking with friends in a bar in Plaka; it had been raining; he was riding too fast, swerved to avoid a bicycle that had swung out in front of him, and then there was a delicate swishing sound as the rear wheel of his 650cc Triumph Bonneville came unstuck from the asphalt. I'm going, he thought, before his bike thudded into the kerb and catapulted him into the air.

He was a doctor. He had always warned his patients against drinking to excess and riding a motorbike without a helmet.

Clara's mother was devastated; she retreated into the depths of their large house and saw no one. As an only child who loved her mother dearly, Clara was distraught at the change that her father's death had wrought and began to devote her life to her mother's care. Her mother passed her days alone in a stifling, dark room made all the darker and more stifling by heavy, velvet curtains that were always half-drawn. She watched television. Clara would bring her meals on a silver tray, with a linen napkin carefully ironed and folded. She would help her to bed, help her to undress, and hold her hand until she slept. It was a pattern that was repeated day after day for years.

In spite of this, Clara went to university to study medicine, but abandoned it after her second year. She had wanted to be a doctor only because her father had been a doctor and she had grown up listening to his stories of saving lives, improving lives, and prescribing antibiotics. Beyond that, she had no sense of vocation at all. So, rather than burden the Greek population with another unmotivated physician, she went to work in a perfume shop in Kolonaki. It was close to her home, safe and undemanding.

She was successful at selling perfume and quickly realised that a woman who entered the shop looking for a cheap scent could easily be convinced that a slightly more expensive fragrance suited her better. Elegant ladies who had been accustomed to the same perfume since their youth could be similarly seduced. And, of course, there were men—husbands and lovers who wished to present their darlings with an expensive perfume that the women in question probably did not like and the men could ill-afford.

Notably, there was Madame Anastasia. Anastasia means "resurrection" and, indeed, she looked like she had been resurrected several times and not always very successfully.

Madame Anastasia was always accompanied by a large man in a grey suit who stood exactly two metres behind her at any given time. He wore dark glasses, would constantly scan the shop, and scowled a lot.

Madame Anastasia favoured extravagant dresses, diamonds—which were clearly genuine—and always a bright pink feather boa.

"You're obviously new here." said Madame Anastasia, dismissively. "You can't possibly know what I want."

Clara thought for a moment.

"You're quite right," she said. "I really don't know what you want."

Madame Anastasia glanced at her and gave a faint smile. She managed to look down at Clara although she was slightly shorter.

"I want my usual," she said, airily.

"Your usual what?" asked Clara.

"Perfume. Don't be obtuse, dear. *L'air du temps*. Nina Ricci."

She reached up and twisted her hair girlishly.

"Parfum or eau de toilette?"

"Parfum, of course."

Clara brought her a bottle and placed it on the counter.

"Thank you," murmured Madame Anastasia. Stroking her boa.

"Have you ever considered something else?" asked Clara, bluntly.

"Never. I have always worn *L'air du temps* and I always will. It's *my* scent."

Yet, when Madame Anastasia left the shop, the bottle of *L'air du temps* was still on the counter and she was perfectly convinced that the new girl understood her wishes perfectly. Whenever she returned to the shop, the fragrance that Clara had recommended always preceded her entrance by at least a few seconds.

In time, Clara learned a lot from Madame Anastasia, but little about her. It was said, by the older members of staff, that she was the mistress of the Minister of Education and Religious Affairs, which seemed at first to be fairly plausible. She was certainly well-educated but rather less religious, as was confirmed several years later when Madame Anastasia gave her the following advice:

"My dear Clara, whatever you do in life, steer clear of the church. Firstly, it is run by men and if that were not enough, it scolds us for being sinful."

As Madame Anastasia never revealed anything about herself, Clara eventually ascribed her supposed liaison with a cabinet minister to pure invention. In fact, the only thing that anyone knew for sure about Anastasia was her name, and only her first name at that.

For several years, she was always accompanied by the large man in the grey suit, whose presence she totally ignored. His appearance, watchfulness and silence suggested that he was a bodyguard although why she needed one was a question that only added to her air of mystery. One day, Madame Anastasia arrived at the perfume shop without him. She offered no explanation for his absence and he was never seen again.

What Clara gained from Madame Anastasia was slowly absorbed over a long period of time. Anastasia was not physically attractive; her features were sharp and almost masculine, accentuated rather than softened by heavy makeup. Perhaps to compensate for this, she was fond of brightly coloured, extravagantly feminine dresses, her ubiquitous pink boa, and diamonds.

Clara and Anastasia could not have been more different. At the time they met, Clara had dressed austerely. Her hair was cut severely short in stark contrast with Anastasia's perfectly coiffed and clearly dyed curls. Although she worked in a perfume shop, and to the despair of the owner, Clara had never used perfume herself, or even much makeup for that matter. On the other hand, she was tall, slim and probably thirty years younger than Anastasia, although that too was as uncertain as everything else that related to the older woman.

Although Clara and Anastasia met only a few times a year, they developed a certain sort of friendship. It was far from a conventional friendship as neither knew anything about the other, or felt inclined to ask. However, Anastasia's imperious approach seemed to soften, while Clara gradually began to adopt some of Madame Anastasia's mannerisms. She started to look down her nose at customers, physically, given her stature, but also metaphorically. Surprisingly few of her customers regarded this as an affront; many seemed to expect it from an employee of a distinguished perfume shop in Kolonaki. She started to address many customers—although notably not Madame Anastasia—as "my dear". This was accepted and valued as a sign of intimacy.

She also began to introduce some colour into her wardrobe. Her first venture was to invest in a Hermès scarf, which used up at least half of her monthly shop-assistant's salary. To the delight of the shop's owner, makeup swiftly followed; eyeliner accentuated her newly adopted half-closed eyes, and she began to pluck and colour her eyebrows into elegant arches.

Her mother was not moving. Clara placed the silver tray with the carefully folded napkin in front of her. She had served her a cup of tisane and a plate of her favourite *loukoumades*. The television flickered meaningless images on the heavy, velvet curtains. On the screen, two men with moustaches were shouting at each other. She heard audience laughter.

A week later, a box was placed on the counter at the perfume shop. It was delivered by a small woman dressed in black who turned on her heel and scurried out before anyone fully realised that she had been there at all. The box was covered in cheap wrapping paper and "To Madame Clara" had been scribbled on the top. It contained a pink boa. Clara took it out reverently, sniffed its heavy fragrance, and draped it around her neck.

As soon as she alighted from the *kaiki,* Clara removed her shoes. It was spring and the concrete jetty was warm but did not burn her feet, although the short walk along the sand and pebble seafront to the family villa was painful enough. Clara welcomed the pain. Birth is painful.

The island did not seem to have changed much since she was a child. A few more houses and a small hotel had been built on the waterfront but the fishing boats rolling and bobbing in the water were exactly as she remembered them. A man in a straw hat was smashing an octopus against the harbour side to soften it. He looked up in surprise as a brightly dressed lady with a pink boa glided past him. She did not recognise him, and thankfully he did not recognise her.

The contractors had done their work well. The contents of the villa had been completely cleared except for the bookcases and books; the house had been painted inside and out, and the garden had been rejuvenated. Her own choice of furniture had been installed, although not where she wanted it. There would be time enough to re-arrange that.

Income was no longer a concern for Clara. Following her mother's death, she had sold the house in Athens and the family estate in Thiva. In the absence of any brothers, sisters or other covetous relatives, this was an uncomplicated procedure. She had used the funds to renovate the villa and purchase an annuity. Although not wealthy, she was now financially independent.

The marble floor of the living room was cool, smooth and soothing. The furniture was foreign. In fact, the bookcases along the wall were the only familiar objects. There was Gray's Anatomy and The Practical Management of Pain. There were also literary works: novels by Kazantzakis and Papadiamantis, volumes of poetry by Giorgos Seferis, a collection of novellas by Lili Zografou, and books by Dickens, Orwell and Steinbeck. There were also children's books and comics, neatly arranged in a manner typical of her mother.

Clara's first appearance in the grocer's shop was not a success. The shopkeeper was ill-mannered and two elderly, black-clad ladies, who had probably been kind and friendly to her as a child, tutted and glared at her disapprovingly. She made her purchases hurriedly and retreated to the villa, angry with herself.

Naturally, when lights went on in the villa, the news was all around the village within hours. Months earlier, there had been a great deal of curiosity when the contractors were at work, but as the workmen had no idea who their ultimate client was, it was a curiosity that went unsatisfied. Now that someone had actually moved in, many people assumed that Clara's mother had returned.

She had not expected a visitor. Clara had been about to take a siesta. She opened the door clad in a silk dressing gown, with no pink boa and no makeup.

In front of her was a small woman of her own age. She was wearing a blue-and-white print frock and her hair was tied back severely. Her only ornamentation was a simple silver cross hanging from a chain. She carried a plate of freshly baked *kourambiedes*. It was clearly a neighbourly gesture motivated by curiosity.

"If you're a Seventh Day Adventist, I'm not interested," said Clara, adopting her best Madame Anastasia tone.

"Clara?" said the woman, her eyes widening.

"Elly?"

Eleftheria did not know what to say or do. She extended her hand and Clara took it in hers. It was soft yet firm. The plate of *kourambiedes* in her other hand wobbled but did not fall.

Clara glanced about her.

"You'd better come in."

Eleftheria entered the villa uncertainly, smiling shyly as she had often done twenty-six years before. Once she was inside, Clara reached out and softly stroked her cheek. The plate of *kourambiedes* slipped from her fingers and shattered on the floor, sending an attractive spray of icing sugar across the marble. The two women embraced, with tears in their eyes.

"I've missed you so much," mumbled Eleftheria with her mouth buried in Clara's neck.

"I've missed you too, Elly," said Clara, stroking her hair. "It's been a long time."

Eleftheria pulled apart and looked Clara in the eye sternly, holding her arms firmly.

"You always understood me."

"You make that sound like an accusation," said Clara, smiling. "If so, I really do apologise. On the other hand, you understood me too."

Eleftheria laughed and released her grip.

"I'm sorry about the mess," she said, looking down at the broken plate and the scattered *kourambiedes*.

"Forget it. Take a seat," said Clara, gesturing towards a sofa. "Can I get you something to drink?"

"No."

She was the same Elly. Always amusingly direct, open and honest.

"I'm going to have a whisky," said Clara, reaching down a bottle of White Horse and two glasses.

"I don't drink," said Eleftheria.

"You do now," said Clara, pouring her a glass.

Clara seated herself next to Eleftheria and took a gulp of whisky. There was an awkward silence.

"Are you on holiday?" asked Eleftheria.

"No, my mother died…"

"I'm sorry to hear that. I remember her as a wonderful woman."

"These things happen," said Clara, dismissively. "She never really recovered from my father's death."

"I knew about your father. He was well-liked here."

"Was he? I don't remember him much. Well, to cut a tedious story short, I sold all the property and moved here."

"For good?"

"For good."

"Why here?"

Clara reached for a cigarette, inserted it into a tortoise-shell holder and lit it nervously. She was not sure how to answer the question because no one had ever asked it before.

"I suppose because my happiest memories are from here."

Eleftheria smiled and nodded.

"But I'm sure you'll agree that it's a bit sad that my happiest memories are from when I was ten years old."

She laughed drily. Outside, the wind was freshening, blowing a billow of bougainvillea flowers across the garden.

"And what about you, Elly?

Eleftheria took a large gulp of whisky, and coughed.

"Excuse me. I told you I don't drink."

"You seem to be learning well," said Clara.

Eleftheria chuckled.

"I married young," she said. "I was eighteen. There's nothing very extraordinary in that. I didn't know what I wanted, certainly not *who* I wanted, but my parents thought it was a good idea to marry Giannis. There wasn't exactly an embarrassment of choice."

"Do I know him?"

"Maybe. He's a fisherman. *Captain* Giannis!"

They laughed. Every fisherman is a captain if he owns the boat.

"He's a good man. He loves me."

"Do you love him?"

Eleftheria rubbed her chin and lifted her eyes to the ceiling.

"Yes, I do love him, but he's not the man I wanted."

It was an unexpected answer. Was Eleftheria talking about unrequited love, or a match that her parents had deemed unsuitable?

Eleftheria seemed to realise that she had gone too far. Perhaps it was the whisky. She brushed a dash of icing sugar from her dress.

"Like I said, he's a good man. We have two children."

"Two?"

"Apostolis and Maria. Apostolis is a lovely boy, very kind although not the brightest. He's doing his national service. Maria is in high school."

Clara smiled and nodded.

"You said that he's not the man you wanted."

"That was silly of me."

"But still."

Eleftheria sighed. She knew that Clara would not be satisfied until she had received a plausible answer.

"Clara, did you ever have a dream when you were a kid? Like being a fireman or a nurse? That sort of thing?"

Clara thought for a moment.

"I might have made a pretty good fireman but you have to be a man to do that. That's strange when you think of it, as women are ten-times better at playing with fire. But no, Elly, I never had a particular dream."

"I did."

"Melina Mercouri and Katharine Hepburn?"

"You remember!"

Clara laughed.

"Of course I remember! You were my best friend. You still are."

Eleftheria reached out and stroked Clara's hand.

"Always."

"So what has this to do with Captain Giannis?"

"He's not Spencer Tracy."

Clara had been about to take a sip of whisky but had to replace it on the table quickly.

"You don't say!"

"Or Jules Dassin, Humphrey Bogart or Peter O'Toole."

"How unfortunate for you! That must have come as quite a shock."

Eleftheria giggled. The whisky had gone to her head and her friend had returned.

Clara stubbed out her cigarette, half-smoked.

"Don't you think you might have been expecting too much, on a small island like this?"

"Of course I was. I wanted to be a famous actress. A strong woman with the world at her feet. Instead I got fish."

They fell silent. The wind had risen outside and a tree was beating its leaves against the window. Eleftheria reached out her hand again and entwined her fingers with Clara's.

"And what about you, Clara. Any men in your life?"

"No."

"You mean not now or not ever?"

"Not ever," replied Clara, uncomfortably. She withdrew her fingers from Eleftheria's grasp, fitted another cigarette into its tortoiseshell holder and lit it.

"So…"

"To be frank, I've never had much interest in men," said Clara, blowing out a plume of smoke. "I've never even been with a man."

"Never?"

"Never. And don't look at me like that. I'm not unique."

"Maybe not, but it's still unusual."

"We're *all* unusual, Elly. That's what makes us so alike. I couldn't care less, frankly."

"So, you're here on your own?"

"No," replied Clara, firmly. "There are two us. I'll be here until one of us dies."

Eleftheria glanced around the room. Although Clara had been in the villa for less than two days, there might have at least been some visible signs of another occupant. Or sounds from the bathroom or kitchen. Perhaps a cough, a rushing of water or a clinking of plates.

"The other person is me," said Clara.

Eleftheria looked at her blankly. Clara stubbed out her cigarette, again half-smoked, and gazed at the frantic tree outside.

"What if you get to my age and you don't like who you are, Elly? I wasted years looking after my mother as she wasted away. I only went to university because I felt it was expected of me. I don't think it was, but that's what I believed at the time. I worked in a perfume shop."

"Many people do far less."

"Fine, if you're happy doing less. It becomes a problem when you do less and feel you were worth more. That's what I felt, Elly. So, I've decided to become another person—a woman who drinks whisky, wears a feather boa, and smokes Sobranie cigarettes through a tortoiseshell holder."

"Like the person I wanted to be?"

A few drops of rain pattered against the window. A spring shower. It would not last long and then the wind would drop and the sun would reappear.

"No, not at all. You wanted to be an actress with the world at your feet. An actress plays a role and then moves on to another. I will be playing the same part for the rest of my life, and there will be no applause, much less an Academy Award. But I'm going to enjoy it thoroughly."

Eleftheria smiled, and nodded thoughtfully.

"My glass is empty," she said.

Clara poured her a generous amount of White Horse. Eleftheria took a judicious sip.

"And does your character have a name?" she asked.

"Clara."

"But that's your name. People will know exactly who you are."

"It doesn't matter if they do. It's not what they think of me that's important; it's what I think of myself."

She paused for the time it takes to fit a Sobranie cigarette into a tortoiseshell holder and light it.

"From now on, Elly, I am *Madame* Clara! You can help me by preparing the ground, if you want. Make up any story you like because it will certainly change entirely within twenty-four hours. I suggest you start with my being the Prime Minister's rejected mistress, although you may find it necessary to work downwards. I'll leave that up to you, my dear. I do draw the line at minor civil servants though."

"The Minister of Tourism?"

"If necessary."

Eleftheria laughed again and slapped her knee, which was not something she usually did. Until Clara arrived on the island, her entertainment had been reading. Now, many of the characters from her books could be distilled into a single joke that would be sure to keep her, and Clara, entertained for many years to come.

"Welcome to the island, Madame Clara," said Eleftheria, raising her glass and spilling her whisky.

"Thank you, my dear," replied Madame Clara. She reached behind her, swept the pink boa around her neck, and blew her a kiss.

Hill 731

Manolis had told him that it would not hurt.

"If you lose an arm or a leg, the shock to your system will be so great that you won't feel it. A paper cut would be more painful."

Socratis and Manolis were not only friends but cousins. They had grown up together, swimming, running, jumping off high cliffs into the water, throwing stones through windows, being chased by angry parents, teasing and later kissing girls, and sneaking their first tastes of alcohol. But by October 1940, they had put childhood behind them and become sober young men. Relatively sober, at least.

Manolis was an intelligent boy. Recognising this, his parents had encouraged him to read as much as he could, not that there was much to read on the island at the time. He was also kind. When other children made fun of Socratis, Manolis was always the first to defend him, and if it came to an exchange of blows, he was not averse to exchanging them.

By island standards, Socratis was a giant. Even when standing rigidly to attention, Manolis barely reached his shoulder. He also had a prodigious appetite, although it was difficult to say whether this was the reason for his size or a result of it. Probably it was a combination of both.

Perhaps the reason for their closeness was that Socratis and Manolis perfectly complemented each other. While Socratis mostly saw only the obvious solution or outcome, Manolis would see gradations of rightness or wrongness and gently point these out to his friend. While Manolis was essentially retiring and studious, Socratis was outgoing and fun-loving. Despite his size, he was a good dancer. He could crouch, hop, skip and glide over the rough earth like a man half his size. He had a ready wit and a loud laugh.

At the age of nineteen, Socratis married Anna. Anna was from a farming family. They owned a small house in the village, which they gave to her as her dowry. Six months after their marriage, Anna gave birth to a daughter, Maria.

In the same year, Manolis married Katerina. Katerina was as vivacious as Manolis was retiring. Her parents built them a small house outside the village. It had a modest olive grove and a vegetable garden.

Socratis and Manolis joined the army on 17 October 1940. They were both twenty years old. They were assigned to the same regiment. Both expected to return to their families before the new year.

In the event, Manolis had been right. It did not hurt. The 81-millimetre mortar shell that blew Manolis apart and threw Socratis ten metres to his right did not cause Socratis any pain. The blast instantly rendered him unconscious.

When Socratis regained consciousness, in a makeshift field hospital not far from the front, he still felt no pain. Through a morphine-laden fog he heard that the surgeon had removed his left leg but, apart from that, he would be fine. The battle on Hill 731 on the Albanian front was a great victory. The Italians had been driven back with heavy losses.

No one could tell him what had happened to Manolis.

Socratis smelled the sweet, musty, mustard-yellow earth of Hill 731 as he drifted in and out of consciousness and the dull ache from his stump ebbed and flowed. He realised later that the blast had driven the earth into his uniform, along with the blood of his friend.

He did not return to a hero's welcome. The German invasion that followed a short-lived victory over the Italians had resulted in Greece's capitulation. Ironically, it was a detachment of Italian troops that occupied the island; perhaps Socratis had even shot at those very men on Hill 731. The islanders had more on their minds than celebrating what were finally meaningless victories.

Although she hoped and prayed otherwise, Anna had not expected her young husband to return from the war. Many men had not. When Manolis's family were informed that he had died heroically in Albania, and yet there had been no word of Socratis, Anna feared the worst. When she finally faced him on the threshold of their home, she saw half a man. He was bearded, long-haired, thin and haggard; his face was pale and his eyes were red; his uniform was torn, bloodstained and filthy; he propped himself unsteadily on a crutch, and a limb was missing. But it was Socratis and she embraced him lovingly before pulling back, nauseated by his stink.

After his return, Socratis found it almost impossible to sleep. He would often awaken after what seemed only a few minutes with a dull pain in the lower part of a leg that no longer existed. And then the terrors would commence. Bathed in sweat, he would toss, turn and thrash until daybreak with the thump and roar of artillery in his ears, the screams and groans, the stench of blood and excreta, the rasping breath of men desperately clinging onto the last seconds of their lives. And he would finally awaken with the agonising knowledge that, if he had only been a few metres to his left, it would have been he who would have caught the full blast of the mortar shell, and Manolis—good, quiet, loyal Manolis—would have been spared.

At first, he and Anna put his night terrors down to fever, but an Italian army doctor found no evidence of infection. In an effort to rid himself of his nightmares, he drank tsikoudia until he slumped unconscious onto his bed. He was dead for at least a few hours but then the effect of the alcohol wore off, he lived again, and the nightmares resumed.

Sleep was not his only problem. Inexplicably, he found he had developed a fear of crowds. In normal day-to-day life, this was not so very restrictive as the island was a wonderfully uncrowded place, but there were often large family gatherings and religious festivals that always ended in raucous singing and dancing to the crazy, hypnotic rhythms of bagpipe and drum. If he could, he would leave the party early, stumping off through the dark streets with a disappointed Anna holding his hand. His fellow islanders would give a collective shrug at his departure. They could understand that the loss of a leg might affect his sleep, and even his dancing, but not that it might lead to unsociable behaviour.

Walking with a crutch was not so difficult, not that Socratis walked very much. He relived his dancing in his daydreams as he sat on a wooden chair outside the door. When the wind made the trees leap and skip, his stump would groan in envy. Even when the war and the civil war that followed it were long over, he could find no rest. He still grieved for Manolis and felt himself a useless burden on his family. There was little enough work even for able-bodied men at that time and a one-legged man with mental issues stood no chance of finding employment. He received a meagre pension that was hardly enough to provide for one person, let alone three. So, Anna found work in his brother's restaurant, where little Maria joined her as soon as she was old enough to carry a tray. This was not the way it should be, Socratis thought. A man should support his family.

When help eventually came, it arrived from an unexpected quarter. Katerina, Manolis's widow, had never blamed Socratis for being a couple of metres too far to the right on Hill 731. In fact, she had welcomed the return of her husband's cousin and best friend. She visited him often and would brew cups of thick, sweet coffee while Socratis sat alone outside the house, staring at the trees. She had tried on many an occasion to convince him that Manolis's death had not been his fault. Socratis would listen, nod his head and smile indulgently, but he knew better.

It was on one of these visits that Katerina put down her coffee cup, took a deep breath, and made a suggestion that she was sure would result in rebuttal.

"Socrati," she began. "Do you know you can have a *periptero*?

"A what?"

Socratis knew perfectly well what a *periptero* was. Greece was full of the small kiosks that sold newspapers, tobacco and sundries. He had bought things from them many times between conscription and losing a leg.

"A *periptero*. You know, it's—"

"I know what a *periptero* is, Katerina. What do you mean I can have one?"

"Do you know how the people who run them come to own them?"

Socratis scratched his moustache. His missing foot had begun to itch, as it often did when he felt uncomfortable.

"No."

"The government gives licences for them to people who have been…well…disabled in the war."

"So that's why there's so many."

Katerina laughed but she could not ignore the bitterness in his voice.

"The government will give you a licence for free and then it's up to you, Socrati. All you have to do is sit in your *periptero,* sell cigarettes and stuff, and rake in the money."

"I suppose it's cheaper for them than providing a decent pension."

"It's better than just sitting outside the door, Socrati."

Socratis thought for a moment, gazing at the trees, which were hushed and waiting expectantly.

"But I will have to build the *periptero* myself. How can I do that with this?"

He patted his stump.

"Besides, it will cost money, and I have none."

"My father will build it for you," said Katerina. "Manolis would have wanted that."

The trees whispered their agreement.

The *periptero* was built at the port. It was modest, even by modest standards. Roughly one-and-a-half metres square and three metres high, it had a narrow shelf that ran around it, a door at the side, three windows at the front with shelving to display wares, and a sliding window where customers could pay. Katerina's father had also topped off his creation with a pyramid roof and sun awnings. It was painted mustard yellow, that being the traditional colour for *periptera*.

One-and-a-half metres square left little room for Socratis, and even less room when tiers of shelves and the cash drawer were added. A slim, able-bodied man would have had difficulty squeezing himself into its narrow confines and it took several hours of sometimes painful practice before Socratis was able to do so.

The *periptero* was officially opened on a warm afternoon in May and was something of a gala event. There was tsikoudia, souvlaki and dancing. For once, Socratis was the centre of attention. He felt uncomfortable with this but smiled, nodded and toasted as the need arose. After all, it would have been ungrateful and ungracious not to have done so, given that the *periptero* was built by his best friend's family and the licence had been granted free of charge by the government.

It is in the nature of *periptera* to not be an immediate success. They are not places where you go to do your daily shopping. Men dropped by for tobacco and cigarettes; women purchased a cheap magazine or chocolate for the children; children would push a few drachmas onto the shelf and Socratis would give them chewing gum at a discount.

This was not a *periptero* on the corner of a main street in Athens or Thessaloniki where trade would have been brisk.

Sometimes, Socratis would sit in his narrow, wooden casket for most of the day with no customers at all.

As if a lack of passing trade was not enough, many people would read his newspapers without buying them. The fact that they were hung on a line outside the *periptero* did not help. They also tended to end up on the ground as the clothes pegs that held them on the line were occasionally stolen in order to fulfil their original purpose of pegging clothes.

Significantly, there were also a few people who were curious about what was happening in the outside world but could not actually read about it.

This was at a time when there were still a few illiterate or semi-literate people on the island. There was no television and not many radios, because there was no electricity. Even when battery-powered radios finally made their appearance, they were considered extravagant luxuries.

Typically, these people would thumb quickly through a dogeared, unsold copy of *Ta Nea* or *Kathimerini*, while tut-tutting noisily.

"Things not going well in Athens, I see."

"Aren't they?"

"Terrible."

And they would replace the newspaper somewhat self-consciously and leave.

Socratis did not know whether things were going badly in Athens or not, nor did he care. Although he had had more experience of the outside world than most islanders, it was an experience that had been short, painful and better forgotten. At least, he had done his best to try to forget it.

This attitude began to change one Sunday evening when Panagiotis, the odd-job-man, stopped by the *periptero* to buy rolling tobacco. Panagiotis's lack of literacy was well known and he went to no trouble to disguise it.

"How did Olympiakos do?" he asked, rolling his first cigarette with the new tobacco and nodding towards the suspended newspapers.

"Olympiakos?"

"The football."

"Oh, *that* Olympiakos," muttered Socratis, for, truth be told, he knew even less about football than he did about Greek politics.

He peered through the narrow window at the dishevelled figure of Panagiotis, who was not much taller than the last child to whom he had dispensed chewing gum.

"Well, let's see, shall we," he said.

He eased himself out of the *periptero*, unpegged a copy of *Ta Nea*, manoeuvred himself back into the *periptero*, put on his spectacles, and turned to the sports pages.

"Olympiakos, Olympiakos, Olympiakos," he said, scanning through the pages. "Ah yes. Here we are. Olympiakos three, Panionios nil. It looks like they've won some sort of cup."

"Who?"

"Olympiakos."

Panagiotis grinned. The cigarette clamped between his lips saluted.

"Nobody buys newspapers," Socratis complained.

Anna was clearing away the dishes. Maria was thumbing through a glossy magazine.

"Nobody?" said Anna.

"Almost nobody. They prefer me to tell them what's happening in the world instead of paying a few drachmas and reading it for themselves. Why, only this evening Panagiotis asked me for the football results, and, like a fool, I told him."

"Which Panagiotis?" asked Anna, scrubbing the frying pan.

"The odd-job-man."

"He can't read."

"I know, but the principle is the same. He's not the first. Most of the people who ask me for news without bothering to buy the paper can read well enough. I went to school with some of them."

For a while, there was silence. Anna put away the frying pan and sat down next to her daughter. Maria looked up from her magazine. By that time, she was married to Captain Costas, a fisherman. Fortunately, his family had waived the matter of a dowry.

"Maybe they just want you to tell them," she said.

Socratis squinted at her. His missing foot began to itch.

"What do you mean?"

"I mean," said Maria, returning her attention to the magazine, "that they might prefer you to tell them the news than to read it for themselves."

"Why?"

Maria shrugged.

"Maybe they're lonely."

Socratis rubbed his stump.

"How can they all be lonely? Some of them are married."

"That doesn't mean they're not lonely," said Anna.

Socratis started to read the newspapers. It was not always pleasant. In his absence, horrible things had continued to happen in the world. There were wars, famines, and Greece itself was in a constant state of chaos, which eventually culminated in a military coup d'état. Under the new regime, the Greek press, rarely impartial in the best of times, was effectively muzzled.

He had started to supply edited versions of the news for those who needed it, but what had happened on 21 April 1967 made this increasingly difficult. When it came to political events, he became uncomfortably aware that he was providing the less literate with an accessible, understandable version of downright lies. Thus, he began to provide his own commentary.

"It looks like Papadopoulos has rounded up a few more anarchists."

"Rounded up what?" asked Panagiotis.

"Anarchists. Perfectly harmless people who don't believe in governments."

"If they're so harmless, why is Papadopoulos rounding them up?" asked Panagiotis.

"Probably because they don't believe in governments."

"Are there a lot of them?" asked Panagiotis, wide-eyed.

"Well, let me put it this way, Panagioti" said Socratis, scratching his chest. "When I was in the army, I met all sorts...royalists, socialists, communists, you name them. You know how many anarchists I met?"

"No, how many?"

"Not one."

Speaking out against the military dictatorship was risky in those days. Even on a small island whose inhabitants tended to favour the Left, you never knew who was listening, or who they might talk to. A wrong word to the wrong person could lead to arrest, torture, and imprisonment or death. Socratis learned to be circumspect.

"You know what they've done now?"

"What?" asked Panagiotis.

"They've banned the miniskirt!"

Panagiotis was aghast. He had seen pictures of girls in miniskirts and rather liked them, even if Colonel Papadopoulos did not.

"Why?"

"They say they're permissive."

"What?"

"Permissive.

"What's that?"

"I think it means doing what you like."

"Ah!" exclaimed Panagiotis, spitting out a loose strand of tobacco. "Is that bad?"

"So it seems," replied Socratis, turning the pages of *To Vima* to the sports section.

Ironically, in the same year that the miniskirt was banned, the press welcomed a visit by The Beatles, who were known to some people on the island, but not to very many. As on previous occasions, Socratis was obliged to make the headlines understandable to islanders.

"They are an English musical ensemble," he said. "From Liverpool."

Panagiotis stared at the photograph on the front page. His cousin Konstantinos had visited Liverpool as a merchant seaman but the four men smiling at the camera did not look like sailors and his cousin had never mentioned them.

"They have long hair."

"They're musicians."

"Ah! Yes. Musicians. What are their names?"

Socratis hesitated. John, Paul and George were easily translated, but Ringo posed a problem. He decided to go for the nearest equivalent he could think of.

"Giannis, Pavlos, Giorgos and Gianko."

"Ah!" said Panagiotis, squinting at the picture. "Which one is Gianko?"

"The one with the big nose."

After seven years, Colonel Papadopoulos and his cronies were ousted from power and miniskirts were back. Even a few men with long hair appeared on the island. They arrived with backpacks, slept on the beach and were not musicians, although some of them strummed guitars.

By this time, the *periptero* was established not only as a convenient provider of news summaries but also of local gossip. In fact, Socratis was so well-informed that even the mayor used him as a source of information, frequently before council meetings and always before elections.

Socratis was not a gossip by nature, and preferred not to know about the intimate affairs of others. However, while it is easy enough to close your eyes, it is impossible to close your ears. And stuck in the *periptero*, as he was, Socratis was a captive audience.

Matters were not improved when the island's first public telephone was attached to the outside of the *periptero*. Socratis could hear every detail of every conversation. This was not helped by the tendency of many islanders to shout down the phone to ensure that their voice was heard at the other end of the line. There were certainly times when highly personal, and sometimes intimate information was bellowed into the telephone at a volume that ensured it was common knowledge within hours.

As the years passed, he was increasingly called on to provide advice on all manner of subjects, most of which he felt very unqualified to supply. To get around this, he devised a simple method of answering every question with a question. In many cases this was successful as the person asking the question invariably had a pretty fair idea of the answer anyway.

A typical question might be:

"Do you think I should let my boy marry Maria?"

To which the first question might be:

"Which Maria?"

"Maria from the corner shop."

"Oh, *that* Maria."

Socratis would scratch his moustache and raise his eyes to the stacks of Karelia, Papastratos, Marlboro and Lucky Strikes above him, as if searching for divine inspiration.

"What do *you* think?" he would ask, after a decent interval.

"Well, I think she just wants to get her feet under the table."

"Is your table big enough?"

And the customer would nod sagely and thank him for his help.

As the only other source of free advice was the local priest, who tended to answer in the form of proverbs, those who found Socratis's Socratic method equally unsatisfactory were pretty much left to their own devices.

In most cases, Socratis's business was fairly easy to conduct. Newspapers and magazines would be picked up from the ferry by any one of a number of children gainfully employed for the purpose. All of the other goods were ordered as required.

Neither were his customers particularly demanding. They did not need to be. After all, with the exception of newspapers and cigarettes, anything that Socratis sold could also be bought at the supermarket up the street, although not quite as conveniently or as pleasantly.

Yet, of course, there is always the exception that proves the rule, and that exception was Madame Clara.

"Sobranie and *Tatler*," said Madame Clara, imperiously, striving to look down on a man who was at least ten centimetres taller than her and, owing to the elevation of the *periptero*, twenty.

It was Madame Clara's first visit to the *periptero*. Socratis stared at her in wonderment through the little window. It was a windy day and Madame Clara was having difficulty in controlling her feather boa.

"Sobranie and Tatler," he repeated. "Is that a new brand?"

"What?" replied Madame Clara, grabbing the stray tail of her boa and looking at anywhere that was not Socratis.

"Sobranie, I know," said Socratis. "It's a British cigarette but pretends to be Russian. They were called Balkan Sobranie until the Balkans went out of fashion."

Madame Clara was impressed. She turned her attention to Socratis, peering at him through the small window. She saw a large man with glasses and a grey moustache.

"Quite correct," she said, with the merest smile.

"But Sobranie and Tatler is a new one for me. Are you sure you don't mean Benson and Hedges or Lambert and Butler?"

"Sobranie are the cigarettes; *Tatler* is a magazine," explained Madame Clara.

"Ah! I see."

He paused to scratch his stump.

"What's a tatler?"

This was a question that had never occurred to Madame Clara. Tatler was unknown to her and had been recommended by a friend in Athens.

"I really don't know. I suppose it's someone who tattles."

"Tattles?"

"It's an English word."

"Ah! So it's a British magazine! Like *Autocar* or *Homes and Gardens*. These I know. So, this is a magazine for tatlers. Or maybe for people who like them."

Madame Clara moved closer to Socratis, and out of the wind.

"Shall we deal with the cigarettes first, mister…?"

"Socratis."

"Mister Socratis."

Socratis made a great show of scanning the massed banks of cigarettes above him.

"Let's see. Sobranie? No. Sorry. Not today."

"Can you order them?"

"Of course."

"What about *Tatler*?"

"What about it?"

"Can you order it?"

"Madame…?"

"Clara."

"Madame Clara, you can order anything here. Even an elephant," he added, stroking his moustache.

Madame Clara was beginning to enjoy this, as was Socratis.

"African or Indian?" she ventured.

"I would recommend Indian. The delivery time will be shorter and they have smaller ears."

"Is that important?"

"Not to me. Perhaps to another elephant."

"Would it arrive?"

Socratis sighed and folded his fingers over the cash tray.

"In the best of all possible worlds, Madame Clara, it would certainly arrive. Right here, at the agreed time, in front of this very *periptero*. Sadly, this is not the best of all possible worlds and we are dealing with the Greek postal service. It is highly likely that it would be held up in the sorting office and returned owing to insufficient postage."

"So you don't think ordering an elephant would be a good idea?"

"All things considered, I would advise against it."

"The *Tatler*?"

"If such a thing exists, I will order it for you.

"And the cigarettes…?"

"…will be delivered next week."

The Sobranie cigarettes arrived within a week, and continued to arrive on a regular basis. *Tatler* took somewhat longer to arrive and was already three months old. Madame Clara flicked through it, decided that articles about aristocratic British families that she had never heard of and public schools that were obviously irrelevant held no interest for her, and returned it to the *periptero*. Socratis declined to refund it, Madame Clara raised her voice and even waved her pink boa threateningly, but finally had to admit that it was her friend in Athens who was to blame for the inappropriateness of *Tatler* and not Socratis.

Socratis retired from his *periptero* at the age of seventy and left its running in the hands of cousin Anna. By that time, electricity had appeared on the island and the little kiosk was illuminated inside and out. A freezer full of ice cream whirred and clattered outside. A silent, red Coca Cola cooler was stocked with soft drinks and beer. At the height of the summer, Socratis's wooden pagoda was the calm centre of a vortex of tourists.

Occasionally, he still had nightmares, but they were not as violent and terrifying as they had been fifty years before. When they occurred, they took on a different form and the awful horror of the victory at Hill 731 was absent.

He would never be able to dance again—at his age, he would probably not have been able to anyway—but he could beat time with his crutch and admire the crouch, hop, skip and glide of young dancers.

It was an afternoon in late summer. A still, treacly heat had gradually trickled its way northward from Africa and descended on the island. There was no refreshing sea-breeze, merely the occasional breath that hardly ruffled the delicate, crimson flowers of the bougainvillea. The trees did not leap and skip; their branches, twigs and leaves waited silently for the wind.

Socratis, Anna and Katerina were sitting in the shade of the narrow veranda, around the battered metal table with its faded plastic top. They had finished their coffee. Anna and Katerina were fanning themselves and chatting about childhood diseases: the whooping cough that had almost killed Anna as a child and the chickenpox that had left scars on Katerina's forehead and carried off her uncle. Socratis was hunched over, leaning on his crutch and gazing sightlessly at the trees.

He remembered that there had been no trees on Hill 731. There were trees, many trees, when he and Manolis arrived there, laughing and joking to dispel their fear, but they were all soon uprooted and shattered by the Italian bombardment. The mustard-yellow earth had seethed and heaved, swallowing the spring flowers.

He and Manolis were crouching next to each other in a shallow trench. He was aware that Manolis was only a couple of metres away, but they did not even glance at each other for there was no time to do so. He clamped his Mannlicher–Schönauer rifle to shoulder and cheek, peered down the iron sight at the green and black figures weaving through the trees and undergrowth far below him. Fire, pull the bolt: fire, pull the bolt; fire, pull the bolt; fire, pull the bolt; fire, pull the bolt. Reload. Fire, pull the bolt.

And nothing.

It was Katerina who noticed. She happened to glance at Socratis over Anna's shoulder. She reached out, softly touched Anna's arm and nodded towards him.

Tears were coursing down Socratis's cheeks. Anna turned, fell to her knees and grasped his arms. She had never seen Socratis cry. Even in his nightmares and deliria, he had never cried. When abject poverty had threatened, he had never cried. Even when he had hurt himself as a child, he had never cried.

"What is it, my love?" she asked.

Socratis stared at her with glassy brown eyes.

"We were all so young," he whispered. "We were. They were. All so very young."

Happy Birthday

The fishing was going badly.

There was nothing new in this but the situation had become serious. Fish stocks around the island had plummeted. Some fishermen had responded by banding together, buying a larger boat and continuing to fish in the Libyan Sea; others soldiered on doggedly in the increasingly vain hope that things would improve. One or two converted their boats to passenger vessels and offered day excursions for tourists. But the island was very small, as too was the market.

There were others who took advantage of the government's offer of compensation in return for destroying their boats. The fishermen called it "cutting", but there was no cutting involved. The boat was smashed with a digger in front of their eyes. And they had to be present whether or not they could bear to watch, for it was only at the time of destruction that the compensation was paid.

Dimitris sold his boat to a Swedish tourist for a very good price. The Swede had wanted a genuine Greek *kaiki* in which to putter around the islands and discover remote beaches, and Dimitris's boat had been colourfully painted and well-maintained.

In spite of the windfall, it had been a hard decision to make. The *Kristina*, named after his grandmother, had been bought new by her husband from a skilled boatbuilder on the island of Symi. The boatbuilder had danced when he designed and built *Kristina* and *Kristina* had danced afterwards.

"What are you going to do with the money" asked Petros over a cup of coffee.

"I will open a restaurant," declared Dimitris.

Petros looked askance at his friend. Dimitris had been a good fisherman but was slightly challenged in most other respects.

"Can you cook?" he asked.

"No, but my mother can cook."

"I know your mother can cook," said Petros, gently. "My mother can cook too but I don't think she would like to work in a restaurant. Have you asked her?"

"No," admitted Dimitris. Now that Petros had mentioned it, he could not see his mother working in a restaurant either. In fact, it was sometimes difficult to persuade her to cook at home.

"Of course, if you had a wife…"

"I'm not getting married just to have a cook!"

"Then I don't think a restaurant is a very good idea. Of course, you could employ a cook but I don't think there are any spare cooks on the island. That would mean getting someone from Athens or another island. It could be an expensive business."

"Maybe a bar then," said Dimitris. "You don't need a cook to have a bar."

"True, but there are already several bars here. You would have competition."

"Pah! My bar will be different!"

"Like every other bar. They all want to be different," said Petros, and took a sip of coffee, "so how is it that they are all very much the same?"

"Are they?" asked Dimitris, who had actually not spent much time in bars.

"Yes. Apart from the colour-scheme and the prices."

"My bar will be different!" repeated Dimitris. But he really had no idea how it *would* be different, until he suddenly had a flash of inspiration. It was a similar flash to when he had decided to sell *Kristina* to the Swede, instead of pocketing the money from the government.

"Happy birthday!" he exclaimed, in English.

Petros put down his cup.

"It's not my birthday."

"No, that will be the name of the bar—Happy Birthday."

"It's a strange name for a bar."

"No, it isn't. Everyone has a birthday, don't they?"

"I suppose so."

"And a name day, or they get married, or they buy a car…"

Petros grunted.

"So, when things like that happen, they will want to celebrate, and where better to do that than in a bar called Happy Birthday?"

"In English."

"Yes, of course."

Petros lifted his coffee cup and took a last sip.

"You don't speak English, do you, Dimitri?"

"No."

In fact, Dimitris did not speak any language other than Greek, and even that was open to question.

"Then let me tell you something," began Petros. "In Greek, we say *chrónia pollá* on all sorts of occasions, including birthdays. But in English, you do not say 'happy birthday' to someone who has just passed their driving test."

"Why not?"

"Because it is not their birthday. Okay, it might *happen* to be their birthday but..."

Dimitris burst out laughing and slapped the table.

"I see what you are trying to do, *malaka*! You are trying to fool me! Listen to me, everybody speaks a little English right?"

"Well, you don't."

"*Almost* everybody. And you expect me to believe that a language that is spoken by so many people has different words for each of these situations? That they say 'happy passing your driving test', for example?"

It was at this point that Petros gave up. If Dimitris wanted to call his new bar Happy Birthday, it was up to him. After all, it was his money.

Although the choice of a name had been easy, the location of the new bar proved more difficult. All of the prime sites had already been taken and Dimitris was obliged to rent a semi-dilapidated house on the outskirts of the village. It was not on a route that tourists generally took, unless they were desperate to get somewhere in a hurry and wanted to avoid the summer crowds on the main street, but it was cheap to rent and it had potential.

"It has potential," said Dimitris, as he strode through the doorless opening and kicked at the fallen masonry inside.

"It certainly has nothing right now," observed Petros.

"You see out there?" said Dimitris, gesturing to the overgrown front garden. "That will be our terrace, where the tourists will sip their cocktails and watch the world pass by."

"What world? Nobody comes here."

"They will come when we are open."

"Wait a minute," said Petros. "Did I hear you say 'our terrace' and 'we'?"

Dimitris turned to him and smiled the disarming smile of an honest fisherman.

"Petro," he said, grasping his shoulder, "did you think I would forget you?"

Petros had rather hoped so.

"You will be my partner. But I will be the boss of course."

It was useless to argue. Petros, who had already accepted money from the government in return for seeing his beloved *Agios Nikolaos* smashed to smithereens, had nothing else to do and becoming Dimitris's partner seemed a small price to pay for a lifetime's friendship.

Dimitris hired builders. His instructions to them were simply "build me a bar", which they duly did, having built bars before.

However, Dimitris had his own ideas about decoration and embellishments. He pursued the theme of Happy Birthday by asking a cousin in Athens to buy a few hundred birthday cards in English, Greek and any other language available. There were not many Greek cards, and there were few cards in other languages, but his brother succeeded in buying a great many cards in English. Unfortunately, Dimitris's cousin's grasp of English was little better than that of Dimitris himself, so the cards sent to the island ranged from "Happy Birthday You Are Two" and "So Sorry I Missed Your Special Day" to "Look Out, It's Christmas" and "With Deepest Sympathy On Your Loss".

Dimitris was very pleased with the cards and posted them all over the interior and even the exterior of the bar. He also bought candles in various colours. Following an unfortunate dress-rehearsal, he then situated these a safe distance from the cards.

The Happy Birthday bar opened at the beginning of the summer and was a resounding success. At least, the opening night was. Dimitris's family was there—his mother, brother and sisters, uncles, aunts and cousins—also Petros's extremely extended family, many friends, and friends of friends. There was a lot of dancing and singing. Litres of tsikoudia were drunk, although no cocktails.

Next evening there was not a single customer. Having written off the evening at midnight, Dimitris and Petros stood behind the bar, trying out cocktails from a recipe book that Dimitris's cousin had thoughtfully sent from Athens along with the cards.

"What you need is a signature cocktail," said Petros, carefully pouring a measure of rum into a shaker.

"A signature cocktail? One that people have to sign for?"

Petros bit his tongue.

"No, Dimitri," he said. "Not quite so life-threatening. A signature cocktail is like our signature—your signature. It is a cocktail that is unique to Happy Birthday."

"Ah. Then it should be a cocktail that people will remember, right?"

"Exactly."

And so they began to experiment. Dimitris and Petros had slightly different opinions on what a memorable cocktail should be. Petros favoured subtle blends of one or two alcohols with fresh juices and perhaps a dash of bitters. Dimitris, who had so far shown little to no affinity with cocktails, favoured three or four alcohols, preferably Greek, and not much else. After two or three hours of trying different combinations, Dimitris was becoming increasingly short-tempered and opinionated, while Petros smiled a lot and became correspondingly slapdash.

Finally, Dimitris poured a large glass of ouzo into the shaker, added equally large glasses of triple-distilled tsikoudia—a Greek spirit noted more for its fire than its subtlety—and tequila. And an ice-cube. He shook the shaker vigorously, poured the mixture into a glass, splashed some cheap Greek champagne over it and plonked a slice of lemon into the resulting concoction.

"Try that," he said pushing the glass over the counter.

Petros squinted at the drink and then at Dimitris, swaying slightly. He removed the slice of lemon and took a sip.

Petros's squint instantly disappeared. He gave a slight cough.

"It's a bit on the strong side," he ventured. "Not unpleasant though. I think you have your signature cocktail, Niko!"

"Is it memorable?" asked Dimitris anxiously.

"Well, I won't forget it. And if anyone remembers it after they've drunk it, they won't forget it either. What are you going to call it?"

"To you," said Dimitris, in English.

"To you too," said Petros, raising his glass. "But what are you going to call it?"

"That will be the name—To You, as in 'Happy birthday to you.'"

"You really don't speak much English, do you, Dimitri?" said Petros.

"No," said Dimitris.

Over the two weeks following its opening, Happy Birthday attracted few customers. Dimitris reasoned that, on a small island, there would certainly be days that were not someone's birthday or name day, but as the days passed, even he started to doubt this excuse.

However, Dimitris's fortunes turned when an ageing Italian returned to the island. Gianluca did not come for the sunshine and the beach, of which he had an ample supply in Rimini. Even less did he come for the excellent Greek food and wines, which he considered definitely inferior to those of Italy. He came for the women.

Twenty years earlier, when he first washed up on the island, Gianluca had been slim, muscular and charming. Twenty years later, his love of good food and wine had taken its toll and his charm was as spontaneous as a politician's speeches on election day. Not that he hadn't somewhat adapted his act accordingly. In his early years, when he claimed to have seduced a girl within half an hour of meeting her, his approach had been direct and to the point. His success rate was also helped by the fact that his prey—usually girls from Northern Europe who liked the idea of a fling with an exotic man in an exotic location—had more or less the same intentions as he. By the time that Happy Birthday opened, Gianluca had been obliged to moderate his style.

Dimitris's new bar, which Gianluca had passed once when taking his clothes to the laundry, fitted his purpose perfectly.

Gianluca had been lucky. It was his only luck after two weeks. He had met two very attractive German ladies in the square outside the *kafeneion*. They were sisters, one much younger than the other. They talked about life, the island, music, books and all sorts of things that Gianluca actually considered very boring but essential steps on the path of seduction. And, at a certain point, he suggested that they moved to a quiet bar that had just opened, where they could continue their serious discussion over a cocktail.

Happy Birthday was certainly quiet. Petros had even decided to entrust the running of a bar devoid of customers wholly to Dimitris.

Gianluca was undecided as to which of the sisters he should try for. The younger, Renate, was more attractive but Sabine seemed more interested in him. He decided to play it safe.

"I'm surprised that you have never heard of Paolo Conte," he said, placing his hand on Sabine's arm and stroking it gently.

There was nothing new in this as he had been doing it all evening, to both sisters, sometimes simultaneously.

"His music is sublime. You will love it. I have some in my room," he continued. "We could listen to it together, if you like."

And he transferred his hand from her arm to her knee. Sabine instantly stiffened and gently pulled her knee away.

"Happy birthday!" shouted Dimitris, as he emerged smiling from behind the bar bearing a tray with three cocktails.

All three of them stared at him, nonplussed.

"Is it your birthday today?" Renate asked Gianluca.

"No."

Dimitris put the tray down on their table and delicately placed a cocktail in front of each of them.

"I think you have the wrong table," said Sabine, slowly and clearly.

Dimitris stood back and beamed.

"To you."

"We didn't order these," said Sabine, pointing at the drinks.

"No English," said Dimitris, smiling happily. And he pulled out a chair and sat down.

"Yes," he said.

"We're the only customers," murmured Renate. "I think these must be on the house."

Sabine too had reached the same conclusion. She also felt slightly relieved that Dimitris had joined them.

"Yes," repeated Dimitris.

"Thank you," said Sabine.

"Yes, thank you," said Renate.

Gianluca grunted a *grazie* and stared at Dimitris coldly. He took a sip of the cocktail and coughed. Renate and Sabine raised their glasses.

"*Gia mas!*"

"*Gia mas!*" replied Dimitris. "Ah, you speak Greek! Now, you must tell me what you think of this cocktail."

His three customers stared at him blankly. Dimitris sighed but kept on smiling. Why did foreigners come to Greece and not speak Greek?

"It's very strong," said Sabine. "Quite an unusual taste. What is it?"

"Yes," replied Dimitris.

"It tastes like drain cleaner," muttered Gianluca, pushing his cocktail away.

Sabine and Renate ignored him.

In fact, Sabine and Renate had suddenly developed a great interest in Dimitris. They managed to introduce themselves and tell him that they were German. Dimitris introduced himself as Dimitris and told them he was Greek.

All of this took some considerable time, during which Gianluca had been sidelined. He glanced about, shuffled on his chair impatiently, took further exploratory sips of his cocktail, coughed, grunted a great deal, glared at Dimitris, and generally tried to attract attention to himself.

It was all in vain. When Dimitris started to tell tales of his life as a fisherman, and Sabine and Renate feigned deep interest although clearly unaware that Dimitris was actually talking about fishing, Gianluca conceded defeat. He recognised a brush-off when he saw one.

"*Scusi,*" he said, rising from the table and making a great show of looking at his watch. "Sabine, Renate, please excuse me but I stupidly forgot that I have a previous engagement. I'll see you around."

He did not even glance in Dimitris's direction.

With his departure, the atmosphere around the table lightened considerably. Dimitris had been aware that the Italian had not seemed happy but had put it down to the cocktail. Not everyone is blessed with a refined palate. It now seemed that Gianluca's presence had not been welcomed by the two pretty German ladies and Dimitris had to admit that he had not liked him much either.

By the time Sabine and Renate had consumed half of their cocktails there was great hilarity around the table. Nobody knew exactly why, not that they troubled themselves by wondering about it. Dimitris disappeared behind the bar and returned with a dish of fresh cucumber, olives and cheese, and a glass of tsikoudia for himself. Thirty minutes later he disappeared again and reappeared with two more cocktails.

"Where did that Italian guy go?" Renate asked Sabine.

"Who? Oh, *him*!"

And they dissolved into laughter, in which Dimitris joined in.

"He said this tasted like drain cleaner," said Sabine, pointing at her drink.

"I wonder how he knew that," said Renate.

Dimitris sat back and laughed when they laughed. He had no idea what they were laughing about, but laughter is infectious and after a second and larger glass of tsikoudia, he chuckled away happily, breathing the night air, listening as the language of Goethe and Schiller wafted around him, and gazing at the bougainvillea above.

After that evening, the success of Happy Birthday was assured. Gianluca never returned but many tourists, and even locals, began to appear. This was due in no small amount to Renate and Sabine's network of friends, acquaintances, friends of friends, and friends of acquaintances. No evening was complete without at least one glass of To You at Happy Birthday.

Petros was amazed. He was doubly amazed when, two years to the day after Happy Birthday opened, Dimitris announced that he no longer wished to run it. It would now be owned and run by Petros. The Swedish tourist who had bought *Kristina* had visited enough secluded beaches and Dimitris bought her back for the price he had sold her for. But he renamed her *Happy Birthday*, and proudly displayed in her tiny cabin was the drinks menu from the bar. It had four headings—"Cofees", "Beers", "Drinks" and "Coctails"—and was artfully decorated with pictures of cakes and candles drawn by his young niece, Kristina.

And on young Kristina's birthday, a September day when the summer sun was waning, Dimitris steered his boat into the calm water beyond the bay, cut the engine, and mixed a glass of To You.

"Happy birthday to you, my Kristina!" he shouted.

He took a sip.

And poured the rest into a thirsty sea.

Rope

(The poem 'Imperceptibly' by Blaga Dimitrova, from her collection Scars, *was translated from Bulgarian into English by Ludmila G. Popova-Wightman and published by Ivy Press, Princeton, 2003)*

There's a bit.

Just poking out of the sand.

Hope it's not too long. Wouldn't want it to be too long. Just long enough to tie together, that's all.

Ease it out. It's just like a snake. It's all wet and there's sand sticking to it, but it'll dry out soon and the length is not too bad. It looks like fisherman's rope, the sort they tie boats up with. Nice and thick. Rough on the outside.

But I need more. More rope. Pretty bits that I can tie together.

What? I didn't hear what you said. No, I'm looking for rope. Not the plastic sort—real rope. I don't care what you think. And you can stop looking at me that way. I clean for you! I clean for everybody.

He has gone now. Good. I hate those smiley old Greek men. They were no better back home. Always busy with their eyes and hands.

There's nothing more on this bit of beach. I'll have to try somewhere else. Maybe on the quayside. Sometimes the fishermen cut off bits of rope and throw them away, don't they? There might be a lot of rope on the quayside. Enough rope to make a big garland. A garland for midsummer! A garland for freedom and escape. A garland to celebrate the fulfilment of me!

But there's nothing here. Plenty of rope but all long in neat coils. Nothing short.

I have a knife; I could cut a bit off, I suppose. No, someone would see me and then I'd be for it. Another bloody Bulgarian stealing, they'll say.

I've never stolen a thing in my life, except a heart maybe and they lock you up for that. They lock *your* heart away. They lock *your* heart in a cold, dark place and leave it to starve.

Hello! Who are you? A sweet little rope hiding under that tarpaulin. A bit frayed at the end… Oh, I see! You're a girl rope with long frizzy hair! Are you feeling all alone? Well, never mind! I've got a friend for you to play with. Isn't he a nice bit of wet, sandy rope? And you're all dry and smooth. You can get married right away. Look, I'm tying the knot! You're twisting and writhing around each other. He's so rough and stiff and stubbly to the touch and you're so beautifully smooth!

I felt his touch.

Now we had better find you some children, don't you think? Married people should have children, shouldn't they? We might even give them names.

But there are no children here, are there, my darlings? We'll have to look elsewhere.

Just look at that seagull. Isn't she beautiful?

Gliding up there, white in the blue. I can feel the air ruffling my pure white feathers. It takes just the slightest twitch of my white wing and I'm soaring away over the island. This stupid island! There's no one to argue with up there. No hate. No pain. No heart locked away in a cold, dark place. Only warm air over white wings. The slightest twitch of a white feather and I change direction. I swoop. I glide.

There's plenty of time to go up to the place. There'll be rope on the way, plenty of rope. And when I get there, the sun will be setting and all will be gold. The sea and the air will turn gold, the hills will turn blue, and I can finish my garland for midsummer. And midsummer will be happy with me.

The street. And the tourists! They spend so much money to get here and then waste their time drinking coffee or beer while they watch people passing. They have coffee and beer back home. And people pass. Maybe even people they know.

I know him. I know him only too well. Always sits here about this time. Mustn't look at him. Mustn't make eye contact. Great, I've passed him and he hasn't seen me.

What do I see? Somebody's cut off a piece of washing line? Did somebody throw you away, my sweet? Never mind. I'm here. And so are your mummy and daddy. Now you can all join together. A happy family already, but I think you need a few brothers and sisters, don't you?

The bars are opening. Soon they will be playing music. It will crash and churn, and then join into one big roar. It won't sound like music any more. It will be the background noise to nights on this island, the white noise for white nights that you accept and ignore.

Some dance to remember. Some dance to forget.

I came here to work and send some money home. Slim chance of that! But what about the people packed into bars or sweating on dancefloors? Why do they travel so far and spend so much money to get here? Because it's warm?

Maybe they think that sunshine and sea will make their pain and problems go away. But life is all pain and problems! There isn't anything else! The boyfriend or girlfriend who thinks you love them and you can't bring yourself to tell them you don't. The parent, partner or child who is going to die, or is dead already. The divorce that hasn't gone through yet. The debts that have to be repaid. The best that you can do is to forget your pain and your problems for a few moments. You can't afford to forget them entirely because sooner or later you will have to face them.

So, maybe you give your pain and problems a holiday. You bring them with you so they get a nice suntan. But they don't go away. You don't leave them here.

He took away my pain. I felt his touch.

Look! A late seagull drifting high above the street! I wonder what you make of us down here. Are you looking for fun too? I don't suppose you know what fun is. Or maybe you don't have to look for it because it's always there. And now you can look down on thousands of people trying to capture what you get every day. Thousands of people looking for fun. And one looking for rope.

No rope here, of course. The streets are nicely swept. Ready for tonight's rubbish.

I'll sit down on this stone wall and smoke a cigarette. No, if I do that, I will have to hold my head up. I'll sit down anyway because I have to think. I'll lean forward and my long black hair will shield my face.

But I cannot think. My head is full of rope and seagulls, caresses and whispered promises. The paving stones are stained and streaked. They will be washed in the morning, but only the winter rain will really wash them clean.

Will I truly do what I promised myself to do? I could go into one of those bars now and spend my last euros on getting drunk. Sit alone in a dark corner and drink vodka. I could stagger back to my room, fall onto my bed and go to work tomorrow. Throw the rope into a rubbish bin.

But I have no more choices. My choices have already been made. Now I will just stare down at myself like a circling seagull and watch my choices play out.

Get up and walk.

Almost out of the village. Now there are only the tourists walking past me, laughing and chatting and looking for fun in their nice, clean, white clothes that show off their new suntans, and with nice, clean, freshly shampooed hair. Forget your pain and problems, my sweet little tourists. Forget again for a night!

And here are two young children for my family of rope! A thin, straggly rope and…well, not a pink one but I think there's something feminine about it. The way it curls and coils. A bit feline. But there'll make ideal children! I'll call them the twins because I found them at the same time. A couple of quick knots and there—done! The perfect family!

But it shouldn't be the perfect family. There are no perfect families. My family of rope needs one more member. A black sheep. The middle child. The ugly one. The runt. Maybe my little black sheep will be at the beach, covered in tar.

Or maybe poking out of a rubbish bin. It will be the weak, debauched rope. The rope that has been abused and defiled. An embarrassment to its family.

My family's getting quite long now. It will have to be long to make a garland for the summer.

The Swedish girls wear crowns of flowers on Midsummer Eve. They look like angels with their blonde hair and shining blue eyes. And they chase after the black-haired, dark-eyed Greek men. Just for the holiday. Just for a bit of fun. And the black haired, dark-eyed Greek men chase after them. The *kamaki*, the harpoons that spear delicate, blue-eyed fish, hunt their prey at the beach or at night and count their catch and boast to their friends when the season has closed. They boast of their catch over glasses of raki and show photographs of the best specimens.

 I am not blonde-haired and blue-eyed. I am dark of hair and eye. I am not a specimen to boast of.

But I felt his touch.

The beach. The beach that faces west. The beach that catches the orphans of the westerly storms—plastic bags, driftwood and rusty cans. Here's where I'll find my black sheep!

The sun is low now, burning its way to sunset. The seagulls have vanished upwards into the sky and the first tiny bats are flitting between the trees. The Swedish girls have vanished into heaven and the dark Bulgarians are out!

Perhaps the glowing sun will show me my black sheep before it plunges the beach into blackness.

And there it is, like a tarry viper on the sand.

You are the proper rope to complete this garland for the summer. You, the black sheep, make this family complete. And now to weave my garland! No crown of flowers for the Bulgarian girl but a loop for the circle of the family and a knot for its union. A loop in which all the family takes part: the stiff, stubbly man; the soft, smooth woman; the two sweet children and the tarry black sheep. No more is needed. The knot for love and the loop for eternity.

And now for the favourite place. The golden place where the sun dissolves into the sea. The seagull's world. You climb a little way through the sweet-smelling thyme and the warmth of the island rises through your feet. You climb over sharp rocks but you do not feel their sharpness. The warm breath of the island takes away all pain.

I felt his touch. It was like the warm breath of the island. It took away my pain.

I felt his touch and then no more.

I smelled him. It was the fragrance of thyme, and of sour wine and cheap cigarettes. I smelled the touch of his skin.

It took away my pain.

But he gave my pain back to me. He locked away my heart in a cold, dark place where the seagull never comes. Cold and darkness in the midst of heat and light. Tears in the midst of pleasure.

I will go. And the space I used to take will be filled with air—a liberation—invisible and spacious. A silent presence, from which someone else, unconsciously, will take a big breath.

Here, at the end of the island, is the favourite place. And there is the sun, kissing and caressing the sea. And here is my gift for the sun and the sunset, my garland for the summer. I will drape it over the tree that strains to join the seagulls at the edge of the world. I will entwine my garland round its trunk and knot it fast for eternity.

I felt his touch.

And the loop of the garland, of my family, I will twine around my neck. The beautiful woman, the loving, devoted man, the two perfect children and the one black sheep will be united in me, in an infinite circle.

Here is the last seagull of the day to salute the sun. Watch it swoop and soar. Watch that impassive face gaze down on the world of men. And suddenly all is purity. All is freedom.

All is hope.

I felt his touch.

I will give the big breath.

Jump.

Lazarus

Martha had been born in a vineyard. At least, that was what she sometimes liked to tell people. It was a joke that she used at boring Burbank parties, usually followed by polite laughter, but there was an element of truth in it. Martha was born and grew up on the island of Martha's Vineyard, Massachusetts, and was named after it.

Her husband Henry had been a moderately successful Hollywood scriptwriter and had earned enough to assure them both a comfortable retirement. They had visited the island before on several occasions—never for very long, but long enough and often enough to fall under its spell. Henry thought that it was an ideal place to retire to while he wrote his first novel and Martha, who had been a librarian, agreed.

Moving from Burbank, California, to a small island in Greece had not been easy. Martha and Henry contacted a local estate agent who sent them photographs of a romantically abandoned house on what was simply referred to as the other side of the island.

Their first viewing explained exactly why the house had been abandoned: prevailing westerly winds had scoured the surrounding land down to scattered stones and smooth bedrock which, if the house had not been so sturdily built, it would certainly have joined.

Despite this shortcoming, Henry at least fell in love with it. This was greatly helped by the weather at the time, which worked completely in the estate agent's favour. Uncharacteristically, there was little or no wind; gentle waves lapped against the pebble beach below; wheeling seagulls added their plaintive selling pitch. They could even savour the sweet fragrance of wild thyme, which would normally have been blasted away to a neighbouring island.

According to the estate agent, the house was about a hundred and fifty years old, making it roughly the same age as Burbank. Apart from an itinerant population of goats, the nearest neighbours were at least a kilometre distant. Having no electricity, running water or sewage system put it on a par with several other houses on the other side of the island, and to add to its ethnic authenticity it had no roof. Nevertheless, to prove beyond doubt that it had once been lived in, what remained of the last occupants' possessions had been dumped in a collapsed heap nearby. There were some broken chairs, the corroded remains of an oil lamp, and a curious lattice of rust that Martha and Henry later identified as bed springs.

But the view was truly breathtaking.

"It's delightful," said Henry. "One hundred per cent Greek. Idyllic. I can write here."

"It really is delightful," agreed Martha. "But it's a wreck."

"It might be a wreck but we can fix it!" said Henry, with archetypical can-do optimism. He knew all about such things, having previously lived in the spacious family home in Encino, a shared warehouse in San Francisco in his hippie days, a flat in downtown L.A. as a struggling scriptwriter, and a condo in Burbank.

"Sure we can," said Martha, not entirely sharing his certainty.

Getting the house fixed up took some considerable time, much of which was spent waiting while the estate agent made sure that the seller was the actual owner and persuaded him to sell at the agreed price a house that he had previously considered worthless and had actually forgotten about but which had suddenly appeared to be of considerable value.

In the first year after purchasing the house, Henry and Martha's attentions were mostly focused on renovating it, which, as Henry had predicted, was possible, though, as Martha had feared, not easy. It was expensively hooked up to mains electricity; a septic tank was installed for the sewage; running water was laid on, although not water that you could actually drink, and there was now a roof. But not much else. Henry and Martha had brought a few sticks of furniture from Burbank, books and records, and a lot of goodwill from their family and friends who had wished them good luck in their new venture and expected to see them back within a year.

Yet there arrived a time when Martha and Henry were sitting on their patio on the battered chairs that they had bought from a local taverna and admiring the setting sun. As it sank to the horizon, they could pick out the grey shapes of surrounding islands. A picturesque *kaiki* puttered into view. A tiny bat flittered around the walls of their house.

"Notice something?" asked Henry, while sipping his ouzo.

"The wind has dropped."

And indeed, it had.

They sat in silence for a few minutes. Henry was first to break it.

"This is why we came here, Martha."

"Yes."

Henry and Martha had never considered producing their own wine; it was very much an afterthought. Grapes had been grown on the island for centuries, possibly millennia, but they were mostly distilled into tsikoudia and wine was rather a by-product. Relatively little was produced, even less was bottled, and none of it was sold commercially. There was a very good reason for that.

They had sampled the local brew on their first visit to the island. The wine list in their favourite taverna was not extensive—in fact there was no wine list at all—and so, one evening, having already tasted the few wines on offer, they decided to try the contents of an unlabelled plastic bottle that was sitting on the zinc counter inside the taverna, ignored by the other customers, including the locals.

"It *is* wine, isn't it?" Henry asked the waiter, who had brought the plastic bottle to their table and poured a small amount into his glass, more out of habit than as an invitation to taste.

"Local wine," replied the waiter, apologetically, and promptly scurried back into the taverna as if he had just thrown a bomb.

Henry held his glass up to the light. On the counter inside the taverna, the wine had been roughly the same colour as malt vinegar. The colour had not changed now that it was in his glass.

He took a tentative sip. The wine was odd. It had a vinegary flavour without being vinegar. It was more like a slightly off sherry, and it packed a punch.

"Well?" Martha asked, preferring to get Henry's opinion before venturing further.

Henry placed his glass on the table.

"It's real wine," he said. "Very real. They've probably been making it the same way since the days of Socrates. Come to think of it, what did Socrates die of exactly?"

"He was forced to drink hemlock."

"Are you sure?"

He paused as the tannins kicked in.

"You know the ancient Greeks never drank wine without diluting it with water first," he continued, grimacing. "They reckoned it was mad to drink it neat. I can see why."

Martha poured herself a glass and tasted it.

"Goodness gracious!" she exclaimed. "That's awful!"

"It's authentic," replied Henry. "Yes, it's awful."

Indirectly, this is how Martha and Henry came to own a small vineyard. They bought it from an elderly farmer who was suspiciously happy to sell it. Although they knew next to nothing about wine production, they figured that their result could not be any worse than the wine they had tasted in the taverna years ago, and producing something better would be a challenge.

They had first considered uprooting the old vines and replanting. Neither of them—and certainly not the elderly farmer—had any idea what variety of grape the old vines were. In fact, he was not very forthcoming about anything related to them. Judging by the thickness of their gnarled trunks, they were certainly much older than the farmer. At least they produced grapes, so Martha and Henry decided to play safe and plant new stock alongside them.

Martha had ordered a few books on viticulture through her sister in Massachusetts, but both she and Henry had been put off by their complexity and they all seemed to have been written with American wine growers in mind. Greece did not get a mention. Finally, they took a leap of faith and ordered twenty pinot noir plants from France. Pinot noir seemed like a safe bet: it was fairly easy to grow, tolerated dry conditions and would produce either red wines or white. The plants took an eternity to arrive and six of them were dead on arrival.

Henry started work on his novel. This meant reading through all of the notes he had made in California over the years, and then making more and more additional notes.

Finally, he rolled a blank A4 sheet into his Olivetti Lettera portable typewriter and waited.

While he was waiting, and while she was waiting for the pinot noir vines to grow, Martha started to take a deeper interest in the island they had chosen as a home. In fact, there was not much else to do.

The written history of the island was sketchy, mostly consisting of anecdotes in the histories of its larger neighbouring islands. It had been overrun by pirates; the pirates were kicked out by the Venetians; the Venetians built a fort; the Venetians left; the pirates reappeared; the islanders left; the pirates left; the islanders returned; nothing much seemed to have happened after that. But what most of these histories seemed to agree on was that the island had once been covered with cedar trees. The trees had been felled for building, shipbuilding and firewood, and none had survived. Except one.

On the north coast of the island, on rocky ground only a few metres from the sea, a magnificent tree rose fifteen metres from the arid soil and spread its branches just as wide. It was obvious to Martha that it was the last remaining representative of the cedar forest that had covered the island millennia ago. Her suspicions were confirmed by asking around locally. Yes, she heard, it is *kedros*—cedar.

"Mary! Is that you?" Martha shouted into the battered public telephone at the port.

"Martha?" came her sister's crackling voice from Massachusetts, with several seconds' delay.

"Listen, I don't have long. Can you send me some cedar seeds?"

"*Cigar* seeds?"

"No cedar seeds! C-E-D-A-R. As many as you can get. And send me anything you can find about growing them."

"Are you okay, Martha?" came an anxious voice.

"I'm fine. Just do it, right? I'm running out of coins."

The seeds duly arrived with a photocopied set of instructions, but even with the aid of the instructions growing a cedar tree from seed was not an easy business.

First of all, she had to "scarify" the seeds—which meant scratching them with a knife—and then soak them in warm water for two or three hours. It was claimed that the seeds less likely to germinate would continue to float, while the more promising examples would sink to the bottom of the water. This seemed vaguely reminiscent of testing eggs for freshness and effectively reduced the hundred or so seeds that Mary had sent to six. Then came "stratification", which meant that these remaining seeds were lightly covered in very damp, sterilised compost. Not having a ready supply of sterilised compost, Martha bought some ordinary compost and steamed it. The pots then had to be kept in the vegetable compartment of her refrigerator for one to three months.

All in all, it seemed like a pretty hopeless task. Why put the seeds in a refrigerator when the temperature on the island rarely fell below freezing? How would that help?

At first, Martha checked on the seeds every week and made sure that the compost was still wet but not soaking. Then she occasionally forgot to check and sometimes added too much water. As the weeks passed, her checks became less and less frequent. Finally, they stopped.

"Hey, Martha! Looks like something's happening with your plants!" shouted Henry, from the kitchen.

"What plants?"

It had now been four months since Martha had put the cedar seeds in the refrigerator.

"Your cigar plants," shouted Henry.

Martha scurried into the kitchen and peered into the back of vegetable compartment. She saw two pale yellow stalks protruding from the pots.

"Well, I'll be!" she exclaimed.

Following the instructions faithfully, Martha re-potted the two seedlings and put them "in a sunny position". Unfortunately, a sunny position in their house proved altogether too sunny for one of the seedlings, which promptly died. Martha moved the remaining seedling to a less sunny position. At first, it too looked not long for this world, but then, quite unexpectedly, it began to grow.

It did not grow very quickly. After six months, it had reached the height of an asparagus stalk and seemed in no hurry to proceed to the level of broccoli. As it had struggled back from the dead, and as her own name was Martha and her sister's name was Mary, she decided to christen it Lazarus.

By the time Lazarus was thirty centimetres tall, the surviving pinot noir vines had grown by a metre and a half, but had so far produced no grapes. The farmer's vines, which Martha had drastically pruned, had large bunches of luscious fruit. Henry was dead.

Henry's death was sudden. He and Martha had fallen into the habit of taking daily walks and she had lately noticed that he had begun to have difficulty in coping with hills. The island had many hills; in fact, the island was mostly hills. They would bring on wheezing and shortness of breath but Henry always dismissed this as indigestion.

"Too many greens and beans," he would say, laughing.

But then, one day, after they had returned from their walk and Henry was setting coffee, as he usually did after those excursions, he suddenly uttered a short gasp and fell. The coroner's report gave the cause of death as a massive heart attack. He was not very old. He had reached chapter six of his novel. Martha gathered together the loose sheets of paper and they were buried with him in the island's cemetery.

Henry's funeral was attended by many of the great and good of Burbank, Hollywood and Massachusetts. In fact, there were so many of the great and good that the island was not able to accommodate them all and many of the mourners had to stay on adjacent islands and fly in by helicopter. This caused much consternation among the locals as, until then, helicopters had only been used in dire medical emergencies.

"Somebody must be very poorly," observed Christos, rolling a cigarette and following the latest flight.

"That makes three today," said Costas. "Unless they brought one back for a second opinion."

The national press also covered the funeral—not because Henry was well-known but because many of the mourners were. He had been well-respected as a scriptwriter but that was strictly within the industry and, apart from a single Oscar nomination for best screenplay, his name had never cropped up in the media. Yet in death Henry had suddenly become more famous than in life, and the very people that he and Martha had come halfway round the world to escape were there on their doorstep.

"I can see why you and Henry came here," said Jad Pickford, gazing dreamily over the hills when the hour after sunset plunged them into warm blueness. He held Martha's hand in his sweaty and not altogether welcome grasp.

"This is real. Authentic," he added, nodding his chiselled features approvingly.

"So was the wine," replied Martha.

Jad decided to build a house. Or rather, have it built.

There was nothing bad about Jad and he was by no means alone in wanting to purchase a piece of heaven. However, thanks to his fame as a film star and the media coverage that Henry's funeral had engendered, the island was now firmly on the international map. Within a few years, there was an explosion of luxury villas built by an army of poorly paid Albanian workers. While making concessions to traditional Greek architecture and planning, the owners naturally wanted somewhat redundant hot tubs, manicured lawns, sprinklers and swimming pools. The fact that the island depended on rainfall for its water was blithely ignored.

In the following years, several of the Hollywood newcomers tried to seek Martha out, but she avoided them on the island as she had in Burbank. It did not take long for them to regard her as an eccentric recluse.

"They've got a nerve calling *me* eccentric," was her only comment.

Apart from cycling into the village to buy food and other necessities, she mostly occupied herself with gardening and taking long, solitary walks across the hills. There was something about both of these activities that brought her closer to Henry, although she was uncomfortably aware that it was walking across the hills that had precipitated his death.

Following Henry's death, Martha had briefly contemplated returning to the United States, but she had become even more attached to the island than before, and more particularly to her house. It still had no air-conditioning and could be bitterly cold and damp in the winter but, thanks to importing several tons of topsoil, the garden quickly became established. Martha had insisted that they planted only species that were native to the island, so she had taken a good look at what was growing locally.

Lazarus had risen from the dead. When the cedar sapling had struggled to a height of some fifty centimetres, Martha transplanted it to the garden. At first, Lazarus seemed uncertain about its new environment. For almost a year, it hung its head as if sizing up the quality of the topsoil and examining the possibilities for extending its roots. Then, deciding that this was probably the best it could hope for, it began to grow again.

It had long been obvious that planting pinot noir had been a mistake. The grape that could produce Gevrey-Chambertin on the temperate, rolling hills of Burgundy struggled in the island's fierce summer heat and its dry soil. But with careful pruning and judicious watering, the anonymous vines that Martha had inherited from the elderly farmer produced big, succulent grapes that burst with aromatic juice.

Since neither she nor Henry had given much thought to processing their fruit, Martha decided to have the grapes taken to a neighbouring farmer who pressed them, fermented them and delivered back the results in large plastic containers. The farmer kept the pomace to be distilled into tsikoudia.

Martha did not taste the wine until the late spring of the year following Henry's death, when two hikers suddenly appeared in her garden.

"Excuse me," said a middle-aged man wearing football shorts and a sweat-stained T-shirt. "Do you speak English?"

"Yes, I do," replied Martha, squinting at the bright sunlight from the shade of her porch. She was surprised at the sudden intrusion and smiled at the idea that such a question was now necessary. But with her grey hair tied back in a bun, her dark brown skin and her simple floral dress she probably looked like a lot of island ladies of a certain age. She set aside her book.

"I'm American."

"Oh, indeed?" said the man, whose wife was smiling frantically and nodding her head. "We are from the Netherlands. We are sorry to come into your beautiful garden but we seem to have missed the path."

To lend force to this, he pulled a crumpled map from his belly bag and waved it at her.

"I see," said Martha. "Where are you headed?"

"What?"

"Where do you want to go?"

"The village."

"The village is over that rise," said Martha, pointing to an adjacent hill. "Just follow the road up from the house."

"This house?"

"Yes, this house."

And then, Martha considered something that she would never have dreamt doing in Burbank, but seemed such an obvious thing to do in Greece.

"Come into the shade. Would you like a glass of water?"

She was reminded of the classic line from Hollywood horror films, usually preceded by a creaking of hinges, a hooded face peering around the door and the words "Come in. The Master has been expecting you."

The man and his wife exchanged looks. The man said something to her in Dutch. His wife replied.

"Thank you. That is very kind."

At least they had not said "We were just driving through to Pasadena but the road's washed out. Can we use your phone?"

"I'll tell you what," said Martha, once the three of them were seated around her simple table, "to hell with the water. How about some wine?"

In the kitchen, Martha opened a plastic container and poured wine into a large milk jug. She set it on the table on the veranda with a plate of black olives and cucumber.

"There!" she exclaimed, pouring the wine into three glasses. "This is our own wine made from our own grapes. Do tell me what you think."

"How nice!" said the man. "I love these Greek traditions!" Although he and his wife regarded their glasses warily.

"It is an unusual colour," he ventured, lifting his glass to the light. "I do not think I have seen brown wine before."

His wife continued to grin frantically although there was now something slightly frozen in her expression.

"Cheers!" said Martha, brightly, and raised her glass.

The Dutch couple raised their glasses and took a sip.

The man grunted slightly and collapsed face down into the olives.

According to the autopsy, the results of which were released several weeks later, the Dutchman had died of a stroke brought on by over-exertion, hyperthermia, dehydration and an underlying heart condition. There was no mention of the wine. Nevertheless, Martha dragged all of the plastic containers out of the house and emptied their contents. She sold her vineyard to the son of the elderly farmer at far less than the price that she and Henry had paid for it.

It is not generally considered polite to die on someone else's porch and undignified to end your life face down in a dish of olives. Martha had been understandably shocked, then angry and shocked, and finally just angry. In revenge, she decided to expand her horizons by coupling her shopping trips to the village with regular visits to a harbourside café where she would drink a cup of coffee, sometimes with a slice of baklava. It was on one of these trips that she was introduced to Dr Michalis Florakis.

Florakis was a professor of Botany at the University of Athens. He was good-looking although slightly overweight, unaccompanied, and on holiday, which is undoubtably why Athena, the lady who ran the café, introduced him to Martha. Florakis, however, was not overjoyed with being introduced to a local gardener when he just wanted to enjoy his beer in peace.

"We seem to have been pushed together," he said in accentless English, smiling and glancing back at the café-owner, who was now occupied with other customers. "Do you really mind if I join you? If not, just say so. I don't wish to impose."

He hoped that she would say that she was waiting for friends.

"No. It's fine. Feel free," replied Martha, gesturing to an empty chair, while wondering where this would lead.

Florakis sat down. He felt very awkward, as did Martha.

"I was told you want to re-establish the local flora," he ventured.

"The what?"

"Plants."

"Oh, yes. The local flora. Of course."

"It sounds like a nice idea."

Florakis took a sip of beer and coughed nervously.

"If I lived here, I would probably do the same," he added.

"I'm just growing native plants, that's all. It would be nice to return the island to the way it was."

Florakis raised his eyebrows.

"That's pretty ambitious, don't you think?"

"Well, my small part of it at least," she said, laughing.

Florakis smiled. He didn't want to be patronising.

"The way it was?"

"Yes."

Florakis leant back in his chair and scratched his head. His shirt was too tight; the buttons described figures of eight across his belly.

"And how was it?"

This was a question that Martha had pondered at some length over the years, but now that Florakis had asked her, she had to admit to herself that she really had little idea how it was.

"Take your time," said Florakis, smiling.

He seemed friendly and genuinely interested, but it felt rather like she was being tested, or interviewed for a job. She sought inspiration in the brilliant bougainvillea that screened the café from the harsh midday sun.

"I heard the island was once covered with trees," she said.

Florakis nodded.

"That's correct. It *was* covered with trees. As I'm sure you know, they were mostly cut down to make houses and boats, or used as fuel. It's sad, of course, but also inevitable, I'm afraid. You can't blame people for wanting to be dry, warm and well nourished. Unfortunately, they went too far."

"They cut down everything."

"Almost everything."

He drained the last of his beer.

"It's much the same with tourism."

"Tourism?"

"Yes. A few hundred years ago, you had an island covered with trees. That was your biggest resource. So you keep on felling trees indiscriminately and what you don't use yourself, you sell. And, for a while at least, you are prosperous. But it's unsustainable, of course. There comes a time when the trees have gone, and so too has your livelihood."

Martha nodded.

"But tourism?"

"I was coming to that," said Florakis, wondering whether to have another beer. He thought better of it.

"Let's go back not a few hundred years but only, say, fifty. About the time when the first tourists arrived here. What did they find? Fishermen and farmers. I think the expression is dirt poor. But for them, coming from the urban West, the island was an unspoilt paradise. They had no idea of the misery that lay behind the white walls and bougainvillea, nor did they care. But the islanders saw a viable alternative to farming and fishing. So, they rented out rooms, and then built hotels and then sold their land so that foreigners could build holiday homes and luxury villas, and claim their slice of paradise. Until finally, there was no paradise left. It had disappeared, like the trees. You cannot sell the same piece of land twice. Gone is gone."

"You make it sound pretty bleak," said Martha.

"It's what's happened. Bleak or not."

There was another awkward break in their conversation. Martha pretended to drink from a coffee cup that was already empty. Florakis was aware that he had become too serious.

"What plants are you growing?" he asked, in a softer tone.

"Well, I've transplanted a lot of wildflowers," replied Martha.

Florakis smiled approvingly.

"And I've also planted oleander, hibiscus, bougainvillea and even a cedar tree."

"A cedar?"

"Yes. It's doing pretty well," she added proudly.

Florakis nodded.

"Well done with the cedar," he said. "But I have to tell you that none of the plants you mentioned are really native to the island. You'll see plenty of oleander bushes here, but they're not Greek. There's a native Greek hibiscus but it's not the one you see in gardens, and it isn't native to the island anyway. As to bougainvillea, well, it comes from South America."

"Oh."

Florakis smiled ruefully.

"I'm sorry to disappoint you."

"But what about the cedar? Surely the island was covered in them? There's still a big one here on the north coast."

"The north coast? Oh, I know the one you mean," said Florakis. "It's really magnificent but sadly it's not a cedar. It's a juniper—juniperus excelsa, to be exact. Yours is an understandable mistake, not helped by we Greeks calling all those trees cedars, which they're not."

"All those? You mean there's more than one?"

"Of course. There are hundreds all over the island. You pass them every day. The one we're talking about is by far the biggest, and it's probably almost a thousand years old, but there are many more—some of them very small. You see, as long as it's left alone, nature can eventually recover without any help from us. The island as a whole is another matter."

Martha looked dejected. Florakis suddenly felt sorry for her. He had not really wanted the conversation in the first place and perhaps he had spoken harshly.

"You did well to grow a cedar," he said, with a diffident smile. "They are not easy trees to grow."

"You're telling me!" exclaimed, Martha. "I named him Lazarus because he rose from the dead."

Florakis laughed.

"I think you like this island, Martha."

"I love this island."

"I'm happy to hear that," he said, in a soft voice. "I truly am. But, may I offer a small piece of advice?"

Martha lifted her empty cup and laid it sideways on its saucer. It was an inconsequential act that she would not have been able to explain at the time. Later, she thought of it as resigning at chess.

"Yes?"

"Always remember that the island is a reality, not an idea. "

He stood up, pushed the wooden chair aside.

"It was a pleasure meeting you," he said. "And I'm sure you won't be surprised to learn that cedars are not an invasive species."

Martha retreated to her hilltop house. She left the island a year later. As she had finally become something of a recluse, her absence was not particularly noticed.

"Of course, not only do you have a fabulous, authentic Greek farmhouse with newly installed air-conditioning but also this wonderful garden," said the estate agent, spreading his arms wide.

"Oh my God," exclaimed the lady. "It truly is a wonderful garden. And you say it was laid out by a Hollywood actress?"

"Yes indeed," said the estate agent. "Although, of course, she wishes to remain anonymous. But just look at these magnificent native plants! You've got oleander, hibiscus, bougainvillea…"

He paused for dramatic effect before pointing to a tree that dominated the plot of land in front of the house.

"And here you have a cedar tree! The last one on the island! It even has a name."

Nereids

"Boat trips," said Captain Nikos, leaning on the bar and scratching his chin.

"Boat trips," repeated Giannis, scanning the basketball results in his newspaper. "Boat trips to where?"

"Around the island," replied Nikos. "For tourists."

Giannis sighed. He transferred his gaze from the sporting pages of *To Vima* to the empty *kafeneion* and back again.

"Sounds a bit boring."

"Boring?"

Nikos looked as if he had heard the word for the first time.

"Why should it be boring?"

"Well, it's not a very big island. You're going to spend the summer going round and round it?"

"Ah!" exclaimed Nikos, significantly. "But you're forgetting the tourists. The tourists will be different."

"I suppose so," agreed Giannis, sighing again.

"Blonde-haired, blue-eyed, big-bosomed girls?" said Nikos, smiling wickedly.

Giannis raised his eyes from his newspaper yet again and scrutinised Nikos. He noted the threadbare cap, the thick glasses, the scrawny neck, the unshaven chin, the missing left hand.

"You do know that there are already bars offering trips around the island, don't you, Niko? There are even one or two people who offer trips around the island without going to the trouble of opening a bar. And they'll even throw in a barbecue on the beach, as much wine as you can drink, and perhaps a game of volleyball. I think your blonde-haired, blue-eyed, big-bosomed girls are more likely to go with them than you."

"Ah!" exclaimed Nikos.

"Get my point?"

"Ah!" repeated Captain Nikos. "But you're forgetting Zorba!"

"Zorba who?"

"Zorba the Greek," replied Nikos, sprinkling tobacco on a cigarette paper and rolling it deftly with his remaining hand. "You've heard of Zorba the Greek, I suppose?"

"Of course," said Giannis.

"Then you know what I mean," said Nikos, slyly, licking the cigarette paper.

Giannis tried to return his attention to the football results, but it was no good.

"No, I don't know what you mean. What the hell has Zorba the Greek got to do with trips around the island?"

"It's simple," said Captain Nikos, calmly lighting his cigarette. "All the beautiful tourist girls are in love with Zorba. They want to go on a trip around the island…with Zorba."

"With Anthony Quinn, you mean."

"I know what they want," replied an unruffled Nikos.

"What they want is Anthony Quinn, not you. Besides, Anthony Quinn is Mexican."

"Mexican?"

"Mexican."

"Then obviously a real Greek can do it better."

Giannis folded his newspaper and tossed it into the rubbish bin.

"Quinn can dance," he said. "You can't."

"I only have one hand."

"True."

Giannis raised his eyebrows and started to make himself a coffee.

"You can't compete with the others," he said, adding a generous amount of sugar. "Face facts."

"Ah!" exclaimed Nikos, once again. "But I'll have Advertising!"

"Advertising?"

"Look here."

Captain Nikos clamped his half-smoked cigarette between his lips and fished in the inside pocket of his work, wedding and funeral jacket. He produced a folded sheet from a school exercise book.

"What have we got here?" asked Giannis, taking it.

"Trips around the island with Captain Nikos. Reasonable rates," he read. "Reasonable sounds a bit vague, doesn't it?"

"I'll discuss the rates before we set off. That's reasonable, isn't it?"

Giannis paused as he was about to add the water.

"How many people can that boat of yours hold?" he asked, peering at the captain over his reading glasses.

"The *Amalia*?" said Nikos, proudly. "Why, the *Amalia* can hold…well…six. Seven at a pinch."

"Including you?"

"Of course not. You never count the crew."

"And how big is the *Amalia*?" asked Giannis, patiently. "Ten feet?"

"Twelve feet!" answered Nikos. "And every foot is solidly built. It's lasted me fifty years and it will last me fifty years more."

Giannis removed his reading glasses and scanned the ceiling of the *kafeneion*.

"So according to my calculations," he apparently read from the ceiling, "that makes two feet per passenger, not counting the extra one at a pinch, crew, or tourists with big bosoms."

"Plenty of room," agreed Captain Nikos. "I might even squeeze in another two."

"Are you insured?"

Captain Nikos chuckled drily.

"Are *you* insured? Have you ever thought about that tsikoudia you serve?"

As it turned out, Captain Nikos's advertising was, surprisingly, a marketing failure. Surprisingly for Nikos, that is. Although the sheet torn from the school exercise book and pinned to the tree in the square undoubtedly received some attention from passing tourists, the lack of a telephone number or even an address, together with the fact that none of the tourists had the faintest idea who Captain Nikos was, ensured a slow start to the new business venture.

This did not come as a complete surprise to Nikos's wife. After forty years of marriage, the long-suffering Maria was more than accustomed to her husband's whims and fancies. These had varied from the planned purchase of a thoroughbred racehorse to the actual purchase of an expensive petrol-powered generator three months before mains electricity was introduced to the island. She also suspected that Nikos's new venture was motivated less by a need to supplement their income and more from a desire to spend large amounts of time with blonde-haired, blue-eyed, big-bosomed tourists, not that she typified them as such.

Be that as it may, what Maria could never complain about was Nikos's lack of inventiveness. He had been born poor—they had both been born poor—but Nikos had always nurtured a desire to better himself. Life together had never been dull. No two years were ever the same.

Finally, Captain Nikos concluded that the only way to effectively drum up trade was to take a direct approach. This meant sallying forth into the tourist area of the square.

Before the first tourists arrived on the island, not counting the Venetians, the Turks, the Italian army and the occasional pirate, the square had been the common property of everyone. In fact, during the day, it still was. However, on summer evenings, the square was now given over to the tourists and the men of the village retreated to a small corner contiguous with the main street. Nobody really knew how this had come about. Some tended to believe that, in the tradition of the Venetians, Turks and Italian army, the tourists had simply occupied the square and driven everyone else out. Others, who viewed tourism with a less jaundiced eye, concluded that the older men of the village preferred the company of like-minded individuals who they could understand to that of young, strangely dressed people who they could not understand.

Nikos did not view venturing onto the square with any great enthusiasm. It meant noise. It meant being jostled. It meant understanding little or nothing of what was being said around him.

On the other hand, it was difficult to ignore the fact that the square contained a good many blonde-haired, blue-eyed tourists—one or two with big bosoms—who would certainly jump at the chance of conversing with the real Zorba. And who might also pay handsomely to be escorted around the island by him.

So, in the end, lechery and greed won. Nikos set his captain's hat at what he thought was a rakish angle and seated himself at one end of the square, although close enough to the locals' section to make a quick escape possible if necessary.

"Perhaps I should have made a sign," he muttered to himself, as he rolled a cigarette. "No, it would look like begging."

He lit his cigarette, clamped it firmly in one side of his mouth and tried to look suitably Zorba-like. This consisted of scratching himself a great deal and grinning unnervingly at any female tourist who made accidental eye contact.

After about five minutes his cigarette went out and his attempts to emulate Anthony Quinn were starting to tire him. A further five minutes saw him stifling his yawns and wondering whether it might be a good idea to give the *Amalia* a lick of paint before the first passengers embarked. The passengers! He saw blonde hair, glistening golden skins in a turquoise sea. He heard the sparkling laughter of young women. A glinting eye.

He was awoken by someone gently shaking his arm. He shuddered.

"Are these seats taken?" asked a blonde-haired young man in a black-and-red T-shirt, in English.

"Eh?"

"Are these seats taken?" repeated the black-and-red boy. He was accompanied by two other boys of about the same age.

Captain Nikos tossed his head and clicked his tongue, regarding the boy coldly.

"These seats…are they taken?" persisted the boy, slowly, pointing at them.

Good God, what was wrong with the lad? thought Nikos. Couldn't he understand "no" when he saw it?

"No," said Nikos, in English.

The boys seated themselves at the same table and started to talk about football. At least Nikos assumed that they were talking about football as he heard the word "Liverpool" repeated several times and they did not look like sailors.

This was not the way it was supposed to be. Nikos wondered whether he ought to have a made a sign anyway: one that said "Seats for blonde-haired, blue-eyed, big-bosomed tourists only". But then some busybody would probably have told Maria about it and he would have been in hot water. Neither did there seem to be any possibility of moving to another table as by now the square was very crowded and some of the tourists were even obliged to stand.

In fact, he was just about to abandon the entire business and re-join his cronies when a girl seated herself on the edge of the adjacent table. She was blonde-haired and possibly even blue-eyed, although it was difficult to tell in the light. And, as she was attempting to make herself comfortable on the edge of the table, her leg brushed against his own. Oddly, the noise of the square suddenly seemed to vanish. Was he still asleep and dreaming? Had the red and black boy and his companions been part of that dream? He thought he heard the sea and the cry of seagulls.

"Sorry," she said in English, and smiled at him, her cheeks dimpling.

Captain Nikos grinned his Zorba grin at her and shrugged his shoulders.

"English?" he ventured, continuing to grin.

"Swedish," replied the girl. "From Stockholm."

"Ah! Stockholm!" grinned Nikos, knowingly. "Holiday!"

This, of course, was open to some misinterpretation, coming, as it did, with no context.

"So, you've been to Stockholm?" asked the girl, misinterpreting him perfectly.

"Stockholm," repeated Nikos. "Yes. Oslo."

"Oslo too!" exclaimed the girl. "My! You *have* travelled!"

"Copenhagen!" grinned Captain Nikos, happy that this mention of Scandinavian placenames was having such a good effect. "Wonderful! Wonderful!"

"I've never been there," replied the girl. "But I hear it's very nice."

Nikos pulled over a freshly vacated chair and the girl sat down next to him. She was wearing a simple, white dress, which was disturbingly short. Now that she had moved out of the shadows, Nikos saw that her eyes were as blue as the shallow waters of the sea, her flawless skin as golden as the hills at sunset. Wishing he was fifty years younger, he decided to take the bull by the horns.

"You been around?" he asked, replacing his Zorba grin with a look of concern.

The girl looked at him oddly.

"Island," said Nikos, crushing his cigarette. "You been around?"

"Oh, I see what you mean," said the girl, laughing. Her laughter was like waves lapping on shingle. "Not really. I'm here with a friend. We were thinking about renting a motorbike."

"No motorbike," he replied, with a dismissive gesture. "Boat. My boat. I take."

"Oh really!" said the girl. "That would be nice."

"All day. Nice beach. *Bagnio*. Swim. Fish maybe."

"That does sound very nice."

"Five thousand drachmas," said Captain Nikos, with his most honest look.

"Five thousand drachmas," repeated the girl, looking slightly concerned. "It's quite a lot. We have to be careful…"

"Take friend," suggested Captain Nikos, good naturedly.

"Oh, I see," laughed the girl, her eyes sparkling. "So, five thousand for the two of us?"

"Two passenger?" said Captain Nikos, with the utmost seriousness. "Ten thousand. Three passenger—fifteen thousand. Four passenger…"

"Twenty thousand?"

"*Endaxi.*"

"That's too much," said the girl, looking crestfallen.

But it was at this point that Captain Nikos demonstrated the business acumen that had successfully taken him from being a young man with a twelve-foot boat to an old man with a twelve-foot boat.

"Four thousand drachmas," he said.

"Two thousand?"

Captain Nikos looked at the girl. She was the most beautiful woman he had ever seen—far more beautiful than the film stars that the barber Adonis has pinned to the wall of his shop. She *did* have blue eyes. And her bosoms, although he did not dare to stare at them directly, were undoubtedly above average.

"Three thousand."

"Done!"

"Eh?"

"I mean yes, *endaxi.*".

The day when Captain Nikos embarked on his first voyage into the tourist industry did not start auspiciously. Firstly, there was a steady force five blowing from the north-west. In the shelter of the harbour, it seemed no more than a gentle breeze and, indeed, for a fisherman, particularly an Aegean fisherman, force five is nothing special. However, force five might be experienced rather differently by two girls from Stockholm in an open boat. And Nikos's boat was very open.

Secondly, Nikos had agreed to meet his two passengers at 10 a.m. This was a time he had thought appropriate as the other round-the-island trips seemed to start then. Unfortunately, Nikos himself tended to wake up at roughly 6 a.m., which meant that he had four hours to kill before departure. So, he had breakfast, if you can call coffee, a cigarette and yesterday's newspaper breakfast. He then had two more cups of coffee at the port while discussing the weather with Costas. Unfortunately, this took him only as far as 8.30 a.m.

By the time the two Swedish girls made their appearance—at a little over 10.15 a.m.—Nikos had downed a beer, a glass of tsikoudia and, as a slight acknowledgement to the weather, two glasses of rum. It was just as well that he did so. Monica, the girl he had talked to the night before, had then been dressed for the evening. However, today she was exposing as much of herself as was permissible within the bounds of common decency. And her companion, Mia, who was also gratifyingly blue-eyed, blonde-haired and buxom, and in every way as beautiful as her friend, had clearly decided to leave common decency to others and was clad only

243

in a very brief pink bikini. Nikos wished that he had ordered a third rum.

"It's a bit small," said Monica.

"Eh?" replied Nikos.

"The boat. Small. Little."

"Twelve foot," said Captain Nikos. "How many you are?"

"Two."

Captain Nikos rubbed his stubbled chin.

"Six foot," he said. "Six thousand drachmas."

Monica and Mia embarked. If they had had any qualms about the *Amalia*'s size, these were soon greatly outweighed by Captain Nikos lurching onto his boat, almost falling overboard, peering myopically at the tiller before grabbing it to support himself, and simultaneously leering.

"Are you all right?" asked Monica, anxiously.

"Eh?"

"All right? Okay? *Endaxi*?"

"Okay. *Endaxi*. Yes," replied a slightly befuddled Nikos.

"He's drunk," whispered Monica to Mia, in Swedish.

"So what?" replied Mia, giving Nikos the sort of look that a barracuda might bestow on a pilchard. Mia liked older men.

"You got food?" said Nikos.

"Food? Yes!" replied Monica.

"I got wine," said Nikos, pointing to two plastic bottles in the scuppers.

"I don't think you'll need it," muttered Monica, under her breath.

Yet the *Amalia*'s departure from the port was everything Monica and Mia might have hoped for. With the Greek flag fluttering bravely from a stick that Captain Nikos had thoughtfully tied to a rowlock, and the ancient Perkins diesel hammering through the pine timber, the *Amalia* swayed picturesquely into the open water.

Once they were out of the shelter of the harbour, the *Amalia*'s progress slowed. The boat began to pitch and roll. However, this did not seem to trouble the two girls unduly. They even seemed to like being showered from time to time, laughing enchantingly as the spray whipped over them.

Yet events took a different turn once they started to round the headland that marks the island's most northerly point, for it is there that the open sea, which extends virtually uninterrupted to the distant Peloponnesus, collides with the warmer coastal currents. Already choppy in the slightest of winds, the waters off the headland had now been churned into a chaotic playground of waves and spindrift.

Captain Nikos realised that he had made a mistake; it must have been the rum, or maybe the prospect of spending a day at sea with two pretty girls. If he had taken the opposite course by the southerly route, the wind would have dropped by the time he made the headland late in the afternoon. Now, on the northerly route with the wind at his back, he had no option but to continue on course until the headland was passed.

There was a definite point at which Monica and Mia realised that the trip would not be quite as sun-drenched and idyllic as they had imagined. That was when the *Amalia* slid down the side of a wave that was roughly the height of an average-sized bungalow and then buried its bows in the water with a considerable boom. Monica and Mia gripped the gunwales. Despite the cloudless sky, the air was cold. Mia grabbed her bag and, much to Captain Nikos's dismay, pulled on a thick sweatshirt over her pink bikini. Her action was swiftly copied by Monica.

Captain Nikos, like all good captains, was immediately concerned for his passengers. However, there was very little that he could really do to ease their discomfort beyond ma-noeuvring the *Amalia* to best advantage. He could not offer words of comfort or sing to them because his voice would not have carried above the roar of the waves, and he could not sing anyway. Rushing to the end of the boat and comforting them more intimately would have been disastrous. Nikos thought it best to keep on grinning like Zorba, which he did. Yet, at the same time, he was regretful that an excursion that he had looked forward to so much had begun so badly. And matters were not helped by the sea itself, which appeared to be mocking him. The waves that rose and fell around the *Amalia* were disturbingly breast-shaped; the troughs reminded him of that delicious curve between hip and rib. In fact, the sea was taking on a mysterious, seductive, feminine beauty that he had never seen before.

Nikos glanced from the sea to his passengers, and was surprised. He had expected them to be green with fear and hanging over the gunwales, but they were not. Although their hair was wet, it had been whipped by the wind into elegant blonde tendrils. Monica's lips were curled into a slight smile as she watched the heaving water around her; Mia gazed at Nikos impassively. For a brief moment their eyes met and Nikos felt the hairs on his neck stiffen. Did her eyes glint and glitter, or was that just water on his spectacles?

To steady himself, Nikos clamped the tiller with his left stump, reached into his pocket and pulled out a lump of hard goat's cheese. As the captain, he felt obliged to offer this delicacy to his passengers but, to his relief, they both shook their heads. Nikos gnawed on the cheese greedily but it did not dispel Mia's gaze. He washed it down with wine from one of the plastic bottles, but her gaze remained with him.

Abruptly, the playground of wind and sea came to an end. The *Amalia* coasted into smoother waters. The sun found its way through the spray and warmed the boat, glistening on the pools of water on the deck and sparkling on the ropes. Captain Nikos removed his spectacles, dried them on his shirt and replaced them.

"That was nice," said Monica, languorously, in English.

Mia smiled and ruffled her hair to dry it.

"Yes, it was," she replied, in Swedish.

As the *Amalia* puttered southwards along the western coast, the pools of water on its deck quickly evaporated to thin rings of salt. Monica and Mia removed their thick sweatshirts and stretched out, luxuriating in the heat.

The Nikos who had left the port little more than an hour before would have been entirely pleased with that. After all, there could be few men on the island who were, at that moment, cruising on a smooth sea with two beautiful, blue-eyed, blonde-haired, big-bosomed, bikini-clad girls on board. Maybe not even the President of Greece was so favoured. And yet... And yet there had been something profoundly disturbing about the nonchalance with which these girls had confronted the rough weather at the headland. There had been something indefinably uncomfortable in Mia's gaze.

"Now *bagnio*," muttered Captain Nikos, as he turned the *Amalia* into a deserted bay. He had meant to shout this with a typically Zorba-like gesture but now his words came out limply, as if this was a routine formula that he had used thousands of times before.

Before the *Amalia* even anchored in the bay, Monica and Mia had stripped off their bikinis and dived into the water. Blonde hair, glistening golden skins in the turquoise sea. They swam like dolphins, laughing and chattering in a language that Nikos did not understand. Their crystal laughter echoed from the cliffs. And then they slid gracefully from the water and stretched out naked on the beach.

Nikos's plan had been to join them, but now he was afraid. These were not creatures from the world of men. He crossed himself and spat to ward off the evil eye. Instead of joining them, he stayed on the *Amalia* and busied himself with cleaning the engine. It did not need cleaning, but at least it was a distraction.

After an hour or two, Monica and Mia swam lazily back to the boat. Nikos helped them to board, but he turned his face away from their nakedness and said very little and avoided their eyes as they completed their circumnavigation of the island. It was safer that way.

Nikos did not return to the square for several weeks. He need not have been so careful as only a few days after their island trip, Mia returned to selling yachts in Stockholm and Monica to her job as a windsurfing instructor. They never returned to the island.

Nikos's round-the-island tours did not stop; in fact, they were relatively successful. But he became more careful in selecting his clientele. With the help of his friend Costas, who was reasonably proficient in English, he adjusted his advertising to emphasise the romantic advantages for couples, favouring those of retirement age, or preferably older. Together, they would putter around the secluded bays on the west coast in calm weather while Nikos pointed out chapels and interesting geological formations. His passengers rarely risked injury by diving from *Amalia* and were never naked. He sometimes remembered Mia and Monica, but never without a slight feeling of terror.

The Saganaki

The Seagull was not quite the oldest taverna on the island, and it was never the best. It had opened sometime in the nineteen-sixties – no one could remember exactly when – with a limited menu consisting of various vegetables and whatever was cooking on the gas stove at the time. This was usually fish soup or stewed goat but occasionally extended to lamb, beef or chicken if they were cheap.

The taverna was owned and run by the Manolas family. In fact, it was the imaginatively named Manolis Manolas who came up with the idea of turning the family home into a restaurant by placing a few tables and chairs on their patio. The tables and chairs did not match but that did not matter; he and his wife Maria had been born at a time when mismatched furniture was the norm.

In the early days, business was as slow as Maria's cooking and Manolis's service. There were few visitors to the island at that time and most of the locals were unaccustomed to eating in restaurants. However, there were just enough customers to assure The Seagull's survival.

Not that the taverna was actually called The Seagull at the time. In fact, it had no name at all and was commonly referred to as Manolis's Place and sometimes just Manolis. It would be a good ten years before Maria persuaded her husband to give the taverna a name. A sign was duly painted by a singularly untalented local artist that featured a seagull at rest. As few of the increasing number of foreign visitors could read Greek, The Seagull was generally known as The Fat Duck.

Although Manolis and Maria Manolas had two sons and a daughter, none of them were interested in joining the family business. Makis was a merchant seaman, Markos ran a betting shop in Patras, and Marina would do as she was told.

As the sixties faded into the seventies, The Seagull underwent several renovations. The sign was repainted more accurately, although The Seagull continued to be called The Fat Duck. A grill was added and souvlaki appeared on the new plastic-coated menu. The tables and chairs finally matched. Some aspects were to remain unchanged: for example, the level of service was always in inverse proportion to how well you were known. New customers could expect swift service; familiar faces could expect to wait. This was a mark of respect.

Marina had two children, both girls. They were put to work in The Fat Duck as soon as they could open a bottle of beer.

Although an increasing influx of tourists was bringing prosperity to the island, and to the taverna, Manolis saw no reason to change his menu. True, he now had a grill and those tourists who did not dare venture into the murky realms of moussaka and pasticcio could enjoy grilled food with the obligatory squeeze of lemon juice and dusting of oregano.

Yet, otherwise, the menu was the same, day in, day out, year in, year out.

Although he had always left the cooking to Maria and the waiting at table to Marina and her daughters, Manolis became increasingly aware that there was an imminent manpower shortage.

Neither he nor Maria were getting any younger, and Maria had arthritis.

Manolis had always been in charge of the cash-desk. This was important work that demanded much energy. In an age before digital payments, the cash drawer had to be kept meticulously open, apart from those times when the tax inspector visited the island, and then he would have to be especially alert, close the drawer after every transaction and even issue receipts. In spite of his age, he felt he could continue to manage this task for a few years more. However, a new cook was essential and there seemed to be no one available. He might even have to employ one.

Help came from the unexpected source of his son Markos. Although the betting shop in Patras was very successful – as betting shops generally are – Markos's son Tassos had no liking for the profession. So, when his *Pappoú* tried to persuade his father to give up his business in favour of a cook's apron, Tassos was quick to offer his services. He had never cooked in his life but he did like the idea of living and working on the island.

"What a handsome boy you are!" said Maria. "Just like your father! But can you cook?"

"Of course he can cook," said Manolis, giving his wife a stern look. "He's a Manolas!"

"Well, you're a Manolas too. If you can cook, you've kept it well hidden for forty years."

"I've had other things to do, Maria. Tasso, can you cook?"

"Not really," said Tassos, who was starting to doubt the wisdom of leaving the relatively cosmopolitan life of Patras. "But I can learn."

"You see, Maria? He can learn."

"Well, you'd better learn quickly, Tasso," said Maria, "because Easter is only three weeks away. You do look so much like your father!"

And she gave him a kiss.

Tassos survived Easter because Maria did all the work. He helped with the preparation of kokoretsi and spit-roasted lamb and counted himself lucky that he would not have to do it again for another year. He bought a book on cookery and learned all the items on The Fat Duck's menu, which was not exactly taxing.

One of the first dishes that he mastered was shrimp saganaki.

In its basic form, shrimp saganaki is a fairly simple dish of prawns cooked in tomato sauce with feta cheese crumbled over the top. The seasonings may differ but the recipe remains fundamentally the same. And it remained the same until Rosencrantz and his family decided that The Fat Duck might be a suitable place for a late lunch or early dinner.

Rosencrantz was French and an artist. His real name, unknown to most, was Georges Marchand. He had a cold.

Rosencrantz scanned the plastic-bound menu assiduously, while his wife and children ordered souvlaki, Greek salad and chips. He sneezed into a linen handkerchief.

"First of all, I would like a tisane," he said, peering at Marina over his spectacles.

"A tisane?" replied Marina.

Rosencrantz paused. Perhaps the word tisane was not familiar to Greek ears.

"Herbs in hot water."

"Oh, I see. Are you sure?"

"I have a cold."

Marina's nephew Tassos also had no idea what a tisane was but herbs in hot water was sufficient explanation, so he boiled up some shop-bought rosemary, oregano and sage, strained the mixture, tasted it, grimaced, added a little sugar, shrugged, and served it.

Rosencrantz sipped delicately. It was not a tisane as he knew it and reminded him vaguely of a sweet marinade, but he nodded appreciatively.

"*Eh bien,*" he said and picked up the menu, by which time his wife and children had, somewhat untypically, been served.

Marina waited patiently, notebook and ballpoint at the ready, as Rosencrantz methodically worked his way through the slightly English translation of the limited menu.

"What is shrimp saganaki?"

"Shrimps in tomato sauce," said Marina. She gazed across the street and yawned. "With cheese."

"What sort of cheese?"

"Village cheese."

Rosencrantz could see that further questioning would be useless. In spite of his cold, he was hungry and in the mood for fish. The only other fish dish on the menu was maridaki.

"What is maridaki?"

"Small fish," replied Marina and held her thumb and forefinger apart by way of illustration. "We don't have."

Marina shrugged her shoulders and gave a lopsided smile which was meant to express infinite regret that, owing to circumstances entirely beyond her control, the maridaki were temporarily unavailable. Rosencrantz ordered the shrimp saganaki.

By the time the saganaki arrived, Rosencrantz's wife was reading. His children were shouting and chasing cats between the tables, which would certainly have been a nuisance to other diners had there actually been any.

Yet the saganaki was worth the wait, his wife's boredom and his children's shouting. It was brought to the table sizzling in its dish. Four huge, freezer-fresh prawns nestled on a fragrant bed of sauce with a generous sprinkling of crumbled feta. The aroma was spectacular.

"Saganaki," said Marina, with no great enthusiasm. "Enjoy."

Which is exactly what Rosencrantz did, mopping up the remainder of his sauce with freshly baked bread. He had not come to Greece for its cuisine, which he regarded as totally lacking in finesse, but here was a dish that was almost worthy of a Michelin star. Almost.

There was something missing. Something that prevented the saganaki from reaching the snowy-white summit of culinary excellence. And he knew exactly what it was.

He beckoned to Marina.

"This dish needs alcohol," he said, smiling.

"Of course," she said, and promptly disappeared into the kitchen, returning with two small glasses of colourless liquid.

"*Merci*," said Rosencrantz. He put one of the glasses in front of his wife, who looked up from her book and shook her head.

"I did not mean alcohol with the food. I meant in the food."

"In?"

"Yes, in."

Marina returned to the kitchen and emerged with Tassos.

"The son of my brother," she announced. "He cook."

She turned slightly and looked at the wall as if she had never seen it before. Tassos smiled at Rosencrantz and leant on the back of his chair.

"You like my saganaki?"

"I like it very much. It is truly delicious, but it lacks a final touch."

"I know," said Tassos, who did not know at all. "A certain *je ne sais quoi*?"

"*Exactement*!"

"And you think I should add alcohol?"

256

"I believe a little would make it spectacular."

"Cognac?"

"Perhaps."

Tassos experimented with the aid of his cookbook. He thought of a flambé, but soon discovered that it was not possible to flambé a tomato sauce. Putting cognac directly into the sauce did not work either; it added an expensive punch, certainly, but made for an unpleasant flavour. To be sure, he tried Greek brandy, which was more economical but no better. Finally, he turned to ouzo. It worked. The slight hint of aniseed perfectly complimented the seafood without spoiling the sauce and the alcohol certainly gave it a lift. Marina tried it. She looked a bit doubtful but finished her plate.

Rosencrantz returned to The Fat Duck, with his family, by special invitation.

"*Magnifique*," was his judgement. "*Superbe!*"

Tassos felt pleased with himself. He felt like a real chef. But the final test would be old Manolis.

Since relinquishing control of the restaurant to his grandson, Manolis Manolas had continued to control the cash-desk for a few months but finally decided that opening and occasionally closing the drawer was too onerous a task for a man of his advanced years. However, he and Maria continued to be frequent visitors to The Seagull, if only because he felt it his duty to keep an eye on the business.

"*Pappoú*," said Tassos, placing the sizzling dish in front of his grandfather. "I want you to try my new shrimp saganaki."

Manolis stared at the dish in front of him. A new saganaki? It looked very much like the old saganaki but he detected a slightly different aroma.

"It smells of ouzo," he said, squinting at his grandson.

"You're so much like your father," said Maria, nodding and smiling. "He likes ouzo too."

This was true.

"Let's see what we've got here," said Manolis. He took up his fork, prodded around, and tasted.

"Pah! What have you done to this? Do you call this saganaki? It's…it's…"

"Awful?" suggested Tassos.

"Awful!" agreed Manolis, loudly.

"I quite like it," said Maria, dipping her bread into the sauce.

But Manolis pushed the plate away. His face was flushed scarlet.

"How could you do such a thing!" he shouted. "How could you defile an innocent saganaki in such a way?"

He stood up from the table.

"I will never eat at this establishment again!" he shouted. "Come, Maria!"

Maria dutifully obeyed, casting a longing look at the shrimps. But she did pull Tassos towards her and whispered "I liked it".

Tassos knew that his grandfather's threat was idle. After all, Manolis owned the establishment – or to be more precise Maria did – and he ate there for free.

So, reluctant to abandoned his new dish, Tassos produced two versions of the saganaki: one, with added ouzo, for the tourists, his grandmother, and the few people on the island who claimed to be connoisseurs, and the other for his *Pappoú* and those who might prefer their saganaki free from sin and as nature intended. Adding the ouzo was simple and nobody was any the wiser. In fact, only Tassos and his aunt Marina were aware that there were two versions.

It was a Saturday evening, the busiest time of the busiest day in the week. It was when locals came to eat out, sing and perhaps even dance, and it was also when Marina's two daughters, Marilena and Melina, helped out at the taverna. This meant laying tables, clearing tables and waiting at tables. It was not the most interesting work and it did not pay well, but it was expected.

Saganaki was by no means the most popular dish on the menu. In fact, most customers never bothered to look at the menu at all and simply went into the kitchen to view what was on offer. So, it was unlikely that two people would order shrimp saganaki in a single evening, and certainly not at the same time. But that is exactly what happened. And it was not as unlikely as one might think, as the two customers in question were Manolis and Maria.

Manolis had not liked shouting at his grandson and had felt ashamed. Tassos had done well in rescuing a business that had now become something of an institution on the island, albeit under a false name. He was doing his best and could not be expected to adhere to a menu that had, after all, been the result of culinary incompetence rather than design. Besides, the saganaki was really not so awful, if truth be told; it was just different.

Maria had not said anything since her husband had stormed out of The Seagull. Although he was sometimes given to outbursts, she knew he would instantly rue them and then agonise for days afterwards. He was a bit of an idiot, but otherwise a good man.

"*Pappoú*?" asked Marinela, notebook and ballpoint in hand.

"Shrimp saganaki," said Manolis, without looking up. "One for me and one for your *Yiayia*."

Marinela conveyed the order to the kitchen. Tassos glanced through the window of the kitchen, saw his grandparents sitting at their favourite table, and nodded.

The old devil, he thought. He's come to make peace, but he can't resist making his point. Very well, he will get his saganaki undefiled and innocent.

The twin versions of saganaki prepared, Melina took them to the table.

Tassos waited. He was grilling lamb chops and the smoke stung his eyes but he constantly glanced through the window to where his grandparents were sitting. They seemed quiet enough. He smiled to himself. There was no point in making a big drama about a dish of shrimps.

It was getting late and The Fat Duck was almost empty. Tassos wiped his hands and left the kitchen. His grandparents had finished eating.

"How was the saganaki, *pappoú*?" he asked.

Manolis did not answer.

"It was a bit insipid," said Maria. "I preferred it with the ouzo."

"The ouzo? There was ouzo in your saganaki, *yiayia*!"

"Listen to me," said his grandmother. "As you well know, my family comes from Lesvos, the home of ouzo."

"Yes. So?"

"So, I know it when I taste it. And there was no ouzo in this."

Her husband chuckled.

His plate was polished clean.

Tomatoes

"Who is he?" asked Christos, stubbing out his cigarette.

"No idea really," replied Costas, lighting his cigarette. "Some rich foreigner. An actor, or so I've been told."

"An actor?" said Christos. "You mean a movie star?"

"I suppose so. Who else but a movie star would build a place like that?"

"Maybe I've heard of him," said Christos. "What's his name?"

"I don't know his name, and if he's a movie star, you've certainly never heard of him," laughed Costas. "The last time you saw a film John Wayne was still a young man."

"I read the newspapers."

"The comic strips."

Christos fell silent and gazed through the window of the *kafeneion* at the rain-lashed square. Costas had a point. He had not seen a film since John Wayne had been a young man. He vaguely remembered a film about a stagecoach and a large group of Indians who were shooting arrows and shouting a lot. In fact, come to think of it, it was always strange that the Indians would chase after the stagecoach, shooting arrows and shouting a lot, while a cowboy would just stand in front of the stagecoach with a gun and tell the driver to throw down the strongbox.

"Well, whoever he is, he has a lot of money," resumed Costas. "Big villa on the other side of the island. I've heard he's even building a swimming pool."

"A swimming pool!" exclaimed Christos, marvelling at the idea before its full significance sank in. "A swimming pool?"

"Why not, if you have the money."

"But he has the sea!"

"The sea's not good enough when you're rich," said Costas, who clearly had an understanding of such matters.

"Not good enough?" exclaimed Christos, who had no such understanding.

"It's like having gold taps in your bathroom. The water that comes through them is the same, but when it comes through gold taps it's better somehow."

"You can't drink water from the tap here anyway."

"Maybe you could if it was made of gold."

On that same day, Panagiotis had spent the morning opening windows. A fellow islander, who worked in Germany during the winter, was returning for the summer and the house had to be aired and the floors washed. In the afternoon, Panagiotis would go to the house of the widow Diamantisis and unblock her drain before watering the tomatoes that belonged to Mr Papadakis. Mr Papadakis had very many tomatoes and it would take a long time, but it would be pleasant work in the sunshine, with no dust or bad smells.

Panagiotis was small in stature, and also in status. Traditionally, his family had been one of the poorest on an already poor island. When his father died, Panagiotis inherited a little, dilapidated house on a barren, unfrequented hillside a few miles outside the village. And because the hillside was both barren and unfrequented, an increasingly self-important municipality thought it an ideal spot to locate the municipal rubbish dump. Naturally, they did not consult Panagiotis about their plans, nor did they inform him of their decision. The first that he knew of what was hailed as "a progressive step towards the future of the island" was when a team of workmen built a metal fence around a large area of land adjoining his house. A few days later, this was followed by the new municipal dust cart with its first load of refuse.

Since the death of Panagiotis's father had been preceded by those of his mother and two sisters, he now lived alone on his barren but now regularly frequented hillside. He did not like the presence of the rubbish dump but he knew that he was in no position to complain. Not only was he the least significant inhabitant of the island but he also knew that many of the people who had voted to site the rubbish dump next to his house were also the same people who paid him to air houses, unblock drains and water tomatoes.

What really perplexed Panagiotis was the metal fence. Why would anyone erect a fence to keep people out of a rubbish dump? He knew that it was a strange world, indeed, but were there people who might break into the dump at dead of night to steal rubbish? Certainly, the fence was not designed to restrict the movement of the rubbish as, thanks to the prevailing wind, half of the contents of the dump was soon more or less evenly spread over the hillside.

But, after all, your home is your home, whatever its location or condition. Panagiotis soon got used to billowing clouds of dust, flies, sun-dried but nonetheless loathsome airborne refuse and the constant flapping and banging of plastic and rusty tin sheeting that now accompanied the sound of the wind sweeping down his hillside. In time, Panagiotis even became quite accustomed to the stink, for, unfortunately, it was not only solid refuse that was deposited. Perhaps he simply blocked it from his mind, in the same way as he blocked out all the other petty injustices that were meted out to the lowest rung on the island's social ladder.

The new, rich foreigner requested Panagiotis's services in the usual round-about way. There was no direct approach and discussion of terms. He was simply told, by Mr Papadakis in fact, who was probably the final link in a very long chain, that the foreigner needed someone to do odd jobs. And so, Panagiotis saddled his mule, scrambled up into the saddle and set off for the palace on the other side of the island.

The foreigner's villa was surrounded by a high metal fence that instantly reminded Panagiotis of the rubbish dump next to his house. However, here there could be no doubt that this fence was intended to keep people out and not in. The driveway that led to the house between two rows of newly planted trees was closed by a large metal gate. At one side of the gate was a small metal box with a button.

Panagiotis dismounted from his mule and tried to open the gate, but found it locked. This mystified him. He could not recall ever having met with a gate that was locked before. What could there be in that house that was so valuable as to justify this high metal fence and a gate that was locked?

Perhaps there was no one at home, reasoned Panagiotis. If so, they would surely be back before very long. It was a simple question of waiting. And so, Panagiotis tethered his mule to the fence and waited.

It was a hot day and there were no trees, so Panagiotis squatted in the shade of his mule and rolled a cigarette. The foreigner had certainly chosen a good spot for his palace for there were no other buildings to spoil the fine view. On the other hand, of course, the foreigner would have to go a long way for his shopping. Perhaps he might suggest that the foreigner bought a few chickens so that he could have fresh eggs and meat without going to the trouble of such a long journey. A cow might also be a good idea, for Panagiotis was quite sure that the foreigner could afford a cow.

Panagiotis was on his sixth cigarette, and the sun was beginning its slow dip to the horizon, when he heard a car. Immediately he stood up and threw away his cigarette for it would not do for the foreigner to see him smoking when they first met. He was anxiously scanning the coast road when he realised that the car was approaching from behind him.

There was a slight click and a whirr and miraculously the gates swung smoothly open as if propelled by two giant men.

And along the drive, followed by a billowing cloud of dust, came a large, black car. It was the sort of car that Panagiotis had seen increasingly frequently when foreigners visited the island. It was a car that was obviously designed to cope with the very roughest of terrain but was rarely, if ever, called on to do so.

The car pulled up alongside Panagiotis and a window hissed down much faster than a man could wind it. The man who had wound down the window gazed at Panagiotis through black sunglasses.

Thanks to his frequent contact with foreigners, Panagiotis had picked up an adequate smattering of English and he now used this to introduce himself to the foreigner and tell him that he, Panagiotis, was prepared to do any small jobs that might be required. In return, he would ask modest payment.

The man in the black sunglasses stared hard at Panagiotis and nodded. He swung the big car round in the driveway so that it was pointing the way it had come and he motioned Panagiotis to follow him. Panagiotis unhitched his mule, mounted it and followed.

Panagiotis was never to forget his first glimpse of the foreigner's magnificent house. Set back against the hillside, blindingly white in the sun, it was the biggest house that Panagiotis had ever seen. In fact, it was the biggest *building* he had ever seen, except for those he had seen in pictures. Bougainvillea, wisteria, oleander and hibiscus were all in bloom. There was a wide, cool terrace. And adjacent to the terrace was a huge swimming pool.

The foreigner got out of his car and Panagiotis had an opportunity to view him for the first time. He was a man of average height. In fact, disturbingly, everything about him was average. Middle-aged, he was neither skinny nor overweight. His hair was an indeterminate brownish colour, flecked with a little grey. His skin was tanned the brown of northerners. He was dressed in a sloppy T-shirt, knee-length shorts and flip-flops. How could a man who did not seem in the least bit heroic have amassed such great wealth?

"It beats me how he did it," said Costas.

"Did what?" asked Christos, brushing cigarette ash from his trousers.

"Got so rich. You wouldn't think it to look at him."

"Can't say I've seen him," said Christos.

"Well, he's nothing much to look at, I can tell you. You've probably passed him in the street and not noticed."

"So what's Panagiotis doing there?"

"Panagiotis?" chuckled Costas. "Cleaning the swimming pool."

Christos took up his tobacco and papers and began to roll another cigarette. It had never occurred to him that swimming pools needed to be cleaned. After all, when his wife cleaned the street outside his house, she used water, and swimming pools are full of water.

"How do you clean a swimming pool?" asked Christos, gluing his cigarette together.

"How should I know?" replied Costas. "More's the point, how would Panagiotis know? Him of all people!"

"I expect the foreigner probably told him," said Christos, nodding sagely.

"I hope he did! I can just see Panagiotis setting to work with a scrubbing brush and a bar of soap!"

Christos chuckled drily and lit his cigarette. So, you cleaned a swimming pool with a scrubbing brush and soap. He had imagined something more technical.

"But what is there in a swimming pool to clean?" he asked, remembering his wife and the street.

"Leaves and stuff. The odd rat."

"Can't be much of a job."

"Probably isn't."

However, cleaning the foreigner's swimming pool was much more of a job than Costas and Christos imagined. For a start, it was well paid. The very average millionaire naturally had little idea of the going rate for odd jobs on the island and was immediately prepared to pay Panagiotis four times what he earned for watering Mr Papadakis's tomatoes and ten times what he received for unblocking a drain. Secondly, the work was easy since the foreigner equipped Panagiotis with a sort of vacuum cleaner and a special brush, which took away virtually any effort that the job might have involved.

Nevertheless, Panagiotis's first attempts to clean the pool did not entirely satisfy the foreigner. He stared at the pool as Panagiotis looked on proudly, brush in hand, and he shook his head. At first, Panagiotis assumed that the head-shaking was a gesture of admiration for his work, which caused him to smile happily. It was after his third visit to the palace that the foreigner told him that if he succeeded in making the pool really clean, so clean that not a scrap of dirt remained, he would get a large bonus.

Naturally, Panagiotis now took infinite care to ensure that hardly a speck of dirt adhered to the side of the pool and that the water was free of leaves, seeds and any other flotsam. The foreigner was very satisfied with this and soon the bonus became Panagiotis's regular payment. What was more, Panagiotis enjoyed going to the foreigner's palace. Surrounded by so much luxury, he felt almost like a millionaire himself. The foreigner had a wife who was every bit as young and beautiful as the foreigner himself was middle-aged and average. She would smile frequently at Panagiotis and sometimes bring him food and drink. It was true that the food was often very strange and the drink was invariably lemonade, but she clearly had a kind heart. Also, the foreigner had told him that if he pressed the button on the small metal box next to the main gate, he could talk to the foreigner or his wife and that they could open the gate for him, without even having to go to the trouble of walking down the driveway.

The overall result of this, was that Panagiotis spent an increasing amount of time at the foreigner's palace. Without giving the impression that he was slacking, he made his work on the pool last as long as he could. He also showed himself willing to do other small jobs, without payment, simply to prolong his stay. He arrived early for work and he left late.

Naturally, this had an effect on Panagiotis's other duties. Requests for help from people who wanted such things as a little gardening, loads shifted or rubbish cleared were answered with either a polite refusal or, more often, a promise that the work would be done the next day. Exactly which next day Panagiotis was referring to was not always clear but since his working hours had always been flexible, to say the least, most people assumed that the work would be done eventually.

More disquieting yet was the indisputable fact that Panagiotis's new duties seemed to be having an effect on other aspects of his behaviour.

"If you ask me, he's getting a bit stuck up," said Costas, after his second glass of tsikoudia.

"Stuck up where?" asked Christos.

"Stuck up! As in above himself. Snobby. You know!"

"Oh, I see," said Christos, not seeing at all.

"We *are* talking about the same Panagiotis?" he asked.

"Yes," said Costas, firmly. "Panagiotis who lives up near the rubbish dump. The same."

Now that Panagiotis had been identified beyond any doubt, Christos could not imagine how a man who was barely noticeable could possibly be called "stuck up". Now his sister Ekaterini was definitely stuck up. She hardly took the trouble to pass the time of day with him. She even put doilies under the plates.

"Uses doilies, does he?" asked Christos.

"Doilies?" exclaimed Costas, while simultaneously retrieving the lighted cigarette that had dropped from his mouth.

"Just a thought," said Christos. "What do you mean he's stuck up?"

"Look," said Costas, in a lowered voice. "Panagiotis is an odd-job man, isn't he? Well, never mind…he *is*. We all know that his stairs don't exactly reach the attic and he could do with a wash, but suddenly he hardly takes the trouble to pass the time of day with you. Spends all his time at that big house on the other side. And he's even started wearing sunglasses."

"Sunglasses!" exclaimed Christos, as if the devil had suddenly been mentioned.

"Sunglasses."

"He's probably got something wrong with his eyes."

"With his head, more like."

Panagiotis had recovered the black sunglasses from the rubbish dump. There were many sunglasses in the rubbish dump, abandoned by tourists because they were scratched or broken, but one pair almost exactly matched those worn by the foreigner. And although they were scratched, they were not broken in any way.

Through his black sunglasses, the interior of Panagiotis's little house looked even darker than usual; however, this was a definite advantage for his imagination could now turn it into a stylish residence that even rivalled the palace. The battered sofa was mysteriously elegant, until he sat on it, and the icon over his bed almost resembled one of the paintings that the foreigner had hung on the wall of his living room.

Panagiotis had considered adopting a T-shirt and shorts but, although cheap T-shirts were easy to come by, shorts were prohibitively expensive. Nor were they to be found in the rubbish dump, or at least not in any serviceable state.

However, it was Panagiotis's appearances in the village that were most remarkable. Gone was the hunched posture and shuffling gait, gone was the deferential air. Panagiotis now strode masterfully down the main street. Although he wore the same clothes that he had always worn, his bearing, and more particularly his black sunglasses, drew the attention of people who had previously not noticed him at all. For his part, Panagiotis now looked people squarely in the eye. It was a proud, almost disdainful look that people might have thought intimidating had they been aware of it. Fortunately, the sunglasses that gave him his air of mystery also totally obscured his eyes.

Nowhere was Panagiotis's new-found pride more evident than in the local shop where he would stop to buy a few necessaries. Stubble bristling defiantly and half-smoked cigarette erect, he thumped his pack of coffee on the counter in a way that suggested that he was actually challenging the shopkeeper to serve him. The shopkeeper had always been more than ready to serve anyone, thumping or not, but he was understandably taken aback with this change in Panagiotis's manner. He was also curious as to why Panagiotis was wearing sunglasses in his shop or, for that matter, wearing them at all. However, once it became clear that he had not actually offended Panagiotis in any way and that the little odd-job-man acted similarly towards everyone else, he soon got used to Panagiotis's new behaviour. After all, another pack of coffee sold was another small step towards retirement.

Yet there was one person who was not quite as accommodating as the shopkeeper, and that was Panagiotis's erstwhile employer Mr Papadakis. Apart from being so well-respected in the community as to earn the title *kyrios*, or "Mister", Mr Papadakis was not at all a man to be meddled with. In his eighty-four years of life, he had defied Germans, browbeaten Italians, cursed Turks and terrorised the honourable members of the municipal council.

Such a man was not about to water his own tomatoes. Nor, out of the pride that had made him the scourge of the island, was he prepared to allow members of his very extended family or his friends to water them for him. The fact that his tomatoes were still alive at all was a tribute to irregular, clandestine watering sessions carried out by torchlight, always with a glance to left and right to ensure that Mr Papadakis had not decided to inspect his crops at midnight. The people who did this—friends and family—roundly condemned Panagiotis for a negligence verging on anarchy but they refrained from confronting him for they knew that Panagiotis's obligation was moral only: he had no contract of employment and was, in fact, paid only when Mr Papadakis remembered to pay him. And it has to be said that their actions were prompted less by the esteem in which Mr Papadakis was held in the community and more from a possible shortage of tomatoes, without which no Greek meal is complete.

This situation might have continued for some time had not fate intervened in the typically interfering way for which it is famed.

It saw fit to intervene on the steps of the shop when Panagiotis, leaving with his usual pack of coffee, found himself face to face with Mr Papadakis, who had come to purchase some liniment.

Actually, had not Mr Papadakis's large frame blocked the door, it is possible that Panagiotis might have passed by without noticing him, as his sunglasses were woefully impractical in the darkness of the shop. However, as if Mr Papadakis's frame was not enough, the worthy octogenarian lent it further force by addressing Panagiotis directly in a thunderous voice accompanied by a severe bristling of his large, grey moustache and matching eyebrows, and with vaguely threatening movements of his walking stick.

Panagiotis tried his best to brazen it out, gazing steely at Mr Papadakis through his impenetrable sunglasses. Sadly, Mr Papadakis was well acquainted with the use of sunglasses and told Panagiotis so in no uncertain terms. He also reminded him of tomatoes and the necessity of watering those fruits. And he did so in a voice that would have made any Turk, Italian or German seriously consider abandoning the island immediately to take up tomato farming in their respective countries.

Mr Papadakis's moustache and eyebrows bristled. Below him, Panagiotis's cigarette drooped. The shopkeeper smiled affectionately and the other shoppers fled as quickly as possible in order to relieve their pent-up laughter a safe distance away from Mr Papadakis.

And so it was that, once more, Panagiotis found himself watering Mr Papadakis's tomatoes. Yet he did so with a very ill will for as he trudged between the rows of plants, hosepipe in hand, his thoughts dwelled entirely on the foreigner's palace, his swimming pool, his garden and his beautiful wife. He cursed Mr Papadakis, and Panagiotis was not a man to curse lightly. To complete his misery, Panagiotis, whose mind was not at all on his job, liberally sprinkled his shoes with water and now squelched rather than trudged between the rows.

Angry and dejected, he sat down among the plants and pulled off his shoes. The soil was warm on his bare feet and felt curiously reassuring.

How had Mr Papadakis dared to tick him off in public and *order* him to water his tomatoes? After all, it was he who had told him of the job at the foreigner's house in the first place! And now that he, Panagiotis, was finally making good money and was being treated with respect, Mr Papadakis wanted to return him to poverty and insignificance. A curse on him! A curse on his moustache! May it catch fire and burn that noble nose! A curse on his walking stick! May it break and bring him to his noble knees!

It was while he was grumbling to himself that Panagiotis became aware of footsteps approaching him. Or rather the unmistakable flip flop of flip-flops. He looked up to see the silhouette of a man wearing a baseball cap, shorts, a T-shirt, and sunglasses.

"Panagiotis," said the foreigner, ungrammatically.

Panagiotis squinted up at him.

"I was told I might find you here."

He paused and shuffled a flip-flop in the red earth.

"Look, I'm not in the habit of tracking down hired help," said the foreigner, "but I'm making an exception in your case. You're a good pool boy."

Panagiotis understood nothing of that, but he nodded his head all the same.

"You haven't showed up for work for a few days. The pool needs cleaning."

Panagiotis understood the last sentence. He had heard it many times before. He said nothing and returned his attention to the tomatoes.

"Nice tomatoes," said the foreigner.

Panagiotis shrugged. He did not know what he was shrugging at, but it seemed the safest thing to do.

"Well," said the foreigner, "if you feel like coming back, we could always use a good pool boy."

Panagiotis did not look up as he heard the foreigner's flip-flops retreating. He rolled a cigarette and began to smoke, spitting loose pieces of tobacco at the tomatoes. He gazed at the hills that hid the foreigner's palace. He thought again of the swimming pool with its glass-like water; he thought of the curious things that the foreigner's beautiful wife brought him to eat; he thought of the small metal box with the button at the gate.

Cleaning the swimming pool had made him a lot of money, which was now safely stored in a tin box on a shelf. He had spent very little of it because he could not think of anything to spend it on. He had a house with strong walls and a roof, and he had even become used to the rubbish dump. He had an endless supply of free tomatoes, not to mention cheap onions, potatoes and more exotic vegetables like aubergines. If he wanted them, he could buy cheese, eggs and meat cheaply from his friends. With the wealth that he had gained by working for the foreigner, he might buy some hens, and perhaps even a pig.

It was all very well to work for the foreigner and wear sunglasses but where had that got him? People he knew well no longer wanted to talk to him, and, he had to admit, they were right. But at least they now respected him more. Perhaps now he was almost an equal.

Panagiotis removed his sunglasses, regarded them briefly with a wry smile, snapped them in two and threw them away. He bent forward, plucked a tomato, and bit into the sweet fruit.

Rain

Dimitra had married relatively late in life. She had not been much of a catch. Her voice was harsh; she had an ungainly way of walking. Although not unintelligent, she was not a ready communicator, which was more a result of laziness than inarticulacy. She had a hard, unpleasant face and a temperament to match.

Why had Giorgos married her?

The reason was simply that they had fallen in love, or rather Giorgos had; Dimitra thought she might be in love and, indeed, tried to be in love, but actually had no idea what love felt like. This was not helped by the fact that Giorgos was not considered much of a catch either. Although wiry and muscular, he had slightly sunken eyes and a weak chin, which he later disguised with a beard. A stonemason by trade, he managed to eke out a steady if unspectacular income despite the fact that most new houses were now built from concrete and brick. It was hard work that gradually took its toll on body and mind.

When they were courting, Dimitra had smiled at him and even laughed at his jokes. Giorgos's jokes were infrequent and not widely regarded as funny, but she laughed at them all the same.

For all that he was not a great catch, Giorgos could dance and sing. While no longer as lithe and athletic as he had been in his twenties, when he could kick his heels up high, whirl into a crouch and spring upright clicking his fingers, his dancing still put younger men to shame. His voice was deep and resonant. When Giorgos sang, you heard the rumble of waves and the soft soughing of the wind in the tamarisks.

In spite of her nature, Giorgos loved Dimitra, but when they were married the dancing and singing stopped.

Dimitra was undoubtedly one of the more respected women on the island, which is to say respected by many of the other women between the ages of sixty-five and death. The reason for this was not her wisdom or exemplary service to the community but rather her deeply rooted religious conviction and her ability to rule her husband with a rod which, if not exactly made of iron, was at least as hard, brittle and cold as a large, sharp icicle.

Dimitra was a frequent churchgoer. Her devotion was beyond question. It originated from her grandmother, who preferred to attribute her sister's recovery from pneumonia to divine intervention, although it was tetracycline that had actually cured her. Her devotion was further intensified by her father, who claimed that his alcoholism, from which he subsequently died, was caused by the Evil Eye.

Alcohol was at the root of Dimitra's gradual dislike of her husband. She had watched her father descend into insanity and had stood by helplessly as his skin turned yellow and blotchy, his belly swelled, and, whether due to the Evil Eye or not, his liver failed.

Giorgos drank. He did not drink excessively and had never been seen drunk, or very rarely at least. Every man on the island drank, so marrying a man who did not drink at all was virtually impossible. Dimitra tried to overlook Giorgos's drinking as she also overlooked his sunken eyes, weak chin and lack of prospects. It was the price that she would have to pay for not being regarded as a dried-up spinster and an object of gossip and ridicule.

For fifteen years following their marriage, Dimitra and Giorgos had not been blessed with children. The more uncharitable souls on the island regarded this as a good thing, for the idea of there being another person who shared even a few of Dimitra's less pleasant traits was almost too painful to contemplate. Even less charitable souls said that intimacy between Dimitra and Giorgos had probably begun and ended with their matrimonial kiss.

Yet they did have a child. Quite unexpectedly, late in their marriage, and to the amazement of many, Dimitra found herself pregnant. It was a condition that left her with mixed feelings. After the first few years of marriage, when it became clear that what she reluctantly regarded as her wifely duty was not going to result in children, that sort of activity had always been restricted to a very few occasions when Giorgos was almost drunk and Dimitra could not be bothered to object. Such coincidences were rare indeed, but one of them resulted in Maria.

Maria was endowed with almost all the qualities so lacking in her mother. She was light of voice and step. She had a fragile beauty that enchanted everyone she met. And she also had a kind nature. However, it was a nature that Dimitra did her level best to undermine.

Although Dimitra had always wanted a child, the reality of having one was disappointing. Child-rearing involved a lot of effort that she would rather have avoided, and she began to resent the fact that Giorgos could go to work, and afterwards to the *kafeneion*, leaving all that effort to her. It was a resentment that gradually replaced the indifference that Dimitra had always displayed towards Giorgos, and which soon developed into a protracted war in which she enlisted little Maria as an ally.

Dimitra's strategy was quite simple. She took every opportunity to turn daughter against father. And her labours bore fruit. If Giorgos relaxed in the shade at the end of a day's work and Dimitra whispered to her daughter "Look at that lazy good-for-nothing! Putting his feet up when there's so much to do around here!" she was rewarded by a scowl on Maria's face and a look of contempt. If Giorgos returned from the *kafeneion* a little unsteadily, Dimitra would hiss "There he goes again, the drunken sot! All our hard-earned money thrown down his throat!". And she was more than gratified when Maria placed a soft, comforting hand on her arm.

If Giorgos had become the Devil, Hell was the *kafeneion*. Admittedly, it was a hell frequented by almost the entire adult male population of the village, including the mayor and the priest, but that did not diminish the fact that it was clearly a place of drunkenness and debauchery. When Dimitra had to pass in front of the *kafeneion*—which unfortunately she had to do every day—she crossed herself and gazed at the ground, with an expression on her face that suggested that she had been munching on raw aubergines. When Maria accompanied her, she imitated her mother exactly.

Giorgos's work as a stonemason meant long hours and returning home with an aching back, a feeling of reluctance, and a layer of fine marble dust over his skin and clothes.

"Where have you been?" Dimitra would shout. "Drinking with your cronies, no doubt. You don't have to tell me—I can smell it on you."

Dimitra was usually too distanced from him to smell anything, not that there was anything to smell save for the musty odour of marble dust and the bad breath that came from an empty stomach. Giorgos would turn on the radio to drown out Dimitra's voice, lower his head over a plate of grudgingly prepared food, and say nothing. What was the point? His wife and daughter hated him. Long before Maria was born, he had learned that his place in the domestic order of things was to work, eat in silence, and enjoy the company of his friends when he could.

Giorgos could accept and perhaps even welcome the icy, black gulf that separated him from his wife, but his daughter's coldness was terrible to bear. If he stroked her head, Maria would shy away with a dark look. If he called her sweetheart, her lips would curl in distaste.

It was not yet Easter. The island was still emerging from its winter sleep, yawning, scratching its hard, parochial feet and preparing itself mentally for the masses of tourists that would invade in a few weeks' time. Some of the tourist shops, cafés and tavernas were already optimistically open, and tables and chairs had been set out in the square in front of the *kafeneion*. Giannis, the proprietor, had even strung row after row of light bulbs across the square, to illuminate the activities of any tourists who might already be on the island and who might endure the evening chill for the sake of an ouzo.

"You're wasting your time," grumbled Christos, squinting up at Giannis as he entered the *kafeneion* carrying his stepladder with a look of satisfaction. "It's too cold to sit out."

"Then look at it this way," said Giannis, wiping his hands on a glass-cloth. "Anyone who sits out here in the evening is definitely mad. If they're mad, we don't want them inside with us, do we?"

Christos thought about this for a moment and decided it made sense. It would also keep the tourist women away from the company of men because everyone knows that the tourist women love to sit in cafés and drink coffee, and sometimes wine.

Yet chilly as the evenings were, the days were already warm. On this particular day, the afternoon was the warmest so far that year. The sky was a pristine blue and a slight breeze gently stirred the top branches of the massive eucalyptus tree that dominated the square. In fact, the dry rustling of leaves, the cheeping of the finches nesting in the tree and the comforting whirr of the massed banks of refrigerators in the *kafeneion* were the only sounds to be heard.

And so, when Giorgos entered the *kafeneion* after listening to the radio over his customary early dinner and announced that a violent storm was on its way, neither Giannis nor any of the other customers felt inclined to believe him.

Giannis himself simply shook his head and returned to his newspaper.

"A storm?" laughed Pavlos, looking up from his cards. "In this weather?"

"They said so on the radio," replied Giorgos. "On the shipping forecast."

"The shipping forecast for where?" said Pavlos. "Greenland?"

"Suit yourself," shrugged Giorgos. "It's what I heard, that's all."

"Better get those chairs and tables inside," Pavlos shouted to Giannis. "And put tape over the windows while you're about it."

This remark drew more laughter from the card-players. In fact, after his first glass of tsikoudia, even Giorgos started to wonder if he had indeed been listening to the shipping forecast for the western Aegean. Perhaps he had tuned into the Greenland shipping forecast for Greek sailors by mistake.

However, by the time the sun began to set, the weather had, indeed, changed for the worse.

At first, no-one noticed it. Even when the first chair blew over outside, nobody paid much heed. Yet it was a squarely built, solid Greek café chair with a rush seat and it takes a fair amount of force to bring a chair like that to its point of disequilibrium.

It was only when Giannis switched on the lights, and happened to glance outside to check that the strings of light bulbs across the square were functioning correctly, that he noticed a difference.

He opened the door of the *kafeneion* and stood on the step, gazing around the deserted square. There was now a strong, steady breeze. Looking up, he saw that half of the sky to the west was hidden by a thick bank of black cloud.

"I told you so," murmured Giorgos sadly. He had suddenly appeared beside Giannis, nursing his tsikoudia.

"Well, if that's your storm, I don't think much of it," said Giannis, without looking at him.

As he spoke, it was as if someone had flicked a switch, plunging the square into a premature gloom that not even Giannis's cheerful strings of light bulbs could brighten.

Then a second switch was flicked.

What happened is still talked about on the island in tones of wonder. From the west came an immense roar, as if a steam train were approaching at full speed. Then, a few seconds later, tables and chairs were sent clattering across the flagstones. Simultaneously there was a brilliant flash as Giannis's carefully arranged light bulbs exploded in a shower of sparks.

"Christ!" shouted Giannis, diving back into the *kafeneion*. Giorgos stood rooted to the spot, open mouthed. Then he crossed himself, tossed back his tsikoudia and followed, closing the door behind him.

By this time, card-playing and tavli had ceased. All of the men in the *kafeneion* gathered at the windows to witness the spectacle. Outside, it was as dark as midnight. Lightning was crashing almost constantly, turning the thrashing eucalyptus into a weird, strobe-illuminated dancer. Rain started to lash across the square as flying debris rattled and skittered along the walls and roofs. Not a light showed in the rest of the village.

Pavlos looked sideways at Giorgos.

"You were right," he said, smiling ruefully.

Naturally, when the storm struck, everyone immediately sought shelter indoors. Within a matter of minutes, the village streets were deserted.

Except for one person.

Dimitra had needed some cinnamon to go in the *stifado* she was preparing and had sent Maria to the shop to buy some. She was on her way home when the storm struck.

At first, Maria had broken into a run in the hope of arriving home before the storm was at its worst. Yet as lightning flickered and crackled overhead, and the street started to run ankle-deep in water, her resolve to get home was rapidly overtaken by a feeling of sheer terror. She beat on the door of the nearest house but there was no answer. The door was firmly bolted and who could possibly discern the beating of a child's hands from the enormous crashing and banging elsewhere? The street was black and rain-lashed, her thin dress was soaking and she was already starting to feel cold.

When her mother first heard the storm, she paid little attention to it. Even when rain splattered against the kitchen window and Dimitra heard a clattering chair in the yard, her attention was more on her cooking. The roar of the gas hob and the noise of meat sizzling in olive oil did much to drown out the noise.

It was only when the lightning cracked and boomed that she grew alarmed. She shut off the gas, went to the front door and looked out. The street had turned into a dark, shallow river shivering under torrential rain.

"Maria!" she shouted, but immediately realised that this was useless. The street was empty of people. There were lights in the houses. Her neighbour Michalis had come onto his balcony to watch the spectacle.

"Michali!" she shouted up to him. "Have you seen Maria?"

His answer was lost in a roar of thunder and wind.

And then the lights went out.

Dimitra grabbed a shawl to cover her head, slammed the door behind her, and ventured into the street. As she plodded forwards, the water grew deeper. At first, it had only come up to her ankles but soon it was washing around her knees and carrying with it scraps of paper, cardboard, plastic, flowers, twigs. She transferred the shawl from her head to her shoulders and wrapped the cold wool around her.

"Maria!" she wailed. But the only response was another skittering crackle of lightning.

It took Dimitra almost half an hour to reach the shop where she had sent Maria to buy cinnamon. The shop was closed and dark, its displays of fruit and vegetables covered with tarpaulin.

There was a warm glow at the end of the street. Giannis had lit oil lamps. The *kafeneion* looked much as it had done before electricity came to the island.

Maria ran up to the door and stopped. She was terrified by the storm, but now she had a different fear. If she entered the *kafeneion*, she would be stepping through the mouth of Hell itself. She huddled against the door and tried to peer through its panes, but the glass was steamed up on the inside. She could make out flickering, shadowy figures, the bright yellow points of oil lamps. Above the roar of the storm, she heard the ringing notes of a bouzouki. A bouzouki! The instrument of rebetiko, the music of the gutter! And then the sky erupted in another blinding flash and, before she was even aware of it, she had turned the handle.

After the first impact of the storm, normal service had been quickly resumed in the *kafeneion*. True enough, the storm was spectacular, but when you have faced gigantic seas in an open *kaiki*, there is little remarkable about a few chairs blowing across a square. Giannis's oil lamps had transformed a *kafeneion* that was usually lit by stark fluorescent lighting. Some of the older men wistfully thought back to the days of their youth, before television and refrigeration.

The only thing that was lacking was music and this want was soon supplied. A bouzouki emerged from the darkness at the back of the *kafeneion* and one of the younger fishermen was prevailed upon to play it. Admittedly, he was no virtuoso but what he lacked in dexterity he made up for in passion. And occasionally, one or more of the older men would break into song, punctuated by crashing from outside.

It was then that the door opened.

Normally, a door opening would not have commanded much attention in the *kafeneion* but, as no one had come in, much less gone out, since the storm struck, and as its opening was accompanied by a howling blast of wind and rain, this simple event managed to draw every eye upon it.

Maria closed the door behind her and turned to face the men, her eyes wide with fear. The men stared back at her in silence.

"Maria?" uttered Giorgos, in amazement.

Amazed as he was, Giorgos was also rather doubtful. The young girl looked a bit like Maria, but it was hard to say as her long dark hair was plastered over her face by the wind and rain. The clothes that he had seen her wearing only a few hours earlier, were dark and dripping. Maria it was.

Giannis was the first to act, descending on the girl with a towel that had been lately used for polishing light bulbs and drying glasses. Pavlos went behind the bar and poured her a glass of brandy, thought better of it, drank it himself and poured a glass of lemonade instead.

For her part, once she had got over the initial terror of entering the first circle of Hell, Maria was surprised to find its inhabitants so welcoming. Although the air was blue with smoke and the oil lamps were casting dark shadows on the walls, the familiar faces of the men in the *kafeneion* showed only a mixture of friendliness and concern. Clutching her lemonade, Maria sat down next to her father.

"Caught in the storm, eh?" said Giorgos.

"Cinnamon," replied Maria, gazing at her glass.

"Ah," said Giorgos, nodding his head.

There were a few chuckles from those who had over-heard, but the rest of the men returned to their cards and tavli. The young man with the bouzouki picked randomly at the strings.

Maria dared to look around her. Uncle Giannis was leaning on the bar, squinting dimly at a newspaper through his glasses. Uncle Pavlos was sucking his teeth and contemplating his next move at tavli. Uncle Costas was blowing on a cup of steaming coffee. If this was hell, it was very unfrightening.

Maria sipped her lemonade and glanced sideways at Giorgos. Giorgos lit a cigarette. He shook the fire out of the matchstick and placed it carefully in the centre of the ashtray before inhaling the smoke. He looked different.

He saw her looking at him. Maria averted her eyes but not quickly enough to miss his smile.

As had happened so many times in his life, Giorgos wanted to say something but found himself unable to do so. He was not a man of many words at the best of times, and the more emotional he became, the fewer words he uttered. They simply choked him. But singing was different. After all, when you sang, the words floated on melody and came easily. They were well-worn words written by intelligent people, and sometimes, occasionally, they could sum up a lifetime of feelings in a brief span.

Giorgos carefully put out his cigarette, turned to face his daughter and, softly at first, almost inaudibly, began to sing.

As he sang, his voice gathered strength. It was an old song familiar to everyone on the island, to everyone in Greece. It was simply called *S'agapo*, I love you, and in that simplicity lay its power. At first no one paid him much heed, but the young bouzouki-player picked up the familiar tune and the men around him fell silent and then, little by little, began to sing with him.

I love you.
I love you because you are beautiful.
I love you because you are you.

I love you.
And I love the whole world
because you are part of it.

The window is closed.
Open it!

The song dissolved to an end. The bouzouki-player smiled shyly. Lightning cracked outside and the rain roared down.

Dimitra was becoming increasingly frantic. She sheltered in a doorway to collect her thoughts. She had tried to open her mother's door but it was bolted. Her mother was frightened of storms despite being almost deaf. No amount of knocking would have produced an answer. Maria might have sought shelter elsewhere—with family or friends—but Dimitra could not knock on every single door. She would have to wait until the storm passed. But how long would that take? And perhaps by then it would be too late.

Giorgos, the drunkard, would be in the *kafeneion*, of course. He would be drinking with his cronies, totally un-aware that Maria had gone missing while buying cinnamon for the *stifado.* And he would not care anyway. Yet, as she thought that, she bit her lip, in the knowledge that it was not true.

Although the doorway offered some degree of shelter, the rain was no respecter of buildings. Whirling gleefully in the narrow street, the wind splashed gouts of water at Dimitra. She wrapped her sodden shawl tightly around her and swayed from side to side as if in grief. If God was punishing her, why punish Giorgos too? Giorgos had not sent his daughter to fetch cinnamon for a *stifado* just as a storm was about to break. Giorgos was not a drunkard. Giorgos was a kind man: faithful, honest and a good provider. He had once been a joyful dancer with a voice that recalled the rumble of waves and the soft soughing of the wind in the tamarisks. She had killed that as surely as the terrible storm had now killed their daughter. She began to weep, rocking back and forth in the cold and wet. And then she stood up, crossed herself and walked out into the storm.

It took her no more than twenty steps to reach the *kafeneion,* but it was not only the water that was pulling at Dimitra's feet. As she grew closer, she could hear talking and laughter and the sound of someone picking at a bouzouki. The oil lamps inside gave the *kafeneion* a warm glow. Then as she put her hand on the door handle, she heard a man's voice singing. It was a voice that recalled the rumble of waves and the soft soughing of the wind in the tamarisks. It was the song *S'agapo* that Giorgos had sung to her many years before. Dimitra paused with her hand on the brass handle and listened until the last notes of the bouzouki died away and there was a ripple of clapping. She heard someone calling "Bravo, Giorgo!"

She opened the door. Directly in front of her sat Giorgos and directly in front of him sat Maria. She was warm and dry. She was holding a glass of lemonade in both hands and was smiling at him happily. As Dimitra opened the door, all eyes in the *kafeneion* turned towards her, but she did not hesitate. As she entered, Giorgos looked at her in amazement and then pulled her into the warmth.

Thanks to the rain, the tears that ran down Dimitra's cheeks were invisible. The rain soon dried, but the tears remained.

Picking flowers with Kristina

The bright hiss of the carbide lamp stopped, and with it the patch of brilliance on the dark water. The only light that now picked out the tiny boat in the blackness was the tiny pinpoint of Gianko's cigarette.

There was no moon. Above him, the Milky Way swept across the heavens in a wash of stars. Around it was the familiar pattern of constellations that had guided his forefathers across the sea.

There was not the slightest breath of wind. Around the boat, the water was black oil. In the clear air, the lights of the village were deceptively close, but otherwise everything was much as it had been for millennia, long before the first men had arrived to eke out an existence from the wild islands.

A dog barked. Gianko heard the whir of a moped somewhere up in the hills. For a moment, he could follow the light of its headlamp. Apart from that, all was silence save for the gentle lapping of the water against the wooden hull of his boat.

He sniffed the air. It smelled of fish, diesel fumes, salt water and tobacco. But he also caught the faint scent of wild thyme and oregano, grilled food, two-stroke petrol, and perhaps a hint of frankincense from the church.

It had not been a bad night's fishing. Two boxes of kalamari testified to the fatal attraction of the carbide lamp and Gianko's skill as a catcher of the white ghosts. The warm night had brought them to the oil-like surface, seeking the tiny fish that the bright carbide moonlight brought forth.

Gianko propped his back against a thwart. He had caught enough kalamari but he was still in no mood to return home. To be a kilometre offshore on a gently rocking boat was much better than to toss and turn in his bed in the airless swelter of the village.

He reached behind him for the water bottle that was still half full of his brother's tsikoudia. The bottle had been refilled many times. Its *Vikos* label had been almost worn off and the plastic now had a dull, scuffed patina.

Gianko removed the blue cap and raised the bottle to his lips. He took a sip.

His brother could make very good tsikoudia, but he was a farmer. Tsikoudia was the single consolation in a life spent bound to the soil. In a good year, his brother's fields would yield lush crops that brought him a comfortable living but there were years when drought or a bitter winter made for hard times.

Yet the sea would always yield a harvest, as long as its moods were respected. For, as was often said by fishermen, the sea is a woman. She can smile and caress and abandon herself to you, but she can also be unpredictable, capricious and angry. You have to exercise caution and respect. Do not be so foolhardy as to imagine that she can be treated in the same way every day.

Gianko laughed and shook his head. He replaced the blue plastic cap on his bottle. The sea is not quite a woman, he thought. As unpredictable as it may appear to be, the sea can still be read and understood while a woman is sometimes unfathomable. Take her choice of mate, for example. We should thank God that women do not choose their men for their looks alone, otherwise precious few would ever get married. Sometimes, the man she chooses seems to have very few advantages on his side. He may not be handsome, intelligent or even manly, but somewhere a woman has seen something in him that is hidden to all others, and no other man will please her.

One day in a warm April long past, he was working on his father's boat. This same boat. His father said that the engine had been running hot. Gianko had never noticed that, but to satisfy his father, he changed the oil and filters, replaced the impeller and tensioned the drive belt. As the *kaiki* had been dragged onto the beach, he also took advantage of the fine weather to re-paint the hull.

"*Kalimera,* Gianko."

He had not heard Kristina approaching over the sand. She was barefoot. He was stripped to the waist and working in the full glare of the midday sun.

"That looks like hot work," she said.

Her voice was soft and yet resonant, like the chiming of a bell at the bottom of the sea.

Gianko laughed.

"It *is* hot work," he replied.

A gust of wind caught her long, dark hair. She reached up and brushed it away from her face. She smiled. It was not a flirtatious smile. Why should it have been? They had known each other since childhood, knew each other's parents, siblings, grandparents, uncles, aunts and cousins. Her smile was slight, the merest curl of her lips.

"I'm going for a walk. To pick flowers. You can come with me, if you want."

Gianko plunged his brush into the jar of turpentine, sealed the lid on the tin of paint, wiped his hands on a rag, pulled on his shirt, and followed her to the hills.

Why did he do that? Why had he just downed tools and walked off with her? They were not even especially good friends. As children, they had teased each other relentlessly. He remembered one Sunday afternoon at a beach on the other side of the island. About twenty of them had walked there and back, setting off in the early morning and arriving home well after midnight. Kristina had taunted him about his skinny body before diving into the water and then turning back and laughing. He had thrown pebbles at her in retaliation, although he did not aim. She did not seem to care whether he aimed or not.

Once, he had called her "Cross-eyed Kristina" and got a sharp slap on the face in return. Kristina had a very slight strabismus that most people, even Gianko, thought quite pretty but was an embarrassment for her as a teenager.

They walked side by side. Kristina chattered about things of no consequence. It was almost as if she wanted to avoid a silence. Not that it mattered to Gianko. He liked to listen to her. Even the most mundane words were suddenly charming, almost elegant, when they were uttered in her soft, dark, clear voice. When she paused, Gianko stole a sideways look at her and admired the shape of her mouth, how it curved so sharply yet so gracefully. How, when she was not speaking, her lips framed the slightest of gaps.

This was new.

Perhaps aware that he was staring at her, Kristina stopped and turned to face him. In all the years that they had known each other, Gianko had never really looked her in the eye. If anyone had asked him, he would have said that her eyes were just brown, but they were not. They were grey fading into brown, and they sparkled with flecks of blue and gold.

Kristina smiled and lowered her head. Then glanced up at him.

"Let's walk," she said.

At the top of the hill was a wide meadow full of wildflowers. There were poppies, asphodel, anemones…showers of red, yellow and blue, multicoloured stars in a green cosmos. Kristina laughed with delight and began to pick them. Only Kristina could smile and laugh from the simple act of picking flowers on a sunny day. It was not a smile for Gianko's benefit.

Gianko stood and watched her, not really knowing whether to help her or not. Until then, picking flowers had been something that only girls and women did but now he felt an irresistible urge to be part of anything of which Kristina was a part. So, he bent down and began to gather blossoms, clumsily and indiscriminately at first but then, increasingly, with a sense of purpose. As he picked, he started to wonder which particular combination of colours and shapes would suit Kristina best.

And then he glanced up. He saw her stooping. He saw the curve of her body, how the warm spring breeze was pressing the thin cotton of her dress against her legs. She must have been aware that he was watching her so closely. Suddenly she straightened up, brushed her hair away from her face and smiled at him, holding a huge bunch of flowers triumphantly aloft so that he could admire both of them. Gianko approached and held out his own small bunch.

"You're very sweet, Gianko," she said, and took them from him, carefully arranging the flowers that he had picked so that they merged into her own.

They sat. Kristina had brought an orange. She bit into it deeply, spat out a chunk of peel and sucked greedily. She smiled and passed it to Gianko. He felt a slight, almost uncomfortable thrill when his mouth met the sweet yet bitter fruit so recently touched by her lips. The juice ran down his chin and he wiped it away with the back of his hand.

He felt clumsy and awkward.

Above them, the stars of heaven were hidden in a cloak of blue.

They sat and talked. They talked about their families and friends and about what they had done or were going to do. They laughed when they remembered the endless teasing, the pebbles thrown into the water and the angry slap. But for everything that was said, there were so many things that were not.

Gianko wanted to tell Kristina about the curve of her lips, about the way the wind had pressed her cotton dress against her legs, about her smile, about the sudden, unexpected delight that he felt in everything she said, in every movement she made, yet there were no words to express this and, even if there had been, he would have been afraid to utter them.

They were sitting close to each other. So close that they were touching. Gianko felt her warmth. Felt that there, next to him, was a truly different person—different to his parents or his brothers and sisters, and different to his other friends. Exactly how she was different, it was difficult to say. She was alien and yet, at that moment, he felt closer to her than he had ever felt to anyone.

The wind blew Kristina's dark hair over her face. Gianko stretched out a finger and brushed it away.

A slight breath of wind shimmered over the surface of the sea. He stubbed out his cigarette on the transom and sniffed the air. The weather was changing. There would be no more stifling heat. It would not be quite so good for catching kalamari but better for sleeping.

He lifted the bottle of tsikoudia, unscrewed the plastic cap, took a sip and held the bottle aloft.

To women! To life!

He cranked the starter. The old diesel engine thudded, drowning the silence. He opened the throttle slightly, leant against the tiller and brought the boat round to return to the village, to home, and to Kristina.